Call Time

Call Time

STEVE JONES

MICHAEL  JOSEPH

PENGUIN MICHAEL JOSEPH

UK | USA | Canada | Ireland | Australia
India | New Zealand | South Africa

Penguin Michael Joseph is part of the Penguin Random House group of companies
whose addresses can be found at global.penguinrandomhouse.com

First published 2023
001

Copyright © Steve Jones, 2023

The moral right of the author has been asserted

Set in 13.5/16pt Garamond MT
Typeset by Falcon Oast Graphic Art Ltd
Printed in Great Britain by Clays Ltd, Elcograf S.p.A.

The authorized representative in the EEA is Penguin Random House Ireland,
Morrison Chambers, 32 Nassau Street, Dublin D02 YH68

A CIP catalogue record for this book is available from the British Library

HARDBACK ISBN: 978-0-241-56140-9
TRADE PAPERBACK ISBN: 978-0-241- 56141-6

www.greenpenguin.co.uk

For Chris. You are always with me.

'Are you gonna shit your nappy?'

'No!'

'Well, don't be a baby then.'

'I'm telling Mum and Dad you swore.'

'That's what a baby would do. We're not pushing our bikes back down that path,' he said, looking back along the mountain trail towards their Auntie's house at the bottom of the valley far below them. 'It'll be easier to take the road through the field there.'

'But Mum said I'm not allowed on the road!'

'There are no cars around, Tom. You'll be fine. It's not like it's the M4,' he said, setting off.

Tom looked at the narrow road beyond the field's gate, following its snaking descent until it abruptly dropped out of view. He squeezed the bike's handlebars.

'Come on, Tom! Last one down's a rotten egg!' he called, opening the gate and mounting his bike.

'Wait for me!' Tom tucked his Dr Who TARDIS T-shirt into his shorts and hurried after his brother.

Soon rapidly moving green filled his peripheral vision. Hot black asphalt flowed beneath sticky tyres. His legs pumped frantic pedals, daring the bike to go faster. He squealed in delight, the climb worth such a glorious descent, his joy caught and scattered by the pine-infused wind he cut a path through. It was a moment of pure intoxication. A moment never to be forgotten, a moment that would come to define his entire life . . . and a moment that would end his brother's.

'*ROBERT!*'

I

Bob Bloomfield shot bolt upright, mercifully pulled from a nightmare whose ending he knew all too well. Gasping for air, in a sweat-soaked bed draped with Egyptian cotton sheets, his racing heart began to slow as he realized he was back in the much-needed security of the present. In the darkness, he dragged manicured nails over a Bavarian teak dipped wooden bedside table, until clammy fingers found the cool reassurance of a bottle of Blue Label whisky (a frequent bedtime companion when dark thoughts lay with him). He swigged greedily before falling into a restless but thankfully dreamless sleep.

His morning routine washed away any lingering thoughts of a dream that had haunted him for most of his life. Cleansing, grooming and breakfast were all practised in solemn silence. No television, music or even the sound of a city coming to life on the streets far below his London penthouse were welcome in an apartment that had become a beautiful temple to emotionless, cold precision.

The only item that jumped out of the apartment's flawless feng-shui was a large cardboard box that rested on a side table next to the front door. Picking up his briefcase, about to head out, he came to a stop. His eyes lingered for long moments on a note that was on top of the box:

> *Here's the rest of your stuff*
> *I don't throw away things that*
> *are perfectly good*
>
> > *Nell*

He made a sad sigh and opened the door.

A short journey from one high-rise to another saw Bob arrive at his place of work. Imagine an institution that championed those that have been dealt an unfortunate hand in life. A place that worked in the best interests of those that don't have the means to provide for themselves. A place of selfless humility dedicated to becoming a beacon of hope and light in a dark and cynical world. Now imagine the exact opposite of that and you are fully up to speed with what FitzSimmons & Bloomfield Entertainment Management represented.

Bob was a good fit. His ruthless professionalism or, as you and I would describe it, the absence of even the most basic decency that enables wider society to function without caving in on itself like a dying star, quickly marked him out as a future thoroughbred of the FitzSimmons stable.

Showcasing the kind of cut-throat detachment that could throw a duffel bag of kittens into a canal without breaking stride, Bob's ascent to company partner and name on a plaque had been quick and devastating for anyone in his path. As he famously told his wide-eyed colleagues at his inauguration, 'And so begins the age of Bloomfield! And it will be an age, I assure you. Do you know why despots seem to live so long? Because heaven doesn't want them and hell is full.' It was a personal maxim delivered with an iron fist and a lupine smile that a silver bullet couldn't save you from.

Stepping out of a lift on to the eighteenth-floor offices of FitzSimmons & Bloomfield's knowingly intimidating central London HQ, Bob strode with purpose, in an outrageously expensive business suit, along a lavishly panelled heavy oak hallway towards his corner office or, as he liked to call it, *'the war room'*.

He returned the standard, 'Good morning, Mr Bloomfield,' from his many employees with a nod and a flash of a smile with spirit-level-even white teeth, which seemed oddly out of place set in his dark, cruelly handsome features. A short, sharp haircut, slightly peppering at the sides in a perfectly annoying symmetrical way, crowned his six-foot-one inch athletic frame.

'Mornin', Mr B,' said a passing company courier, one of the many men and women employed as a rapid delivery system for countless time-sensitive documents.

'Good morning, Arvin. Oh! Whilst I have you, I need you to take a script to . . .' Bob began, but was immediately shut down when Arvin raised a gloved hand grasping the aforementioned script.

'I just leave your office. Package received and en route,' Arvin replied with a grin.

'How could I ever have doubted you? You're the best!' Bob said, bowing in contrition. 'By the way, I was wondering, where are you from, Arvin? I can't place the accent.'

'Albania.'

'Of course! *Taken*, that's where I've heard it.'

'You are right!' he replied with a laugh. 'Liam killed many of my countrymen. We hope for revenge in *Taken* four.'

'Fingers crossed. Well, from human trafficking to the traffic of London. You be careful out there my friend.'

'*Lamtumirë*, Mr B,' Arvin said, departing with another laugh.

Satisfied an important document had been dispatched, Bob turned to continue his march to the 'the war room' when suddenly the sound of excited possibility brought him to another full stop. Hushed voices from the company kitchen, just beyond his view around the corner, caught his ear.

'. . . it's fancy dress, so it's up to you to dress for sexual success,' said junior assistant Chloe Huxley, addressing a gaggle of giggling workmates about a party she was throwing that very evening, 'but then again, there will be a hideous amount of bubbles available, so maybe don't try too hard.' More excited laughter.

'Zip and dip,' he smiled to himself.

'I read the brief,' Bob said into the microphone of the minuscule hands-free device looped around his ear.

'So, what did you think?'

'Well . . .' he began, enjoying the silent expectation of the caller on the end of the line. Stretching the moment, he took the time to rest his handmade brogues upon a sprawling oak desk that you could have sailed the Atlantic on. Which was apropos considering the surrounding dark wood panelling gave Bob's corner office the intimidating impression of being in the captain's quarters on a whaling vessel. 'You are without doubt the country's most beloved motivational self-help guru. It is high time you got a book out there. You're ready.'

'Why am I sensing a "but", darling?'

'You're my favourite client, Monty, you know that, so if we're going to do something, it has to be right.'

'Has to be right? The time has never been more right! Mental health is one of the most pressing issues of our time. This is going to be the must-have book for training one's mind to cope with the complex challenges and pitfalls our society now presents. I assure you, this book will benefit people greatly.'

'You misunderstand. I'm with you. Mental health has never been more important . . . or lucrative. I'm all for this book and its contents. It's the title I'm finding a little problematic.'

'Oh. What's wrong with the title?'

'Mind Camp?'

'And? It's a great title and an accurate representation of what the book will be, essentially, a psychological dojo, a boot camp for the mind. I intend to train people, equip them with the right tools needed to . . .'

'Not much of a history buff, Monty?' Bob interjected.

'No past, no future, only the present, darling.'

'That's great. What I'm going to do is ask you to write down the following and then pop it in a Google search, OK?'

'*All right.*'

'Mein Kampf. That's M-E-I-N, K-A-M-P-F.'

'*What is that? Foreign?*'

'German, I think.'

'*I'm assuming it's a book of some kind. What's it about?*'

'Let's just say, you wouldn't want to read it on the tube.'

'*OK,*' Monty replied, sounding more confused than ever.

'Like I said, pop it in Google and then get back to me. We'll talk more.'

'*Got it, darling. Will do.*'

'Perfect. Speak soon, superstar,' he said, tapping his headset to end the call. 'Fucking idiot.'

Satisfied his client was about to learn an important lesson, his mind moved on to the next problem in need of a solution. After a short time, he reached for the intercom that connected him to his secretary. 'Miss Pennypacker . . .'

'*Mr Bloomfield, you've cut me off at the pass. I was just about to buzz you.*'

'Everything OK?'

'*Ian Sommer from* The Print *has been in contact again regarding Mr Thacker's recent alleged dalliance with a glory hole in the changing rooms at Debenhams. Mr Sommer urged me to tell you, I quote, "With or without an official response, we will be going ahead with the piece. It's in the public's best interest to learn that one of its most beloved game show hosts, who trades heavily on his family man image, is, in fact, less than wholesome. So, a line or two from FitzSimmons and Bloomfield would be in Mr Thacker's best interest." End quote.*'

'Sommer is a piece of shit.'

'*What would you like to do?*'

'I'd like to send him a noose and a how-to guide.' He pondered his next move before coming to a decision. 'OK, I want to go scorched earth on this one. Let's fire a DEFCON 2-level email across his bow. Take this down, Miss Pennypacker.'

'*Yes, Sir.*'

'Dear Ian, the allegations regarding my client are wholly false. Roger Thacker is a national treasure on and off the screen. He is a man who has entertained this great nation for decades and campaigned tirelessly for its well-being through various charitable endeavours. The allegation that he engaged in such a base act in . . . where was it again?'

'*Debenhams.*'

'. . . in Debenhams, will be contested in the most vigorous manner possible. We ask you to cease and desist with any article that might impugn his good name.

'Furthermore, *Ian*, the man who owns your rag, my dear friend Tony, is but a phone call away. I recommend you load this bullshit article into a cannon and shoot it into outer space as soon as is humanly possible. Otherwise, I will personally see to it that you end up living in a cardboard box under a bridge in Vauxhall. Signed, lots and lots of love, Bob Bloomfield.'

'*I'll get this to him immediately.*'

'Thank you, Miss Pennypacker. Also, can I ask you to remind me to speak to Thacker and warn him that the next glory hole he puts his dick through, I'll be waiting on the other side with a sledgehammer.'

'*I'll put it in the diary.*'

'Excellent. Now, the reason I was calling you, would you send for one of the juniors?'

'*Of course, Mr Bloomfield. Who would suit best?*'

'Dealer's choice ordinarily, but I think what I have in mind might suit Miss Huxley's skill-set best.'

'*As you wish, Mr Bloomfield.*'

'Oh, and Miss Pennypacker, one last thing . . .'

A short while later there was a rap at Bob's door.

'Enter,' he commanded. The door opened and Chloe Huxley obeyed, her petite frame wrestling with the heavy old oak door, robbed of its creak by Miss Pennypacker and a can of WD40.

'You asked to see me, Sir?'

He didn't offer her a seat. He sternly gazed at his computer, apparently absorbed in a communiqué of epic importance. He began to fake-type with a flourish. A good thirty seconds went by before he addressed Chloe. 'One minute,' he said, holding a finger up, before starting to fake-type again. She waited patiently, rocking ever so slightly on pumps almost completely buried in the fur of the not-at-all-fake bearskin rug she was standing on.

Out of the corner of his eye, he watched her surveying the room. She seemed to be enjoying the Who's Who of superstars mounted and framed on the far wall, caught forever in a moment in time with the man who made them – Bob Bloomfield.

Relatively new to the company, she was younger than he remembered – twenty-six? Twenty-seven? He noted that her long red hair was strikingly incongruous in the predominantly mahogany expanse of his office, as was her pale complexion and light green eyes. He thought to himself that she had more of an appearance of a woodland nymph than a stomp-on-your-balls Entertainment Manager. *The poor whelp won't last long in this business.* He slammed his laptop shut, and she snapped to attention.

'Now, Chloe is it?'

'Yes, Sir.'

'Excellent. I wonder if you might deliver a rather important message to Mr FitzSimmons for me?'

'Not a problem.'

Bob took a sheet of paper out of his desk drawer and began to write. 'A little sensitive – I'd rather not email it; the walls have digital ears and all that. Think you can handle it?' he smiled.

'Of course,' she said, with a dutiful nod.

A moment later, Bob finished his message to Mr FitzSimmons, which was in fact wordless. Its sole content was a crude stick figure receiving a blow job from a fish. He folded the paper and put it in an envelope.

'Don't worry, he'll know exactly what it pertains to. How are you settling in by the way? I know this place is about as organized as an Italian airport, so I do hope we're not working you too hard?' he said with a friendly chuckle, handing her the envelope.

'Everybody's been fantastic and I enjoy the work, so it's a win-win,' she said, visibly flustered by the inquiry.

'Excellent! Here we like to work hard and play hard, so make sure you . . .' The intercom buzzed into life. With an apologetic roll of his eyes and a shrug, he pushed 'answer'. 'Speak.'

'Sorry to disturb you, Mr Bloomfield, but the Save the Children people have been in touch and they regret to inform you that the benefit you were speaking at this evening has been cancelled.'

'Oh, balls! I was looking forward to doing my bit for those little cherubs. Did they mention why it's been cancelled?'

'Apparently, one of the STC execs was kicked to death by a horse at a dressage event yesterday.'

'Ummm . . . OK . . . thank you, Miss Pennypacker.' He quickly ended the exchange whilst making a mental note to have a word with his secretary about her ad-libs.

He blew out his cheeks. 'Crazy,' he said, still looking forlornly at the intercom. 'Well, that puts me at a bit of a loose end this evening. God knows I wanted to help those kids. Such a shame.' Coming out of his sad reverie he turned his gaze back to Chloe, who'd been watching, silently impressed. 'Gosh, I'm sorry Chloe, look at me keeping you from the grind,' he said, with a chuckle. 'If you wouldn't mind getting that note to Fitz.'

'Of course, Sir.' She turned to leave but made it only as far as the door. Giving in to an impulse, she swivelled around to see Bob staring into space, comforting himself by gently stroking the back of his head. 'Feel free to laugh in my face . . .' she began.

Bob's rhythmic stroking stopped. *There's blood in the water.*

'. . . but I'm throwing a bit of a thing at my place this evening,' she concluded, through an apologetic squint.

'You're too sweet. But I couldn't impose.'

'You wouldn't be, honestly. There'll be loads of people there. It's going to be great fun. But, there is one important detail . . .' That apologetic squint again. 'It's fancy dress . . . but, of course, you wouldn't have to . . .'

'Fancy dress is one of my passions!' Bob replied, with an insincerity Chloe seemed oblivious to.

'Really? Well, that's that, you're coming . . . Sir,' she added quickly. 'I'll leave the details with Miss P, and feel free to bring a friend. The more the merrier.'

'Well, all right, I certainly will. Thank you, Chloe.' As she reached the door, Bob exclaimed, 'Serendipity!' She smiled and the door closed.

He leaned back in his chair. 'Too easy,' he said, reaching for his personal phone. Accessing his contacts, he skimmed through to find the number he wanted. It didn't take him long, such was the meagre body count of his social circle. Scrolling past Mum and Dad (written in his phone as John and Judy), past various names of women who had come and gone, he finally arrived at *Scotty*.

2

Bob arrived at the townhouse residence of the Pickers-Gills. At least, he thought he had. *These family cages all look the same to me.* He threw another cursory glance up and down the well-to-do street. *Balls to it.* He walked up a short path to a front door. It had been a while since Bob last visited his BFF.

Exhaling and breathing through the nose, finding his centre, he pushed the doorbell, but instead of ringing, he heard the beginning of Tchaikovsky's 1812 Overture on a ten-second loop, softly reverberating from within. *OK, this is definitely the place.* The twee sound sent his eye-balls rolling three hundred and sixty degrees in his head, asking his brain en route why he was here in the first place. It whispered back, *you are lonely, Bob.* A contemp-tuous sneer cracked his handsome face. *Piss off!*

The door opened.

The lady of the house, Kirsty Pickers-Gill, was immaculately dressed in a 'just pottering around' outfit straight out of the pages of *Tatler*. In fact, her quintes-sentially English jet-black hair and blue eyes wouldn't have looked out of place on the cover of the magazine, such was her classically refined beauty.

Bob regarded her with begrudging appreciation. He had never had an issue with how she looked. He appreciated beauty and elegance as much as the next man. It was the fact that she was immune to his charms that bothered him. For Kirsty possessed a superpower most people didn't have in their armoury – *she knows I'm full of shit* – and Bob hated her for that.

Tall, and taller still due to the hefty period doorstep she stood on, she was eye level with him. 'Hello, Bob,' she said, the words sounding like the oral equivalent of a pair of turds being flushed down a toilet.

'Please Mrs Pickers-Gill, can Scotty come out to play?' he said, in the voice of a twelve-year-old.

'Oh, sweetheart, I wish, but you're one of those human garbage kids from the caravan park. You'll be dead from meth or homeless with only a smack hound for a friend by the time you're eighteen. I can't have you drag my Scott down with you. Now, off you go and play on the train tracks.'

'There's that wonderful snobbery bought and paid for with Mummy and Daddy's money. Like my grandmother used to say, better to die honest, than live a lie.'

Throwing her head back in laughter, a frustratingly pleasant timbre, she shot back, 'Spoken like a broke old trash hag!'

'Really?' Bob said, his features darkening. 'You know the thing that really sticks in my craw about you lot with your . . .'

'*That Bob, Kirst? Bring him to the kitchen. I'm getting ready, I won't be long,*' a man's voice called from within the house.

The voice took the wind out of both their sails. Defused, for the moment, with a sense of mild shame, they blankly looked at one another wondering who would make the next move. Kirsty turned on her heels. 'Come in,' she said, walking away into the dim light of the hallway.

Closing the door behind himself and shaking off the feeling of being trapped, Bob made his way to the kitchen. En route, he glanced up a staircase; playful young voices out of sight floated down mellifluously to his ears.

Passing a large, bright living room, he saw children's toys dotted around and throws on couches with too many cushions. A perfectly distressed side table presented a framed newlywed picture of the Pickers-Gills beside a mountain lake, staring into one another's eyes adoringly. *Don't look at things you don't deserve, Bob.*

He entered the kitchen, a broad welcoming room. A family table took centre stage, appliances hugged the walls, the fridge doubled up as a makeshift gallery dedicated to abstract, colourful scribbles. Bob smiled at a picture of what looked like a purple monkey with massive testicles, though his smile quickly vanished when his eyes came to rest on Kirsty, leaning against a work surface, arms crossed, watching him with a displeased look upon her face.

'Scotty going to be long?'

'He's putting on his fancy dress. I see you've come as a selfish arsehole.'

'What?'

'You're not wearing fancy dress, Bob.'

'I am. I'm going as a rich, successful Entertainment

Manager.' He spun on the spot, showing off the sleek lines of his Savile Row suit.

'Infinitely worse than a selfish arsehole.'

'What's the problem, Kirsty?' he asked, nonchalantly resting one glute on the corner of the family table.

'Where is this evening going?' she said, through gritted teeth. 'How wrecked are you going to get my husband? And get your arse OFF MY TABLE!'

Bob jumped up like a scalded cat. 'Jesus Christ!' *How does Scotty cope with this woman?* Chastened, he stood in the middle of the room, definitely not touching anything. 'He's a big boy, Kirsty, he can make his own decisions. A night out with his best mate isn't going to put him in the Priory.'

She whooped a hollow laugh. 'Best mate? You don't know what friendship is. He doesn't hear from you for months on end and when he does, you get him so blitzed it takes him a week to recover. You can't keep dropping in and out of his life when it suits you.'

'God forbid he busts out of Shawshank for an evening now and again.'

'You're so childish!' Pushing herself off the work surface, she began pacing whilst running her fingers through her thick black hair. 'I don't know how to communicate with you.' Eventually, she came to a stop in front of Bob. A little too close for his liking. 'Look, I know you've been through a lot,' she said, speaking in a more measured tone. Alarm bells started to ring. *Shields up, Bob!* 'But Scott has responsibilities,' she continued. 'He has a family. You're not kids any more. I know he was there when you needed him, but you have to move on, that was a long time ago. I'm sorry for what you had to go through . . .'

'I'm going to stop you there, Oprah. You know nothing about what I've been through, OK. So, save your *Good Will Hunting* speech. I know it wasn't my fault . . .' An unexpected quiver of emotion caught in his throat.

'Oh, Bob,' she said, placing a comforting hand on his upper arm – *SHIELDS UP, GODDAMN IT!*

'What are you doing?' he asked.

'I'm trying to comfort you.'

'No. You're staining my £3,000 suit with some kind of gross lavender hand cream you use to fight the signs of ageing.'

She looked at him for a long moment before removing her hand. 'Ahhhh!' she exclaimed, before resuming her pacing. 'You're a monster! You always have been. Even in school you were insufferable, tormenting me whenever you could.'

'Can you hear yourself? I "tormented you in school"? And I'm the one who needs to move on apparently.'

'Oh, I have no doubt that it was all just good fun for you. The popular "swot" with glasses and a "dirty" name was fair game.'

'Your maiden name is Cummings! That's crack to kids. What was I supposed to do? Anyway, that's all behind you now, Mrs Pickers-Gill,' he said, stifling a laugh.

'Materially rich, spiritually empty,' she said, with pity in her voice. 'You're heartless, Bob. Always have been, always will be.'

'Whatevs.'

'You go have your night, Bob. Just remember, he'll be coming home to me. I'll be right here waiting for him,' she said with finality.

Before Bob had a chance to keep on digging, 'YEAH, BABY! SHAGADELIC, BABY!' proclaimed Scotty, literally jumping into the room dressed as a frighteningly accurate Austin Powers. A shocked Kirsty and Bob scanned the package – the wig, the ruffles, the blue velvet suit, even the thick-rimmed glasses and the neglected horse teeth, were all present and correct.

The juxtaposition of the perpetually laid-back Scotty (making him perfectly qualified to cope with Bob's mania) and this comical dervish resulted in a simultaneous burst of laughter. An astonishing feat in and of itself.

'Do I make you horny, baby?' he asked, in a flawless Powers twang, as he jigged his way over to Kirsty, the final steps taken in the form of a sexy bunny hop. He took her in his arms, gave a seductive cat's purr and kissed her deeply. Bob watched this slice of domestic bliss the way a chimpanzee might examine a Rubik's cube.

'GROOVY, BABY!' shouted Scotty, coming up for air as Kirsty blushed. 'You're next, Daddy-O,' he teased, dancing his way over to Bob, whilst whistling Quincy Jones's 'Soul Bossa Nova'.

'Great energy, but could you be more of a cliché?' Bob said, stopping Scotty in his tracks.

'What? Come on, this is vintage. It's a classic,' he replied, breaking character. His own voice contained the faintest hint of an American accent due to an early childhood in New York.

'Hackneyed, Scotty, we're better than this.'

'Well, if you'd given me more notice I might have lived up to your expectations,' he replied, a little crestfallen. 'I haven't been to a fancy-dress party since 1998, and this was state of the art back then. Anyway, I think it's highly impressive that it still fits,' he said, grinning at Kirsty.

'You own it,' she smiled back.

'Yeah, baby,' he growled in Powers mode. He turned his attention back to Bob. 'And you are going as what, Patrick Bateman?'

'Your wife and I have already covered this,' Bob said. 'Speaking of *witch,* Kirsty, it has been such a joy to catch up. Great to see you're doing so well.'

'The pleasure's been mine. Great to see you are the same old Bob Bloomfield.'

The lashings of false civility were not lost on Scotty. 'OK . . . *and break!'* he mocked. 'I'll be back . . .'

'Wrong outfit,' Bob interjected.

Ignoring him, Scotty continued, 'I'll be back . . . by twelve, one at the latest. Give the kids a goodnight kiss for me, OK.'

'Will do,' she said, straightening his glasses and brushing some of the synthetic hair out of his eyes. 'Have a great time and be careful. I love you.'

'Love you too.'

'Love you three,' she cooed.

'I'd *love* to get going,' Bob added. 'I'm sure you'd

prefer I throw up in the back of the taxi than here in this beautifully maintained kitchen.'

'Pay no mind to this sad, bitter man, my love. He's just jealous you chose me and not him,' said Scotty, gently ribbing his old friend.

'So true. You're a very lucky man. What I'd give to be in your shoes,' said Bob, grappling Scotty away from his wife and into the hallway.

'Don't wait up, baby!' he exclaimed, back in Powers mode, dancing towards the front door.

'See you later, Austin,' she called after him. 'Bye, Bob,' she added, giving him the middle finger whilst mouthing the word 'Arsehole'.

'Cheers, Kirsty. Take care,' he replied, mouthing 'Cummings' and making an obscene gesture with his hand.

3

After a short cab ride, where most of the journey was taken up by Bob arguing with the 'erratic' driver – 'If you use your horn fifteen times on a single journey, the chances are that the "clueless dickhead" is you' – Scotty and Bob arrived at Soho Square.

'What's your record for days going by where you don't argue with anyone?' asked Scotty, straightening his ruffles whilst surveying the square's ants' nest of activity.

'Well, that would coincide with the number of days where I don't come into contact with people.' They both laughed. It was an easy laughter, the kind that could only be shared by friends who knew one another intimately.

Knowing who Bob was was something almost entirely exclusive to Scotty. There were those who had known him for over a decade and still didn't know how many sugars he had in his tea (three). But Scotty had been there before the barricade went up, before Bob was shown how brutal life could be. He was there when Bob's smile didn't come with a caveat.

'I jest of course. I love my fellow man. I'm a proud participant in this great experiment we call society.' As they walked around the grassy little park's periphery, right on cue, Bob bent down to fill the cup of someone begging for change.

'You seem to forget I've known you for a long time, Bob. You give change to homeless people because you don't like carrying it. You think it ruins the line of your suit.'

'Objection your honour – supposition?'

'Annoyingly – sustained,' said Scotty, before breaking into more of that easy laughter.

'Here's a question. Was Austin Powers a thing in China? If not, then the employees of the restaurant we're heading to are going to think this,' he gestured to Scotty's dandified attire, 'is you.'

Powers mode – 'If they can't handle me at my groovy-grooviest, then they don't deserve me at my eaty-eatiest, baby!'

'You berk.'

The Mayfly was a classic West End Chinese eatery. Classic in the sense that it seemed to have no idea it was based in the centre of London.

It was a piece of China carved out of the mainland, hermetically sealed and shipped to Britain. The only tweak to what would have been a professional and courteous service, was The Mayfly's wonderful and fully warranted, unapologetic and frequently rude disposition that it had been forced to develop over time, as a result of the multitude of drunken louts that poured through its doors when the sun went down.

Inside, a no-nonsense floor plan of communistic tables and chairs was at odds with the flora and light show above. Lengths and lengths of plastic lotus and orchid flowers linked the flickering paper lanterns hanging from the ceiling. The overall impression was of Santa's grotto in a prison canteen.

'I didn't have you down as the nostalgic type?'

Bob peered over his menu. 'Explain?'

'This place . . .' He gestured around the restaurant, 'This is one of our old stomping grounds. We used to come here and load up on carbs and MSG before hitting the town.'

'I have no idea what you could possibly mean,' Bob countered. He placed the menu on the table and an ever-widening mischievous grin grew on his face. 'SBOD!' he exclaimed, loud enough for the surrounding diners to turn in alarm.

'Bob . . .'

'SBOD!'

'Bob . . .'

'SBOD!

'BOB! We're not getting SBOD. We're two men in our forties. I have three kids. This is *not* gonna be a "Super Black-Out Drunk" evening.'

'Come on! Whatever happened to Captain Shagger and his loyal wingman, Pickledick? We were biblical!'

'Marriage and fatherhood,' Scotty replied, straightening his fake glasses, 'and I never cared for that nickname.'

'You stick your dick in a jar of pickled eggs, what do you expect?'

'Not my finest hour.'

'What? It was awesome! My God, she's got you wound up tight.'

'Here we go,' he said, wearied by a charge he'd become accustomed to from Bob. 'But let's go through it again. I'm very happy. It's a great marriage. There's a lot of love and a lot of trust. I can do what I want, Kirsty can do what she wants.'

'Not where Captain Shagger's concerned.'

'Believe it or not, she was all for this evening.'

'Really?'

'Yup. She said it's nice to see me stepping out for a quiet drink with such a successful, responsible, handsome man like yourself.'

'Yeah, sure,' he said, laughing. 'What did she really say?'

'She said, if I wanted to spend my time with an arsehole, that was my choice.'

'Yeah, sure.' Laughing harder, 'What did she really say?'

'OK,' beginning to laugh himself, 'she said if I wanted to spend time with a vicious, malicious . . .'

'Great name for an album,' said Bob.

'. . . vicious, malicious arsehole, whose sole purpose is to manage the most shallow, vacuous, self-absorbed narcissists in our society, then that was my choice.'

'There she is!' Both now laughed hard as a waiter placed two pints of lager in front of them.

'How is work by the way?' asked Scotty.

'Did you see in the press that everyone's favourite TV presenter, drunk out of her mind, crashed her Range Rover into a Greggs?' Bob asked.

'No, I did not.'

'Then I guess work's going fine,' he said, with a wicked grin. 'When it comes to bullshit, I'm a visionary. You? How's the exciting world of high finance?'

'Oh, you know, numbery.'

'A toast – to all the numbers!' proclaimed Bob, raising a glass.

'Hear-hear!' said Scotty.

They chink-cheered and drank.

'OK, so I admit there is an element of nostalgia, sat here in this restaurant,' said Bob, wiping his mouth, 'but there are practical applications too. I'm pretty sure I've seen a fancy-dress shop around the corner.'

'So, you're planning on dressing up?'

'Wouldn't leave you hanging, buddy.' Observing Scotty's fancy dress, realizing he was almost used to it by now, he asked, 'You are going to take those teeth out to eat?'

Scotty popped them out and dropped them into his glass of water. 'Yes, Sir.' His smile was now transformed to a set of white transatlantic teeth that almost rivalled Bob's.

'What about the glasses and wig?'

'You don't eat with your eyes, Bob. And I'm enjoying having hair. It's been a while,' said Scotty, to more laughter. 'How's Nell?'

'Nell?' Caught by surprise, his laughter suddenly stopped. 'You would have to ask her. That ended.'

'Why?' asked Scotty, dismayed. 'Too beautiful? Too intelligent? Too funny?'

'All qualities that I'm sure I could find in someone who doesn't feel the need to periodically grill me with: Where is this going? Do you want to get married? Do you want to have kids? Why don't you just chain me to a radiator and be done with it.'

'You don't think they're legitimate queries for a man who recently entered his late, *late*, forties?'

'What kind of a man remembers the date of another man's birthday?' asked Bob, frowning.

'A considerate one?'

'Look, they are legitimate queries. I'll give you that. But I literally said at the start of the relationship, I don't want marriage. I don't want kids.'

'Why not? Aren't you lonely?'

'Nope. I'm free.'

Scotty tilted his head to one side and narrowed his eyes. 'And you're happy about that?'

'I am. Tonight is a celebration,' replied Bob, taking another hearty swig.

'Then why do I get the feeling I'm watching a man drown his sorrows.' Bob's smile dimmed. 'I've known you a long time. This is classic Bob.'

'What do you mean?'

'As soon as anyone gets close to you, you push them away.'

'That's not true.'

'Said the single forty-nine-year-old.' Bob was stumped into silence. 'I want you to be happy, Bob. I'm just not sure you do,' Scotty said with a sigh.

'You know you're really bumming me out, Scotty. We're supposed to be having a laugh.'

He granted Bob a reprieve and changed the subject. 'How are your parents?'

'Oh yes! That's a better subject. Let's move on to that,' he said sarcastically. 'Why don't you tell me how your mum and dad are? How are the kids?'

'Mom's great. Dad's still cancer-free, so that's great. And the kids are an absolute joy. Although it's no picnic having a six-month-old again.'

'A what?' Bob was gobsmacked. 'You have a baby?'

'Yes, Bob. I mentioned it. We now have three children.'

'I didn't know,' he said, suddenly sheepish.

'We haven't seen you for eighteen months. You don't answer my calls or texts.' Even though Scotty was as calm and composed as he always was, Bob could tell he'd disappointed him greatly.

'Shit, Scotty. That's . . . that's bad. I'm sorry.'

'Woah! The unicorn of Bob Bloomfield's lexicon, the elusive S-word. This is almost worth you missing Chester's birth.'

'Well, I am. You deserve better.' They looked at one another, slightly embarrassed by the heartfelt exchange.

'You named your kid Chester Pickers-Gill? Wow! You know we don't need chimney sweeps any more?' Bob said, attempting to bring back some levity to the evening.

'Easy now. It's Kirsty's grandfather's name.'

'I'm kidding. He can be anything he wants to be, even prime minister – in 1890.'

'Bob!' scolded Scotty, through more of that easy laughter.

'Ready to order?' snapped a Chinese waiter, who might have been standing next to their table for some time.

'Oh, excuse us. Yes, we're ready,' said Scotty, picking

up his knife and fork and beginning the ritual of cleaning them with his napkin, a sight his old friend had become accustomed to over the years.

'Meh,' said Bob, ignoring the menu, 'I'm not hungry, let's just drink.'

'I'll have the number two, and so will he,' said Scotty, rolling his eyes.

'Number two?! Sounds delicious,' said Bob, beaming at the waiter. 'And more beer, my good man!'

After an extremely good meal, and a frustrating volume of lager for the poor waiter charged with the responsibility of keeping their glasses full, Bob and Scotty stumbled out of The Mayfly.

It wasn't a completely smooth exit because (if you had asked the waiter) Bob had been drinking like he had a liver transplant on speed dial, and Scotty's protests of 'I'm OK,' and 'I'm taking it easy,' had become less and less frequent as the meal went on. The end result was two men with limited coordination, zero inhibitions and a reduced life expectancy.

Joining the late evening throng of merrymakers, Bob, squinting up and down Wardour Street, took a moment to get his bearings. 'OK,' he said, swaying precariously, 'here we go. Let's have it. Fancy dress. Let's do this.'

'You don't have the faintest clue where we're going, do you?' said Scotty, equally uncertain of their next move.

'Do I look like a man who lacks direction? Details are my currency,' replied Bob, setting off with a surprisingly assured strut.

'Well, all right, baby!' said Austin, who followed in his footsteps.

Like a river, Soho's main thoroughfares move with a purpose that's difficult to counter. Side streets and alleys go by unexplored. Dark voids, inhospitable maws that most people avoid through common sense or instinct.

But Bob Bloomfield was not most people. By fate or design, he was expected that evening. Following a beacon beyond his understanding, Bob guided Scotty away from the throng, the sound of civilization fading in their ears as they ventured into one of Soho's opaque ventricles. Narrow walls closed in as they penetrated further and further into the murk.

Bob's confidence waned as silence enveloped them, darkness now all but complete. 'I could have sworn there was a . . .' he faltered, as a red glow suddenly entered his peripheral vision. 'Oh, here we go.'

Turning a corner they had not registered until now, red neon illuminated their path to a sign that announced: *Always in Style*.

A blinking arrow, shrouded in wafts of steam hissing from a nearby grate, pointed to steps leading down to a subterranean door.

'If I'm going to be murdered, please don't let it be dressed as Austin Powers. I'd hate for that to be my legacy,' Scotty drunkenly slurred, adding 'not groovy' and grinning his crooked smile for good measure.

'Don't be such a baby. There's absolutely nothing to be worried about.'

RING, RING!

'JESUS CHRIST!' Bob and Scotty screamed in unison, jumping back against the alley wall, narrowly avoiding a collision with a speeding bicycle.

'*Sorry, boys!*' a female voice apologized in a heavy cockney accent, disappearing into the dark as quickly as she had appeared.

With shocked faces, red in the neon light, they looked at one another . . . before bursting into laughter, 'You crapped yourself!' said Scotty, between gasps for air.

'*I* shat myself? Look at the blue velvet He-Man, over here,' said Bob, hands on knees laughing.

'He-Man? Come on Bob, it's the twenty-first century. We prefer to say Them-Person.' With that, Scotty held aloft an imaginary sword and proclaimed, '*I HAVE EQUAL POWER!*'

'Now, that's the kind of dynamite social commentary that justifies thirty-odd years of friendship.'

'Love you too, buddy,' said Scotty.

'And I . . . like you very much,' said Bob, pulling away from the intimacy of the moment. 'Let's get old Bobby B a costume.' They descended the steps to *Always in Style*.

4

Inside, a multitude of candles was the illumination of choice. But their potency had been dulled somewhat due to their flickering edges being lost in a sepia haze of smoke that filled the air. The smoke's origin was a long, thin pipe that protruded from a mouth that billowed sickly sweet wisps into the ether.

The pipe and the mouth belonged to an extremely old man who sat behind a counter adjacent to the entrance of the windowless room. A burgundy dressing gown covered his withered frame. A fez of the same shade (under which spider-web hair crept its way down to his narrow shoulders) rested upon his head. A similar tuft of fine hair, which looked like it might blow away in a faint breeze, sprouted from a chin that was part of a face that was barely more than a skull painted dirty pink.

Sunken eyes, which could not be seen, looked down at a paperback book he held in his pipeless claw. He appeared not to have noticed his two customers, even though their presence had been signalled by the dainty chime of a small doorbell above their heads.

Frozen at the door, the heat and smoke adding to their already discombobulated state, they regarded the interior beyond the old man. Every available surface was

covered with bric-à-brac, figurines, clocks . . . curiosities –
and that was just the parts they could see: what might lie
in the deep shadows out of the candlelight's reach?

Holding their breath, the solemn space somehow
demanding it, they noted that the only sound that could
be heard was the ticking of innumerable clocks, time
passing in a place where it appeared to have stopped.

Bob approached the counter. *'Ahem.'* The proprietor registered neither the cough nor Bob's looming
presence. *What's the deal with this waxwork?* Following
the proprietor's cadaverous gaze, Bob read the title and
author of the book – *The Present* by Mitch Mainee. Its
cover featured a picture of an empty hourglass.

'My good man,' he persisted, deciding to go for an
ice-breaker, 'I'm looking for a creature about yay-high,'
he held his hands about a foot apart, 'covered in brown-
and-white fur, hates sunlight, picky eater, answers to the
name of Mogwai?' He and Scotty giggled like the pair of
drunks they were.

'Firstly, he *is* a Mogwai. He *answers* to the name Gizmo.
Secondly, he is *not* a picky eater,' said the old man, without
looking up from his book, enunciating each word as if
addressing children. *'Timing* is the prime concern when
considering his diet,' he concluded, in a voice that had
smoked for a long, long time.

The giggling stopped. Bob, wide-eyed, turned to
Scotty, 'Impressive *Gremlins* knowledge.'

Scotty nodded in agreement. 'Do you mind if we take
a look around, Sir?' he asked, far too loudly, assuming
the old man was hard of hearing.

'Feel free,' he replied, devil-may-care, still not finding them worthy of his gaze.

Happy to take their leave, they headed quickly into the dust-covered riot of oddities.

'All right, Mr Ben, what have we got?' whispered Bob. 'Actually, it's more like *Steptoe and Son*, in here,' he said, correcting himself, looking around at a rag-and-bone man's heaven.

'I don't get either of those references,' said Scotty, in the same hushed tone.

'Oh, I forgot. The first few years of your life were all *CHiPs* and *The Love Boat*, back in the US of A,' he said, as a glimmer of light caught his attention on a nearby shelf.

It was a snow globe, doubling as a bookend for some illustrated books about sundials. Picking it up, he peered into the ornate setting within, and saw a vast mushroom cloud erupting in the middle of a bustling metropolis. A candle's flickering flame inches away added a disconcerting realism to the scene. 'Game over,' he said to himself. Deciding to leave it unshaken, he carefully replaced the globe, letting it resume its role of bookend.

'Bob, come take a look,' said a soft voice from somewhere within the shop's dark recesses.

Squinting, the light becoming dimmer the deeper he went, Bob followed the direction of the voice. 'Where are you?'

'Over here,' whispered the voice again. Bob moved cautiously towards where he thought 'over here' might be, his beer-sodden eyes struggling to adjust to the voids between the candlelight.

'You're getting closer,' – barely audible – 'and closer,' – verging on a hiss.

He stopped, realizing the candlelight had gone. 'Scotty?' Nothing.

His head started to swirl. Disorientated, he now stared blindly at a black wall. The tick-tock of the clocks had stopped, and a cloak of silence fell upon him. He spoke into its nothingness in a voice more panicked than he would have liked. 'This isn't funny,' he said. There was no response.

Long moments went by until suddenly the silence was broken by what sounded like a giant snake uncoiling.

Dread filled his chest, cold fingers grasped at his soul. He was a boy again, lost in the darkness, fearing a menace he couldn't see. He needed the light; he'd give anything to see the light again! He took a step backwards and turned. There was light there . . . but not the light of life. It was the kind of light you see before death.

Blindingly bright bone-white skin stretching over a freakishly long face was framed in a wreath of black. Blue veins cascaded over a bulbous, hairless cranium. Green gangrenous eyes with grey slits where pupils should be watched him hungrily. Dread held him in place as if frozen, as a screech split his ears, emanating from a mouth filled with rotting, yellow, razor-sharp teeth. It took Bob a moment to realize his own screams were intertwined with the demon's as its dreadful malice bore down upon him. Instinctively, his hands assumed a defensive posture, shielding his gaze from the unbelievable nightmare before him. The demon, its unholy screech turning into mocking laughter, knew that there was no escape for its prey.

Bob's final scream was drowned out as his destroyer spewed a shrill victory cry. 'DO I MAKE YOU SUICIDAL, BABY!? YEAH, BABY!!'

Everything stopped.

The realization that he'd been played, the immediate sweet relief that his mortal soul wasn't about to be dragged to hell, was replaced by indignation just as quickly.

'YOU MASSIVE PIECE OF SHIT!' he bellowed as Scotty removed his death mask, lowering the torch he'd used to highlight its evil glare, becoming once again the PG face of an international man of mystery.

'Shhhhh!' a deliriously inebriated Scotty implored through tears of laughter, gesturing back towards the shopkeeper. 'Your face, man!' That same face now more angry than scared. 'What? I thought you wanted some fun?' he said, still laughing.

'Not the kind that gives you a fucking heart attack!' said Bob, a smile now threatening to break out on his face.

'It's just like being kids again,' said Scotty, waving his frightful disguise. 'The last time I heard you scream like that was when your brother pushed you off that wall and you broke your arm.'

The smile that had threatened to break out on Bob's face vanished. 'What!? What are you talking about? Tom didn't push me,' he said, suddenly vexed.

'Yeah, he did.'

'He didn't!' Bob insisted, becoming even more agitated. 'We were just kids playing around. It was an accident.'

'If you say so,' replied Scotty, still chuckling, oblivious to Bob's consternation. 'Come on, Janet Leigh. I've found some potential duds.'

As Scotty headed off with the torch in one hand and the object of Bob's terror, now an innocuous sheath of flaccid rubber, in the other, Bob stood rigid, confused by the exchange. After long moments, he shook his head as if to reset the swell of uncertainty he felt. He then took a calming breath before heading in the direction of the torch's light.

'All right, this is it,' announced Scotty, as Bob arrived.

'Oh, joy. Oh, rapture. A landfill somewhere is missing its fill. It's a jumble sale, Scotty!' came his lacklustre response as he eyed the moth-eaten garments jammed on a clothes rack dimly lit by a handful of precariously placed candles. Scanning the surrounding area he saw a large trunk – *looks a bit more like a coffin* – filled with accessories: hats, scarves, wigs and the like. Completing his disappointment, he observed a series of wall-mounted shelves stacked with electrical goods – outdated cameras, phones, games consoles – once cherished possessions, now strewn haphazardly, forgotten and left to their antiquated shame in the dusty dark.

'This is where I shall "*Pretty Woman*" you,' said Scotty, tossing his horror mask back into the trunk.

'I was kind of hoping to get laid this evening? Slim chance of that happening if I go as a bus station vagrant.'

Scotty laughed. 'I'm no Mary Quant, but I think I can rustle something up.' And with that, he started to rifle through the clothing rack.

'Careful you don't rustle up a dose of smallpox going through that old shit,' said Bob, but Scotty was already too immersed in the hunt to respond.

'Oh yes! Inspiration strikes!' he said, excitedly pulling a black leather jacket from the rack. 'Take off your jacket and tie.' Scotty slid the leather on to Bob's frame, and then hung his suit jacket and tie on the rack.

'Oh, mamma. I like where this is going. Fits like a dream actually,' said Bob.

'I told you, O ye of little faith. Looks good against that pink shirt too,' he said, popping the jacket's collar whilst loosening a few buttons to reveal a generous offering of chest hair. Satisfied, he reached into the trunk. 'Now, where was that . . .' he asked himself, rummaging in the tat. 'Eureka!'

'The shirt's salmon,' scowled Bob. 'And what the hell is that?'

'The hairy cherry on the cake.' An excited Scotty was clutching a brown bouffant wig.

'That's going nowhere near my head,' Bob insisted.

'Don't be such a baby. You don't know how lucky you are. Imagine the hell of putting on a wig against a bald head. That's when shit gets real, my friend.'

'And then you have to go through the hell of taking it off and becoming bald again,' Bob scoffed.

'Why did it have to be me who went bald? Why not you? I so wish it was you.' He spun Bob around, made him crouch a little, and fitted the luxurious pelt on his head. 'Oh, sweet Jesus,' he gushed at his creation, ushering Bob to a nearby mirror. Peering over his shoulder, he introduced Bob to his reflection. 'There's my baby boy. You look like a real piece of ass.'

'Which part? The hole? Who am I supposed to be? Tonight, Matthew, I'm going to be fifty per cent of WHAM?'

'You're kidding, right? Don't you see it? The chest rug? The black leather? The beautiful shag of hair?' Bob stroked the wig, still unsure, 'You're the freakin' Knight Rider, man!'

'Well, I'm not much of a Knight Rider without the car, am I? Unless our friend here has a black Corvette out the back, I'm just a tit in a wig.'

'You don't get it, do you? Fancy dress is all about using your imagination. All we need is something to symbolize your connection to the car and you're good to go, *Michael,*' he said, in the voice of KITT, Michael's faithful crime-fighting car. 'And just so you know, KITT is a black Pontiac Trans-Am, you slow-witted boob.'

'All right, Mr Wonderful,' Bob said, watching Scotty engage in the hunt once again, his prey this time hidden amongst the old tech.

'No, that's not right,' he said, dumping a Speak & Spell back into the disorderly mess.

Bob was content to watch him, enjoying the feeling of being fussed over by his friend. Although he couldn't resist pushing the 'door open' button on an ancient grimy microwave. '*Ping*!' he smiled. 'Ahhhh, you can't beat roast chicken in a microwave.'

Beside him, Scotty had found something. 'Oh, that's close.' Then he thought better of it. 'But no cigar.' He tossed back a Sony Walkman.

Suddenly, he came to a halt. '*My precious*,' he hissed, charmed by something he'd found on the top shelf. 'Yes, yes and thrice yes,' he added, pushing aside anachronistic pieces that wouldn't find a home this evening. 'Meet the Knight Industries Two Thousand's latest communications device. Sleek, portable, sexy and fully electronic. KITT is now just the push of a button away.' On cue, he pushed a button that illuminated a display. 'Woah! It's still got a bit of juice in the tank,' he laughed, blowing dust off the contraption before hitting the off button and holding up the large, matt-grey eighties mobile phone, inches from Bob's face.

'Fully electronic, you say?' He snatched the old piece of junk out of Scotty's hand, shaking his head. 'Christ, this could be the shittiest fancy dress costume ever assembled. It makes no sense.'

'Makes no sense? The man fought crime with a talking car.'

'Yeah, fair enough,' Bob said, conceding the point. 'This is what I'm going to do. I'm going to go along with this farce, just to prove to you I can get laid even whilst looking like I've just stumbled out of a coke party at Gordon Gekko's house. This, for me,' – indicating his attire along with the phone – 'is a challenge, and I accept that challenge.'

'That's the spirit, Lovejoy!' said Scotty, with a wide grin.

They erupted into laughter. 'Come on. It's time we left this creepy dungeon.'

'I concur,' and they made to leave, but not before Scotty added, 'Hey, your jacket and tie?'

'Leave it.'

'Really?'

'Yeah. I don't want to carry it around all night, and it's almost out of season anyway.'

'Wow, Mr Big Time.'

The old man prised himself away from his book now that an exchange of goods and money was on the cards. For the first time, with his cloudy, milky-white eyes, he beadily regarded Bob and Scotty. 'Umph,' he grunted through a cloud of smoke, seemingly unimpressed, and then got to business. 'One Chez Verne durable, equine thread hairpiece,' he said, hitting a sequence of buttons on a cash register that clearly yearned for a time before decimalization. 'One Dr Lloyd's faux black leather jacket.' Again, surprisingly quick fingers stabbed at the till. 'That it?'

Bob was about to say yes, when he realized there was something bulky in his faux leather pocket.

'Oh. And this . . .' he said, producing the matt grey mobile. 'Sorry. I forgot it was there.'

For a fleeting moment, infinitesimal really – maybe it was a trick of the candlelight, maybe a wisp of smoke breaking formation – but he could have sworn the old waxwork looked . . . surprised. *Nah, it was nothing.*

'One cordless communications device.' Consulting the till, he announced, 'That's £300.'

'Three hundred quid!?' Bob guffawed. 'I've never paid so much money to look this bad,' he added, with a playful look to Scotty. 'But, my unusual friend, I'm feeling generous.' He took the money from his wallet and placed it on the counter.

The old man gave a mirthless chuckle. 'Are you feeling *brave*? That's the question,' he asked, whilst running a finger over the bundle before placing it in the till.

'Am I feeling brave?' Bob repeated, perplexed, as Scotty looked on, both enthralled and relieved that this powwow didn't involve him.

'Yes, brave? There's nothing more heroic than a heroic coward. There's nothing heroic about a fearless man. Wouldn't you agree?'

'What fortune cookie did you crack that nugget out of?' Bob said.

'Fortune?' he pondered to himself, before continuing with slow clarity, 'Yes . . . good. Interesting. Can one manifest one's own fortune?'

'Well, life's a box of chocolates. You never know what you're going to get,' Bob said, beaming his self-assured wolf's grin.

'If you're an idiot, yes. Or you could just read the inlay card that comes with the chocolates,' the old man replied. With a faint smile, he continued, 'We're born into the light, we live in the light, and we die into the light. That is an undeniable truth that cannot be altered . . . most of the time.'

'That's a lot of talk about light for a man who can't pay his electricity bill,' said Bob, stealing a glance into the candlelit gloom.

'Darkness strengthens the light.'

'Cosmic, baby,' a grinning Austin chipped in, revelling in this tête-à-tête.

Bob's focus stayed with the old man. 'If I may, I'd recommend a Chalkduster font, set on a field of lavender, at dusk, and you've got yourself another flawless inspirational Instagram post there,' he said, hoping to bring this curious interaction to an end.

The old man raised a quizzical eyebrow. 'What . . . is an Instagram?'

'OK. Well, this has been great,' Bob concluded, deciding this *was* the end. 'Mr Pickers-Gill, shall we?'

'Yup, time to skedaddle. Thank you, Sir. Great store, great . . . ambience,' he said, slightly bowing.

'I'll be sure to pass that on at the next shareholders' meeting,' said the shopkeeper.

They hurried towards the door, under the old man's watchful gaze, both suddenly eager to end this chapter of the evening.

Scotty was the first to exit and feel the sweet relief of the cool evening air. Bob, just behind him, without looking back, exclaimed, 'Continued success,' with a casual wave of his hand, before hearing an eerily accurate Gizmo falsetto. '*Bye, Bye, Bobby.*'

His hand on the doorknob, he stopped dead, and turned.

The old man's stare was fixed upon him. A smile

slowly formed around the ever-present pipe, spreading like cracks on glass. Long, brown, nicotine-stained teeth revealed themselves, crowded in a mouth that seemed too small for them.

A coldness ran along the ridges of Bob's spine. *I'd like to go now, please.* Bob slammed the door to *Always in Style* and hurried up the stairs.

5

After a longer than hoped for journey that saw their beer buzz diminish significantly, the sound of tyres on gravel announced their arrival at a much bigger than expected south-west London country home. Beyond the winding drive, the main building's true extent was concealed by darkness, but it was evident from the many windows visibly blazing with light that it was big – very big.

'Well, well. Miss Huxley is from money,' Bob quietly observed.

The drive eventually opened up into a large forecourt, overlooked by the house's mid-eighteenth-century facade, which was littered with high-end cars.

'Woah. It's like the Gumball Rally,' said Scotty, excitedly. 'Aston, Ferrari . . . oh man, that's a Lamborghini Aventador, 740 horses, V12 engine, 0–60 in 2.9 seconds, top speed 217.5 miles per . . .'

'All right, Rainman, relax.'

As they came to a halt, the sound of gravel giving way to rubber was replaced by an aggressive bass line originating from inside the house. Seizure-inducing lights flashed through windows that vibrated precariously, the days of chamber music a distant memory for the wafer-thin period glass.

Vacating their car, the raucous sound of music and

drunken hollering was suddenly undulled without the German-manufactured soundproofing. They stood before the impressive Neoclassical edifice, noting its beautiful, simplistic symmetry and towering columns that supported a temple-like pediment with a crest at the centre.

A nod and an unspoken *pretty nice* passed between them as they made the short walk to stand beneath the facade in front of a large, shiny, black door. Bob extended a manicured finger and pressed a brass nipple. The chime was lost amid the cacophony. After a polite twenty seconds, Bob repeated the procedure, holding the bell for a full minute until the door was eventually opened, revealing a vision that was worth the wait.

In a purple-and-gold bikini, bound in chains, a woman stood in the doorway against a backdrop of partygoers revelling in a phantasmagoria of sound, light and dry ice. 'You're late,' she said coolly.

Boys before a childhood fantasy, it took them both a second to engage their brains. 'Better than never, Princess Leia,' said Bob, recognizing the fantastically accurate costume . . . apart from its only inaccuracy: a long, red, braided ponytail.

'You got it!' she squealed, breaking her cool, and revealing that she was a little tipsy.

'Got it? I can almost smell Jabba's pleasure skiff,' added an entranced Scotty.

'Well, aren't you a sweet nerd for saying such a thing,' she giggled, turning her attention to their own get-ups. 'So, you . . . are Austin Powers.'

'Oh, behave,' he growled seductively, flashing his crooked grin. 'The shagadelic force is strong with this one.'

'Perfect!' she cried, with a clap of her hands. 'And who is Austin's friend?'

Bob struck a dynamic pose for her scrutiny, but somehow it came off more seventies' cologne model than crime-fighting hero.

'You're . . . ummm . . . George Michael?' she offered.

Bob gave Scotty an *I told you so* stare.

'No. I am *a* Michael, though.'

'Michael . . . Jackson?' she said, to Scotty's snickering amusement.

'So close,' said Bob, becoming a little agitated, 'but, this Michael is from the eighties, when that Michael was black. I'll give you a clue.' He removed the mobile from his jacket pocket, put its antiquated bulk to his ear, and attempted his best Michael Knight impression. '*KITT, go pick up my parents at the airport.*'

'What is that?'

'Really?! Michael Knight. The Knight Rider!'

'No, I mean what is that you're holding to your ear?'

'It's a phone.'

'It's massive.'

He shrugged. 'That's how they used to make 'em in the eighties.'

'I was born in ninety-six,' she said, before swivelling to address a bloated, gyrating Elvis who was screaming her name from the top of a sweeping staircase. She screamed back, laughing wildly.

'I forgot the phone died out as a form of communication in ninety-five,' growled Bob.

'Easy now, big fella,' said Scotty, as her attention snapped back to the tardy pair. 'Aren't you going to introduce me?'

'Of course, how rude of me. Scotty, allow me to present – by night, she might be a Princess, and property of the Hutt cartel – but by day she is an *invaluable* member of the FSB team, and goes by Miss Chloe Huxley.'

'Lovely to meet you, Scotty,' she said, with a playful curtsy and another drunken giggle.

'Thanks for having me. Love your place.'

'My place?' she snorted. 'This is Mum and Dad's, who are in St Moritz. When the cat's away,' she added, fixing her gaze on Bob. 'Great you could make it, Bob.'

'Oh please. Bob's my father's name. Call me Mr Bloomfield.'

'Oh sorry.' Suddenly mortified. 'I didn't mean to . . .'

'Relax, Chloe. I'm just messing with you,' he grinned. 'I'm not your boss tonight . . . I'm Michael Knight.'

'I'm still not sure who that is.'

'I'll send you the VHS.'

'A VH what?'

'Oh, for fu . . .' he began, finally at his wits' end.

'Ha-ha! Well, look at us, *Jabba*-ring away,' interjected Scotty, attempting to rescue Chloe from further torment. 'What do you say we head in and join the party?'

'Good idea,' she said, still apparently a little confused by the whole thing. 'It's chilly out here, and I'm not wearing much.'

She turned and entered the fray.

After a heartbeat taken to admire the turn, Scotty looked to Bob and mouthed *be nice*.

Inside was not as you might expect a large eighteenth-century country home to be. Yes, the standard sweeping staircases were present, but the expected exotic artefacts from far-flung places, oil paintings of old inbred English gentry, grandfather clocks that have been telling semi-accurate time for generations of privileged sons and daughters and bastards, were all missing. Ordinarily, all of the above would have been on display in all their dusty glory at the Huxley residence . . . but not tonight. Tonight, those clichés had been put into storage and replaced by an entirely different set of clichés – music, dance, drugs and sex.

Admittedly, these particular old English walls would have seen their fair share of music&dance&drugs&sex back in the day, but it's unlikely there would have been a laser light show, a Dubstep DJ called Praxis, and a city banker named Jeff dealing drugs out of a snakeskin briefcase in the basement.

'Holy shit,' said Scotty, surveying the mass of fancily dressed human depravity he was about to be part of.

'A dab'll do ya,' said Bob, viewing the same scenes of abandon and hedonism. 'It's Pacha in the countryside,' he shouted over the music.

'Pacha. Yeah, totally . . . what's Pacha?'

'Sorry, I forgot you're married with children.'

'You like?' shouted Chloe, handing Bob and Scotty a flute of champagne acquired from a passing server.

'It's adequate,' sniffed Bob, quaffing the golden fizz.

'It's awesome! Thanks again for having us, Chloe,' Scotty quickly added.

'You're very welcome. I'm going to circulate, so I'll drop in from time to time to see how you're doing,' she said to both of them. But it was Bob who got her last word. 'Stay out of trouble . . . Sir.' With a wink and a smile, she made her way into the crowd. Before the celebrators swallowed her up, the pair availed themselves of one last look at her scant form bathed in blue and red flashing lights, her chains reflecting momentary incandescent bursts through the dry ice stirred up on the throbbing dance floor, adding an almost celestial quality to an already unbearably alluring costume.

'Wow,' said Scotty, just as the last flash of Chloe disappeared from view.

'I concur.'

'She's a bit young for you though. Won't you get tired of people assuming she's your granddaughter?'

'I resent the implication, Sir! Our relationship is strictly one of a professional nature.'

'I'm not sure she sees it like that.'

'I'm not a maniac, I don't cross the streams.'

'Then why are you here?'

'Heavens to Betsy,' said Bob, with a pitiful look 'You poor bastard, you've been out of the game so long, Look around you.' He gesticulated at the packed dance floor and surrounding pockets of animated partygoers, a cornucopia of recognizable heroes and villains from past and present, chugging booze, keying sniff, flirting, popping pills, necking. 'These people don't work for me,' he finished with a cocked brow.

'Ohhhh,' Scotty said, Bob's scheme now becoming apparent. 'You sneaky bastard.'

'Nope. Just an old romantic looking for love,' said Bob with a huge grin, looking out at the sea of human possibility before him. Suddenly, his eye was caught by a man that stood by the stairs talking to a woman in a Barbarella costume. Bob's smile collapsed. The poet fedora hat, the ridiculously long scarf . . . the man was dressed as his dead brother's childhood hero.

Colin Baker had been the successor to Peter Davison. Those were the actors of Tom's era. But it was Tom Baker (possibly because they shared the same name) who he had loved with a fanatical intensity that almost seemed to worry his parents at the time. That had been the Dr Who for him.

'All right! Are we doing this or what? SBOD! SBOD! SBOD!' Scotty shouted over his shoulder.

By the time Bob turned to face him, he had already recovered his smile. But behind it, dark thoughts were gathering. He needed to vanquish them immediately.

10.49 p.m.

'Merry Christmas,' Bob wheezed, his face contorted in exquisite agony, as the fine white crystal powder liquified and dripped into his throat, delivering its bitter promise, numbing all it touched on its journey to multiply the dopamine in his brain circuits.

Extracting the rolled-up fifty, he pinched his nose and sniffed one more aggressive toot, making sure his snout wasn't harbouring any stubborn Bolivian guests. Satisfied, he stared at his reflection in the bathroom mirror. He studied the deepening lines of his face, the fine red broken veins in his cheeks and around his nose, the tell-tale signs of a life lived, for better or worse, staring back at him. 'Materially rich, spiritually empty,' he said to his reflection. 'I'd rather eat a hot bowl of cobra venom soup, than be you.'

A wave of sadness crashed over him.

'GET A GRIP!' he yelled into the mirror. Bouncing on the spot, he rolled his neck and shadow-boxed a few uncoordinated jabs at his reflection. 'An eagle doesn't look back. An eagle *never* looks back!' After splashing some cold water on his face, he straightened his wig and popped his collar.

'It's all good, Bobby,' he said, his composure returning.

'Are you OK, Sir?'

In the corner of the spacious bathroom, drafted in for the evening's festivities, surrounded by breath mints, cologne and washcloths, sat an old, smartly dressed toilet attendant. He'd been sitting there the entire time (apparently not worthy of discretion), watching Bob with equal measures of disbelief and concern.

'Never better.'

'Sometimes life doesn't turn out as we had hoped,' he said, with a nod to his paraphernalia.

'Do you want to know how to remedy that?'

'How?'

After taking the washcloth offered by the attendant, and dabbing his face, Bob said, 'Abandon hope.' And then dropped the rolled-up fifty into the tip tray.

11.05 p.m.

'It's a wonderful outfit. Very handsome. I've seen a few in my time and this is a cracker.'

'Thank you,' said the man dressed in an inflatable penis costume, who had been cornered on the stairs for far longer than he would have hoped, his ascent interrupted by an energized Bob's descent from the bathroom.

'Urinals.'

'Excuse me?'

'Urinals!' he shouted over the music into his bemused victim's ear as it protruded awkwardly out of his costume's engorged purple helmet. 'That's how I've seen a few in my time. I'm six-one – I get a lot of peripheral penis at the urinals. It's not something I can avoid,' said Bob with an embarrassed shrug.

'Lucky you,' the man replied, whilst frantically searching for his friends and an exit strategy.

'I'm not gay though. Just so you know.'

'Oh. I assumed you were.'

'Why?'

'Because you've been talking about penises at me for what feels like a long time, now.'

'Not gay. But I wish I was. Now there's a community that's mastered the art of no-strings. Lucky bastards.'

Deciding he'd finally had his fill of Bob, the penis man said, 'I'm going to go find my friends,' adding, 'excuse me,' but it was more of a request than a parting gesture. He stared blankly at Bob, waiting for a response.

'What?'

'You're standing on my balls,' he said, gesturing to where his feet should be. Looking down, Bob observed two huge hairy, rubber testicles, trapped beneath his size twelves.

11.40 p.m.

'We have a populace that's been infantilized to a point where they can't see the wood for the trees. Baby doesn't care what Mummy and Daddy are doing. All baby cares about is baby. All thoughts of society have been jettisoned. Self-aggrandization, self-importance, self-consumption are the new rules of engagement.' Preaching from within a cloud of cigarette smoke, a commanding, fast-talking, twenty-something female (dressed as a Ghostbuster, her name tag 'Tully' stitched into the fabric) stood before an enthralled group who were sat around her on bean bags in a converted dining room, where party patrons could seek conversation and respite from the flashing imagery and 120bpm.

Brushing a wayward strand of hair from her eyes, she took a quick sip of a dark liquid from a no-frills plastic pint glass (explaining her purple teeth) and continued. 'Our government has ceased to govern. Their own interests comprise the daily agenda without a second's thought for the misery and poverty beyond Whitehall. Those are the inconsequential problems of people they will never meet.

'What does reality TV teach us? Bad behaviour is an asset and will be rewarded. Got a sex tape? Here's the keys to the kingdom. Got a moral compass? Sorry, a sense of right and wrong isn't marketable, you're not going viral. Civility gets you nowhere!

'Film is just as stupid and insidious. They used to throw propaganda leaflets from aeroplanes for free. Now they call them superhero movies and charge you thirty pounds a head to watch them. Sleep easy baby, the bed bugs won't bite because Captain America will save us from the Nazis. Iron Man, what a *hero*. Batman, such an *inspiration* – if only Rosa Parks had sat at the front of the fucking Batmobile maybe then this lobotomized generation would know of her courage.' The gathering broke into applause, but Tully silenced them with a raised cigarette-holding hand. 'Our sporting "heroes" are not worthy of the title. Do I see a team that represents my country, or do I see a team comprised of a rapist, an adulterer, a drug user, a racist, a sexist, a homophobe . . . a man who sleeps with his own brother's wife!? These people do not represent me!

'We have forgotten what truly matters, my friends. It's not material wealth, it's not celebrity and it's definitely not keeping Britain British. Here's the simple solution – cast out fear. CAST. OUT. FEAR. We need to look beyond this little island and its outdated jingoistic bullshit. We need to come together on a global scale! We need to accept and respect each other's cultures and religions, or we die. Don't listen to the naysayers. It is possible to maintain your own identity even whilst integrating with other people's, regardless of one's chosen beliefs. When we achieve this, I believe we will say goodbye to every negative we have ever known. Say goodbye to reality TV, say goodbye to celebrity magazines, say goodbye to the fucking newspapers.' A wave of applause erupted from her transfixed disciples. She allowed them their moment, using the time to inhale and exhale her nicotine. 'And I promise you,' she continued, as the clapping subsided, 'experiencing different ways of life – language, music, food, art – will enhance the path you've chosen to walk.'

'The best thing, for me,' interjected Bob, who had been leaning against the fireplace watching Tully's grandstanding with an arch expression on his face, 'about a multi-cultured, multi-faith society is that there's always going to be someone who will work in Tesco's on Christmas Day. I don't mind putting in a shift at my local corner shop on Ramadan. I'm a team player,' he concluded, as the whole gathering watched him take a large gulp of whisky from the tumbler in his hand.

'That's an incredibly insensitive thing to say,' a twenty-something male, dressed as Snow White, suggested from the comfort of his Union Jack bean bag.

'Is it, princess? You lot need to chill out. Politics and diversity? You do realize you're at a banging house party, yes? You sound like you're about to storm Nuremberg.'

'Hey, boring guy by the fireplace,' said Tully, annoyed by the continued interruption, 'wake me up before you go-go, yeah?' she said, to the laughing delight of her acolytes.

'Actually . . .' Bob began, flustered by her put-down, 'I'm Michael Knight.'

'Fuck off, grandad!'

Bested, he retreated to pastures new.

12.31 a.m.

Bob and Scotty were wrestling their way through a bottleneck built up in a hallway that led to the bar. They shovelled handfuls of food snatched from a passing waiter's tray into their mouths.

'Whoopsie!' said Bob, reaching down to the sticky floor to pick up his cheese-and-pickle on a stick hors d'oeuvre. Dusting it off, he quickly popped it into his intoxicated mouth. 'Five-minute rule!' he declared, catching the eye of an attractive woman's approximation of Mia Wallace, on a similar pilgrimage to the bar.

'I think you mean five-second rule,' she corrected.

'Health and safety gone mad,' he replied with a grin. 'Man, that's good cheese. Who doesn't love cheese? Let me ask you this. Don't you think food and sex need to progress? Why are we stuck in this fruit and cream realm? What about some nice Manchego?'

She laughed, 'Ew, gross!'

'How about some Dairylea?' slurred a smashed Scotty.

'Who are you? The spy who shagged cheese?' she quipped to Bob's laughter.

'YEAH, BABY, YEAH!' screamed Scotty in delight.

1.30 a.m.

'IN OR OUT?!' someone amongst the frenzied group shouted, offended by the light from the hallway pouring in around Bob, highlighting their contorted flesh, an orgy of mayhem liberated from the pile of costumes discarded on the floor.

Startled more than offended (Bob was well accustomed to the sort of group dynamics better suited to darkness), he stepped back into the hallway, quickly closing the door, to give the question of 'in or out?' serious consideration. That was when someone asked in a familiar voice, 'Having fun?'

'Muchly,' he said, turning to face a surprisingly fresh face. 'Nice of you to drop in, Chloe.'

'I see you've taken the tour,' she said, looping her arm through his and gently guiding him back towards more wholesome climes via small clusters of people dotted about the hallway. 'Where's Austin?'

'I left him on a couch in a state of low defensive readiness.'

'A what?'

'He's drunk, completely smashed in fact. So, I decided to explore – pull back the curtain, as it were.'

'And did you like what you saw?'

'Oh yes. It's quite the commotion.'

'The night's young,' she said, gesturing over her shoulder. 'I wouldn't commit to that, just yet. But I bet I can take your evening to the next level,' she added, running a lime-green fingernail along her collarbone, and then down to the curve of her breast.

'Chloe . . .' he said, alarmed, 'I don't think that's a good idea . . .'

'*Relax*, Mr Bloomfield,' she laughed, reaching into her cleavage. The sturdy construction of the princess's gold bikini provided a secure resting place for a perfectly rolled, extra-fat, skunk-filled spliff. 'I meant this.'

'Oh. Marijuana? The old Moroccan Jazz Cabbage. It's not really something I've ever done,' he said, with oodles of faux innocence.

'Yolo! You only live once, right?' she said, firing up the B-class sheath.

'Actually, there's no empirical evidence that confirms that.'

'So, is that a yes or a no? I don't want to get in the way of you living forever,' she said, raising her voice to compensate for the increased volume of the music as they were now stood above the dance floor below. After a moment or two of hesitation, he answered her question by snatching the fat blunt.

'To good health,' he toasted, sucking at its lipstick-smeared roach, filling his chest with the dense, potent psychotropic. He held its smoky cargo for over a minute in a pair of lungs better suited to Olympic swimming, before slowly exhaling a cloud stripped of its contents. 'Is that how it's done?'

'Well, aren't you full of surprises,' she beamed, genuinely impressed by his aggressive 'first-time' usage. Weed might not have been Bob's first drug of choice, but he did have a small collection of *very* expensive Moroccan bongs, along with a smorgasbord of his actual first drugs of choice, in a hidden cabinet behind his comprehensive bedroom mirror. 'You're a bit of a mystery to us underlings at the office, you know?' Chloe added, deciding to venture a little deeper into the abandoned mine shaft that was Bob Bloomfield's life.

'What do you need to know, beyond: I'm your boss?' he replied flatly.

'Where did you grow up?' she asked, ignoring the curtness of his reply and retrieving her joint.

'Earth.'

'Very funny. Where in England?'

'South.'

'OK,' she said, deciding to move on to a more general line of questioning, 'are you a cat or a dog man?'

'Dog.'

'What's wrong with cats?'

'Nothing. Yes, I admit cats do fantastic work with the blind and law enforcement, but I'm just more of a dog person.'

'I think cats get a bad rap.'

'OK. Well, you let me know when a cat has a statue erected in their honour, and we'll talk some more on the subject. Next question.' He was starting to enjoy himself for reasons he couldn't quite pinpoint.

'Do you have a party trick?'

'I can fart the alphabet.'

'Ahhhh! That's disgusting!' she laughed. 'What music are you into?'

'Anything that was discovered on a talent show.'

'Really? I like the oldies, myself. What's your favourite film?'

'Anything with my boys Vin Diesel and Jason Statham.'

'So, you're an action man,' she cooed. 'When's your birthday?'

'March 12th.'

'You're a Pisces.'

'Apparently.'

'Now we're getting somewhere!' she said, as if she'd just split the atom. 'Pisces means you're sensitive, intuitive, and self-sacrificing by nature. But most of all . . . a bit of a dreamer.'

'Really? You know who else was a Pisces?'

'Who?'

'Osama Bin Laden. Not really an exact science is it, astrology?' He felt the first wave of the reefer's caress lapping against his mind.

'What?! Shut up!' Chloe hee-hawed, giving him a playful punch on the shoulder.

'You shut up!' Bob giggled, returning the playful tap to her bare shoulder. *Oh shit, here it comes!*

He was correct.

Whisky and cocaine were being substituted from the field of play. It was an early shower for those unable to adapt to a game that was about to change, and he could feel that change intensifying. A tingling warmth trickled down his spine like hot molasses. More evidence of the impending inter-dimensional shift.

'I'm starting to feel . . . really nice.'

'That's why it's a miracle herb,' said Chloe, looking upon the glowing joint with awe. 'It can even make a twat like you nice,' she said, with three quick, hard tokes.

He watched her imbibe, transfixed.

The lights from the laser show on the dance floor below strobed to a decidedly aggressive bass line. The effect slowed her actions, giving her a staccato, robot-like look. In Bob's pot-addled mind, she took on the aspect of a hologram, much like Princess Leia, à la 'Help me, Obi-Wan Kenobi. You're my only hope.'

'*Help me Obi-Wan, I'm high on dope,*' he said, through a thousand-yard stare. Running the words over and over in his mind, a pressure began to build within him. What started as the slow rhythmic caress of a feather duster sweeping the inner lining of his stomach, soon erupted into an exquisite rush of laughter.

After what seemed like an eternity: his eyes streaming, his stomach aching, his face throbbing from the exertion of using muscles unfamiliar with the joy of laughter with such abandon, the strobing slowed, bringing Chloe's delicate features back into focus. It was then that he realized what had just happened.

'Hold on. What? Did you just call me a twat?'

'Did I ruin your buzz?' she asked, unabashed. 'Don't get paranoid. Ride the wave. Here, take another hit.' He cautiously accepted the offering. 'There you go. Let those hard edges melt away,' she purred, watching him take another large suck.

Am I paranoid, or is this girl messing with me? he thought, holding another Olympic-sized cloud in his polluted lungs.

'OK, I have to circulate. I must continue my hostess with the mostest duties. I'll catch up with you later.'

'You're leaving?'

'Just for a little while.'

'OK,' he said, scoping his surroundings like an impala in open terrain.

'You'll be fine,' she soothed, sensing his reticence. 'Have a wander and enjoy the world with your new ganja eyes,' she added, with more than a hint of mischief in her green ganja eyes. 'One last thing, if you really are hell-bent on avoiding me this evening. Just so you know, I'll be in the room with the lights *on*. I like to see that shit.'

Be it through the heady cocktail of drugs and liquor, or the outrageous level of candour on Chloe's part, Bob, for the first time, was rendered speechless by someone he considered a subordinate. Wordlessly, he offered her back the reefer.

'Keep it,' she said casually, before walking away.

She's definitely messing with me.

2.03 a.m.

'SBOD!' The volume of DJ Praxis's music was once again an issue. 'Super black-out drunk!' he shouted into the ear of Little Red Riding Hood, her red cape (all the

65

more vivid against her ebony skin) and thigh-high boots had alerted his lupine senses from across the room. 'I suppose the irony is you never know if you're SBOD until the next day. I have no way of knowing if I'll remember this chit-chat tomorrow. That's the tragedy,' Bob slurred, with a quick toke of the joint that had taken up residence in his right hand, the left being the fixed abode of a whisky glass once again (yes, he had made the executive decision that whisky did indeed have the legs to re-enter the game, even at this late stage of play).

She placed a blonde pigtail over her ear, a buffer to Bob's deafening ramblings. 'Why don't you try not getting so drunk?' she said, more annoyed than curious.

'Where's the joy in that?'

'Memories?'

'Wait a minute, Red. Are you trying to tell me you are not drunk?' he asked, squinting through bloodshot eyes at his watch (Franck Muller, Master of Complications, one of ten ever made: £10,000) 'at 2.05 a.m.?'

'Yes, I'm sober. This is ginger ale,' she replied, indicating the drink in her hand and gesturing to her friends making up the semi-circle Bob had infiltrated.

'I could do with a crystal-clear memory in the morning to tell me how all this went,' he said, attempting his most winning smile, which unfortunately came across more stroke victim, than come hither.

'I can tell you right now. It's not going well,' she said, her face a picture of embarrassment for this heavily intoxicated man, whose asinine intentions were clear to all. 'You're old and weird,' she went on. 'So, I think I'll use my excellent memory for more important things, like remembering to buy toilet roll.' The semi-circle laughed at her effortless take-down.

A man dressed as Keith Flint of The Prodigy (the words 'party starter' emblazoned in fire on his chest) added, 'You do have a weirdly good memory. Did you know that she can remember every number in her phone?' he asked the gathered group, who had already lost interest in Bob.

Just too damned wrecked to compute the rebuff, Bob persisted. 'You can remember all the numbers in your phone? That's amazing. My memory's shit with stuff like that. Although . . .' He took a moment to burp into his hand. 'Excuse me. I can remember the first phone number I ever had when I was a kid. Of course, back in those days that was what you would call a "landline".'

'Riveting. It's been fun, Jeremy Clarkson,' said Red, eliciting a last laugh from her group.

'I'm Michael Knight, guys. Check me out!' he declared, fumbling the eighties house brick from his jacket pocket. He clumsily poked at its sparing amount of buttons and its green display sprung into life.

Blinking into the green glow of its now active screen, he attempted to marry up the multiple images of the phone's buttons that swirled a drunken dance in his vision. Slowly, as ash fell upon the digits, he punched the old number into the seasoned phone. When completed, he celebrated with a toke and a mad chuckle into the fiery glow of his joint, 'Okey smokey. KITT, ring 0175 6634.'

He pushed his best guess at the dial button and the display announced – *Calling* . . .

'Holy shit!' exclaimed Bob. 'It's ringing!' An update intended for Little Red Riding Hood and Co., but they weren't paying any attention to him. The cold shoulder was still very much in effect. 'Guys! It's . . .'

'*Hello, Bloomfields*',' a tired young voice answered.

Hearing his surname immediately grabbed Bob's attention.

'What's that? Who's this?' he said, trying to mute his surroundings by jamming a finger in his free ear, whisky sloshing from his glass into his wig. 'Did you say *Bloomfield?*'

'*Yeah,*' the voice confirmed, sounding just as confused as Bob.

'And this is 0175 6634?'

'*Yeah,*' he confirmed, stifling a yawn. '*It's really late. I gotta go back to bed.*'

'Wait, woah, woah, woah. Just a sec . . .' Bob left the periphery of the dance floor in search of a quieter spot. He stumbled his way as quickly as his rubber legs would carry him back to the bean bag room, remembering a narrow staircase at the back with a secluded nook out of general sight. Privacy secured, he continued, 'Is this 231 Grove Hill?' A long pause followed Bob's inquiry, a slight crackle in the connection filling the void. 'Hello. Still there?'

'*I gotta go to bed. I've got football in the morning,*' he said, his voice now shifting from tired to suspicious. '*I'm not supposed to talk to strangers.*'

'Hold your horses. I don't think I am a stranger. Do you live at 231 Grove Hill? Because if you do, that's where I used to live.'

'*We live at 231.*'

'Mental!' Bob whooped in amazement, shaking off a little drunkenness in the process. 'We must be related. Are we cousins? Do I know your parents? Did my parents sell you the house?'

'*I don't know,*' he replied, sounding overwhelmed by the cross-examination.

'How long have you been there?'

'*Forever.*'

'So, since you were born?'

'*Ahhh . . . yeah, I think so.*'

'How old are you?'

'*I really need to go to bed.*'

'Just a minute more. What difference is a minute going to make? What are you, nine? Ten?'

'*I'm twelve!*' he said, clearly offended.

'All right, we got ourselves a big boy,' Bob chuckled. 'Do you think you could stay up a little longer or does baby need his beddy-byes?'

'*I can stay up as late as I want,*' he declared defiantly.

'My man,' said Bob, draining the last of his whisky. 'Now, let's figure this out. What's your dad's name?'

'*Dad's John,*' he said, sighing irritably.

The unexpected answer threw Bob momentarily. 'Did you say John? J-O-H-N?'

'*Yeah. John Bloomfield.*'

Bob's face lost its sloppy drunk and happily high

air. 'Weird. That's my father's name,' he said, his brow knitting furiously. 'What's your mother's name?'

'*Judy.*'

'Mine too,' he whispered, feeling his pulse quicken, each beat clearing the drunken-drug addled fog of his mind, edging him a little closer to sobriety. *What are the chances of another family moving into our old house, with the same surname . . . AND Mum and Dad have the same Christian names . . . billion to one.*

'What's your name?' he asked. Time seemed to slow down as he prepared himself for the answer.

'*Robert.*'

Bob's world started to spin.

The tumbler slipped through his fingers, shattering on the floor.

'*So, we're related? You know Mum and Dad?*' asked the boy. But Bob couldn't hear him. A pressure was building in his ears, drowning out everything apart from that one word: *Robert.*

He brought the simmering joint before his eyes, noticing the golden cherub getting precariously close to his fingertips. A few thoughts simultaneously occurred in his rapidly clearing mind. *What is happening? I must be high as eagle dick. Where's Scotty?*

The last question took precedence. Peering out from beneath the stairs, he frantically searched the space before him, expecting to see Scotty's smiling face with a phone pressed to his ear. 'GOT YOU!' But he was nowhere to be seen. *He's in no fit state to pull off a wind-up of this magnitude anyway.*

The pressure in his head reached its zenith, popping like a balloon, leaving a high-pitched buzzing in its wake. When it eventually cleared, a voice spoke from the phone. *'Hello . . . you still there?'*

'Yes,' he answered in disbelief, 'still here . . . Robert.' He dropped the joint to the floor and crushed it beneath his heel, broken glass splintering and grinding in the process.

'Why do you wanna know all that stuff?'

'I had to be sure,' he said, cautiously, his mind scrambling to get a grip on the reality of what was happening, 'but now I know. I'm a family friend.'

'So, you do know my Mum and Dad?'

'I do. Your dad's middle name is Andrew and our . . . *your* mother doesn't have a middle name.'

'That's right!' he said, sounding impressed for the first time. *'Do you know my middle name?'*

'It's John.'

'Wow! Yeah, like Dad. Do you know Tom's?'

A lead weight dropped on Bob's chest. The air left his lungs with such ferociousness he was pitched forward, doubled in agony. He reached out and steadied himself against the underside of the stairs, fearing he could collapse into a broken heap. He hadn't heard his brother's name spoken without pain, sorrow and regret in thirty-seven years. He forced himself to breathe, feeling the warm rise of tears in his eyes. 'Henry,' he said, trying to keep emotion out of his voice. 'How is he?'

'He's in trouble.'

'How?'

'He got into a fight in school, so Dad grounded him.'

The memory of the incident pushed through the alcohol and drugs and began to form in Bob's mind. 'Some boys tried taking his ball from him.' He hadn't seen the altercation but he could recall his father angrily handing out the punishment.

'*That's right. How did you know that?*' the boy asked in wonder.

'It's always something like that when you're in school, isn't it,' he said, as he considered his options for a moment. 'Sounds like Tom gets into a bit of trouble now and again?'

'*Yeah, he does. Tom gets angry really easy,*' said Robert, with a gentle laugh.

'You need to watch his back. Look after him.'

'*I do.*'

'Are you sure? I know how annoying little brothers can be. Do you pick on him a bit, now and again?'

'*I don't,*' he said, too quickly.

'You don't? Well, that's great. When I was your age, I had a little brother and I bullied him terribly. Not only did I bully him, but I bullied kids at school too. I don't know why, but I always felt worthless and I thought if I could make someone else feel the same way, I'd feel better.' He paused, hearing the boy's faint shallow breathing down the line. He sensed he had a captive audience and continued. 'The funny thing was that hurting people never made me feel good. It made me feel worse. But I kept doing it because I didn't know any other way. And then one day I ran out of people to hurt . . . there was no one left. I was on my own. And it was then I realized, when it was far too late, that I'd been hurting myself the most all along. I wish I could speak to my younger self and tell him that there's a better way to live. Do you know what I would say to him, Robert?'

'*What?*' he asked, softly.

'I'd say, I don't want you to end up sad and lonely, like me. So, I'm going to give you the best advice anyone has ever given you. And if you do what I tell you, you're going to be happy. The quickest way to happiness is to make other people happy. Compassion, caring, helping people, that's where true happiness lies. You have to appreciate people, respect who they are, don't be judgmental, be humble when the hand of friendship is offered. You have to open yourself to people. If you want someone to like you, be likeable.' Bob's words led him to think of his own evening up until that point: the toilet attendant, penis-costume guy, Tully and her disciples, Little Red Riding Hood and his host, Chloe. 'Instead of belittling people, your new mantra, your new mindset is this . . . you're going to ask people: "How are you? What can I do for you? Do you need help?" That's the key, three simple words: How. Are. You? *Help* people. Don't push them away. Lower your protective shield and take a chance or you will end up on your own. You don't have to become what I am,' he pleaded, trying to calm the urgency in his voice. 'Does that sound like good advice, Robert?'

'*Yeah . . . it does,*' he replied, his voice trembling.

'I'm glad you agree. I'm proud of you.' *It's time, Bob.* 'Do you trust me?'

'*I think so.*'

'Good, because there's something I need to tell you. It's going to be hard for you to hear, but you have to believe me or something terrible is going to happen.'

'*OK,*' Robert said, sounding nervous.

'It's going to be OK. You can handle this, Robert,' he began, feeling the weight of the moment bearing down on him. 'You and your brother Tom . . . are going to . . .'

'*What the bloody hell is going on!?*' asked a distant voice on the other end of the line.

'Robert, listen to me . . .'

'*Who are you talking to this late?!*' That voice again, a woman's voice, angry, much closer now, looming.

'NO! ROBERT STAY WITH ME!' Bob shouted into the phone, 'ROBERT!' But it was no use, he had lost him.

'*I was getting some water and the phone went. It's OK, he's a family friend,*' Bob heard him say to the woman.

Bob knew her voice well. Its strident pitch had been a permanent feature of his childhood.

'*GIVE ME THAT PHONE NOW!*' There was a thud as the phone changed hands. '*HELLO, who is this . . . WHO IS THIS! WHAT HAVE YOU BEEN SAYING TO MY S—*'

He yanked the phone from his ear as if it were a hot coal, before repeatedly hitting its buttons with such force its flimsier modern counterpart might have shattered. All illumination on the display abruptly ceased, returning the phone to its previous state of lifeless, innocuous antiquation.

'What just happened?' he said, breathlessly jamming the phone into his pocket as his heart thumped like a battering ram against his chest. He exited his nook-sanctuary. 'I need a drink.'

Eyes wide in disbelief, he wandered confused and scared, feeling like he had just followed a rabbit and tumbled into a deep hole.

Frantically he pushed past people who now looked distorted and ugly, dancing and screaming like fevered hallucinations in their strange masquerade costumes.

Whisky. Must find whisky.

Mercifully, clearing the suffocating crowd, he found a bottle of old faithful . . . and then set course for his favourite place . . . annihilation.

6

His eyes opened and there was music playing. It was an unsettling sound that made his brain anxious for reasons he couldn't remember as yet. That brain's outer casing, his dense throbbing head, was nestled in a deep white pillow. It took a moment for his vision to focus and flip the horizontal image of the clock's digital message of the hour.

Two thoughts occurred, one of them troubling:

1. 9.00 a.m. is later than Bob would generally get up (no matter what time he went to bed).
2. It was not his clock.

The troubling answer as to who the clock's owner might be came quickly and devastatingly.

A pale arm reached over him, and he watched in horror as a lime-nailed hand pressured the clock and Jefferson Airplane into silence, the white rabbit instantly disappearing down the hole. Retracting the elegant appendage, the clock's owner gave a satisfied moan of pleasure into the quietness, before wriggling her warm body into a spoon around Bob. He felt hard breasts compress against the muscles of his back and short, tight legs tuck under his bare buttocks. *Bob, you soft-skulled moron!*

Transforming from a spoon to a man full of instant

regret, he broke formation. Sitting on the edge of the bed, the full panorama, highlighted by searing light pouring in through two huge curtain-less windows, was revealed to him.

Disorientated and ravaged by excess, he found himself in a large bedroom with a fireplace still nursing its smouldering remains. The brightness of the light streaming in through the windows was enhanced by the room's contents, which were all white – white bed, white chest of drawers, white chairs, white cupboards, white vanity station.

In fact, the only items breaking the room's *One Flew over the Cuckoo's Nest* loony-bin continuity were Bob's clothes, draped over a shabby colonial chair (the bouffant wig resting on top of them like a watchful guinea pig), numerous exhausted condom wrappers, a plentiful collection of empty green champagne bottles and a lonely blue bottle of Johnnie Walker Blue Label (missing its contents), perched on his white side table.

'Huxley reporting for duty, Sir,' came an enthusiastic declaration behind him.

'Oh shit, no,' he said, turning slowly to see Chloe's smiling face propped up on her elbow. Green eyes (far too alert for the hour) peered out from behind a mess of red hair, cascading over naked shoulders, all the more vivid against the white of the bed sheets.

'Oh shit, *yes*. Bravo you and Brava me.'

'Chloe . . . this was a mistake.'

'Well, you were mistaken *many* times. You kept telling me you were in love with me,' she said.

'I . . . I . . .'

She burst into maniacal laughter. 'I'm fucking with you. Jesus. You're so serious all the time.'

He got up to retrieve his trousers. Slipping them on, he watched her with a growing sense of unease.

'Let's do something,' she grinned back at him. 'How about breakfast, my treat?'

'Chloe, this was a mistake,' he said, buttoning up his shirt. 'I'm your boss and old enough to be the guy your mother is having an affair with.'

'If you're not hungry we can skip breakfast. But I want to see you again.'

'And you will, at work on Monday. Where I expect our professional relationship to resume, and no mention of this . . . ever,' he said, attempting a tone of authority, only to be undermined by the effort to flatten his chaotic bed hair.

'If this is a discretion thing, then you needn't worry. I won't tell your wife.'

'My wife!?' It was now Bob's turn to laugh. 'I'm not married. You might want to think about cutting back on the weed.' He slipped on his jacket. 'Now, if you will excuse me, must dash, I have some work to finish up at the office,' he concluded.

'I bet you do. Someone has to save the children. And those pictures of stick figures being fellated by fish aren't gonna draw themselves . . . Sir.'

Observing her impishly confident grin and bright, piercing green eyes, it was at that moment that Bob finally realized he had severely underestimated Chloe

Huxley. Be it through poor judgment, complacency or arrogance, the manipulator had allowed himself to become the manipulated. What Chloe's end game might be at this stage he had no clue. But he definitely had cause for concern.

'I should . . . go,' he said, hurriedly turning to leave.

But Chloe had other ideas. 'You sure I can't interest you in . . .' she lifted the bedsheet.

After a millisecond of hesitation he made a break for it.

'MR BLOOMFIELD!'

Jesus, what now? He turned.

Pressed against her ear, she held an antiquated eighties mobile phone. 'Call me,' she said.

He reached out and, with a devilish grin, she placed the phone in his hand.

'I know we need it to sustain all life on Earth,' he said, squinting through an insufficiently tinted window, 'but does the sun have to be *so* bright?'

'Heavy one?' asked the chauffeur, the rear-view mirror filled with his smile.

'An evening of significant weight, yes,' replied Bob.

Aching for the solitude and recuperative powers of his penthouse apartment (he had no intention of going to the office – *'I have to work'* was his standard response when extracting himself from the dreaded sleepover or the, even more bone-chilling, breakfast date), he sat in the comfort of a reclined leather seat watching the world go by in a blurred hum of Saturday morning activity, when suddenly the silence was broken by a buzzing from his inner jacket pocket. Removing his iPhone, he looked at the screen: *incoming call KIRSTY*.

After declining the call with the kind of speed a bullet leaving a gun would be proud of, Bob saw that this was one of six missed calls from Kirsty over an eight-hour period, and this information made him laugh, a jubilant laugh, a laugh that lifted his spirits considerably.

'Good news?' asked the driver, his grin once again filling the rear-view mirror.

'Not for a dear friend of mine,' he said through more snorts of laughter. 'Scotty, you maniac, she's going to eat your heart. But that's what happens when you marry a Disney witch. Poor bastard.'

7

17
18
19

Watching the numbers escalate, Bob felt the poison, the doubt, the insecurities, ebb away.

20
21
22
23

He'd arrived.

The doors silently parted, revealing an opulent corridor. Along its elegant length were a beautifully elaborate herringbone wooden floor, grey ashen walls sporting gently lit, framed pencil drawings of various creatures from the animal kingdom, an ottoman that had never been sat on and a black bust of a handsome Roman perched atop a slim plinth. All very familiar and welcome sights to him, but the most welcome of all was the door at the end of the corridor to his apartment. With a smile, he exited the lift, each step making him feel lighter, his burdens left far below.

Reaching the thick, red Jarrah wood door that was the portal to his sanctum, he held his iPhone over a small cylindrical sensor embedded in the doorframe. A satisfying soft beep signalled he was permitted to enter.

As the door closed behind him, he leaned his shattered carcass against the cool wood. Closing his eyes, he breathed deeply, basking in the moment, rejoicing in its cold assurance of serenity: *Goodbye cruel world – hello peace and tranquillity.*

'WHERE THE FUCK HAVE YOU BEEN!'

'CHRIST ALMIGHTY!' he screamed, his brittle head hitting the back of the door with such force he could only assume stitches would be needed. 'KIRSTY?! What the . . .?!? You scared the shit out of me,' he said, reflexively feeling the already rising welt on the back of his head. Thankfully his fingers showed no traces of blood. 'What are you doing?'

'I've been calling and calling you!' she seethed, waving her phone at him to punctuate the point. Throwing the phone on to the couch, she placed both hands on her hips, the poster girl for beautiful indignation in jeans and a white T-shirt, smack bang in the middle of Bob's living room for reasons he could not fathom.

'Yes, I noticed,' he said, perplexed.

'Where were you? Why didn't you answer?'

'Why didn't I answer?' he echoed in disbelief. 'Listen, Kirsty,' he rubbed at his eyes, as if hoping to erase the nightmare that stood before him, 'I don't know what this is, but you've crossed a line coming here. Not cool after the night I've had. You're freaking me out big time. That aside, believe me when I tell you, I have no idea where he is. As I've stated in the past, he's a big boy, and he can look after himself. You need to get a grip. This crazy frothing-at-the-mouth, wife-on-a-warpath thing is gross, and beyond the pale. So, in closing, if you don't mind, off with you demon to the house that Mummy and Daddy built.' With that, he stepped aside and opened the door he was recently assaulted by, signalling with a stern hand the empty rectangle by which she should exit.

Crossing the room, to his great relief, she seemed about to take him up on his offer. At least that's what he was led to believe, until she came to a full stop and closed the door with a finality that was as baffling as it was alarming.

'You should be in the corridor now. Yet you're *still* here.'

'Robert,' she said, losing her angry edge and shifting to concerned and confused, 'you have no idea where who is? Who can look after himself?'

'*Robert*? Who are you, my mother?'

She repeated the question. 'You have no idea where who is?'

'Ummmmm, your idiot husband.'

'Ummm, he's here.'

'He's here?' said Bob, his eyes darting around the apartment. 'When? When did he get here? Oh! Wait a minute, he put you up to this?' he said, feeling the penny drop. 'Of course, he's got the only spare, that's how you got in. You pair of tinkers! What a stitch-up. All right you evil bastard, you can come out now!' he shouted into the apartment, brushing past Kirsty.

'Robert,' she said, grabbing his arm, 'I don't know what you're talking about. You're starting to scare me.'

'Wow! So, you're staying in character, you're properly committing to this?' he said, noting the confusion and concern still etched on her face. 'Very impressive, Miss Dench. Stellar work. I gotta say, I didn't think you had it in you, but this is a first-rate wind-up. Although, and I know those that can't create, critique, but I must say, you keep calling me Robert – it's *weird*, it takes me out of the performance. That's my only production note. Apart from that, you're very good. Do you have representation?' he asked, whilst attempting to detach her hand from his arm. 'I get it, I've been punked. Well done. YOU CAN COME OUT NOW!' he yelled into the apartment.

Tightening her grip, she yanked his arm, *hard*. 'Robert, for fuck's sake, STOP!'

'Hey! What the hell, Kirst?'

'*Please* . . . please stop. What's going on? Where have you . . .' her sentence trailed off as she registered that the material she gripped so firmly was not one of Bob's omnipresent suits. 'Why are you wearing a leather jacket?'

'Didn't you know? I'm playing Danny Zuko in this little farce,' he laughed, finally separating his arm from her steely grip. 'OK, enough's enough, let's bring the curtain down, shall we. It's the final bow for all principal actors,' Bob clapped his hands together in sarcastic applause. 'This is all a bit much after a SBOD evening, don't you think? PICKLEDICK!' he said, raising his voice again, and heading to the dining room to begin his search.

'Stop shouting. You're going to wake him.'

Bob came to a halt. *Bingo!*

'Wake him? Having a little nap is he?' He followed Kirsty's eyes to his office door adjacent to the living room. 'Such a baby!' he cried, vaulting over a couch before barrelling through the door. The interior was steeped in darkness. He flicked a switch, calling out 'Wakey-wakey, dipsh—' *What the hell?*

The location of the light switch and the dimensions of the room were second nature to him, but everything else was alien. A room that was once a mini version of his corner office at FitzSimmons & Bloomfield had been converted to become less Wayne Manor and more Clown Academy.

'Where's my stuff?' said Bob, slack-jawed, now truly unsettled by the complexity of the prank.

'What stuff?'

His 'stuff' – chair, desk, computer – all gone. Leather-bound encyclopaedias filling the entire south wall – gone. A stuffed eagle owl in a bell jar – gone. A mounted flintlock musket – gone. Cherished objects of power – all gone.

Beneath his feet, where he once felt the solid support of a dark hardwood floor, was an inexplicably soft, garish, jigsaw carpet made up of every colour of the rainbow. Pulling his sickly gaze away from its offensive cheer, individual objects began to take shape within the haze of this saccharine hellscape.

A large, fluffy, stuffed ladybird lay prostrate in the middle of the room, seemingly offering its black-and-red bulk as some kind of chair. In the far corner (where the owl once haughtily surveyed its kingdom), spilling some of its multicoloured spherical guts on to the carpet, now resided a triangular ball pit. Not far from the pit of balls, lying on its side and bringing Bob's retinas to the brink of despair, was a bright yellow horse on wheels. *What am I looking at?*

But all of these items, strange and exotic as they were, paled in comparison to what occupied his field of vision at the north wall of his 'office'. Beneath a paper chain of letters tacked to the wall that spelt out the colourful words, B.A.B.Y.B.O.Y was a crib . . . with a sleeping child in it.

A tsunami of goosebumps broke out in a chilling surge across his body. *This is all wrong.*

His vision retracted to a solitary point in the distance: the crib filling the minuscule dot. He was aware that Kirsty was still speaking to him or, rather, worriedly grilling him, but the words reached him dulled and incoherent as if he was trapped beyond a wall of glass. *Am I dreaming?*

The answer: there were three people in the room and only one of them was dreaming – the child. His mind raced to the soundtrack of his heart hammering in his chest. *Whose baby is this? Is it one of hers and Scotty's? Where's Scotty?*

'ROBERT!' the glass shattered, finally getting his attention and that of the now fully awake and crying infant. 'What's wrong with you? Have you taken something? You can tell me. I won't get mad,' she said, reaching into the cot to retrieve the child.

'Is that one of yours?'

'What?'

'The kid. Is it one of yours?' he asked. All colour had now abandoned his ashen face.

'One of *yours*?! This is our *son*, and you're scaring him, and your wife.'

'WIFE!' he laughed, but her stony face soon halted the action. 'I'd really like this to stop now. Enough, Kirst. Please . . . this is not possible.' He pointed at them both with an outstretched hand. '*This* is not a situation I would get myself involved in.' A glint on his waving hand caught his eye. Raising it for closer inspection, like a crazed magpie, he noted his fourth finger now sported a thick band wrapped around it like a golden boa constrictor.

He brought the quivering finger in question closer still to his eyeball, rotating it in disbelief. 'What the . . .' He attempted to remove the unwelcome manacle but it wouldn't go beyond his clammy knuckle. The tan line and indentation beneath inexplicably suggested that it had been there for quite some time. Panicking, in an effort to lubricate and free himself, febrile to the point where you might have suspected the Eye of Sauron was watching him, he jammed the finger in his mouth.

Kirsty, holding the now somewhat mollified child, watched the bizarre display in horror.

Flustered and consumed with self-doubt, Bob quietly

conceded, 'I'm having some . . . issues.' Returning the hand to his side, he was horribly aware of the weight of the ring. 'Could I have a cold glass of water, please?' he asked, in the hope of satisfying two pressing needs: slake his now raging thirst, and give himself a moment to think, away from the scrutiny of her glare.

'I've never seen you like this before. Should I call someone?' she said, trying to keep her voice level. 'Do you want me to phone for a doctor?'

'No. I mean, I don't know . . . maybe . . . can I just have the water first?'

Giving him a deeply suspicious sideways glance, she placed the child, now appeased to the point of unconsciousness, back into the crib and switched the light off. 'When I come back, you'd better have some answers,' she warned, before marching off to the kitchen.

The light from the living room poured in around him, illuminating the crib in a dim rectangle. He looked down on the child's peaceful features, so at odds with his own twisted and confused consciousness. *What is happening? Think!*

He was looking at the ring once again, his hand shaking uncontrollably, when a thought bloomed, discernible as a small patch of light in a mind muddied by the aftermath of a 'super black-out drunk' evening. Something Kirsty had just said triggered a memory. *'Should I call someone? Do you want me to phone . . . do you want me to phone . . .' PHONE!*

Reaching into his jacket pocket his fingers tightened around a cool casing *(a flash of smoke exiting a cracked mouth crossed his mind).* Holding his breath, he removed it and scrutinized its outmoded ridiculousness *(a flash of a green inviting glow)*. He lifted a finger to push a button, any button . . . but stopped short *(a flash of a young voice – 'Hello, Bloomfields'')*.

'Oh. My. Fucking. God.'

8

This has to be a dream?

On the verge of hyperventilation, he stared at the phone and the sleeping baby. *Is it possible? Could this ridiculous contraption have somehow changed my life?*

He looked down at his trembling hand and braced himself. He took a deep breath and slapped his face with a ferociousness that would make a WWE star proud. Wincing through the pain, he slowly opened his eyes . . . and the phone and child came back into focus. *This can't be happening?*

From the kitchen, the distant clatter of ice tumbling into a glass broke the spell and spurred him into action. *First things first, get out of this room.*

Closing the door to his office, playroom, kid's bedroom – *whatever the hell it was!* – he scoured his mind for a game plan more expansive than exiting a room. But it was a vacuum, an empty cavern containing nothing but the emotions of confusion, despair and fear. *Shit, shit, shit, shit . . . think, you dumb lump of meat!*

But it was no good, his brain had blown a fuse. Inspiration eluded him as he heard footsteps heading his way. He stuffed the phone back into his pocket just as she entered the living room, a glass of iced water in hand.

'Start talking,' she said, handing him the water before adopting an all-too-familiar cross-armed stance.

'Just gonna have a little sip . . .' He began to methodically gulp the cool liquid, savouring its life-restoring properties whilst giving himself some time to think. Meanwhile, Kirsty looked on, becoming more and more agitated with his obvious stalling.

'Well . . .'

He gulped some more.

'Robert . . .'

Still gulping.

'ROBERT!'

Still gulping . . .

'Oh, for God's sake,' she grabbed the glass out of his hand.

'Ahhhh,' he sighed, wiping a drop from his chin, 'I needed that. Where were we?'

'Where were we? *Where were you!?* I want some answers and I want them *now!* I haven't slept a wink because I've been worried sick you were lying in a ditch somewhere. And when you do eventually get home, you're spouting nonsense like you've had a bang on the head. What happened to you? Why are you wearing a jacket that's as eighties as acid rain? *Where were you?*'

He stared at her blankly. *Say something, Bob. Anything, just say something . . .*

'Drugs,' he blurted, finally deciding that he might as well go with the truth, or at least part of the truth. 'You were right. It was drugs. That's all I can think of. Has to be. I remember leaving the office and heading to the pub

94

for a couple of pints. Then I woke up about an hour ago lying on my office sofa, wearing this stupid jacket. I must have picked it up somewhere. I can only assume some prick spiked my drink with some kind of hallucinogenic. Only now am I starting to feel normal again . . . after that water.'

'Jesus,' she said, unfolding her arms. A good start. 'That's terrible. Why didn't you call me as soon as you saw my messages when you woke up?'

'Well, as you just saw . . . I was off my tits.'

'Who would just randomly do that to someone?'

'There are some sickos out there,' he nodded, pleased his story appeared to have stuck.

'You look like shit,' she said, moving towards him. Bob's reflex action was to step away from her. '*Easy*. It's OK,' she assured him with what sounded like genuine concern. Bob stopped his retreat. She gently rested a palm on his brow. 'You're on fire. And you're sweating buckets.'

'Drugs,' he said again, strangely enjoying her cool palm on his clammy forehead. 'I don't know why people do them.'

'Well, you must be getting on, because I can remember a time when you could handle your drugs,' she said with a withering glance. Having no idea what to do with that information, he simply grimaced like a moron and shrugged. The gesture seemed to trigger something inside her. Her face lost any remaining signs of scepticism and broke out in a motherly smile. 'You idiot. You know, if you weren't the perfect husband, I'd have a hard time 'believing you,' she said, brushing some dank hair off his forehead.

'Yup, that's me, the perfect . . .' He felt the wretched word form in his mouth, hatching like a spider's egg in a rat's nest. ' . . . *husband,'* he managed finally, pushing it out in a gulped whisper. 'I still feel a bit strange. I should probably freshen up and have a shower or something. Try and shake off the feeling that my brain's been thrown into a wood chipper.'

She switched back to concerned. 'Are you sure you shouldn't ring the police and let them know where and when you think this happened?'

'No!' He said, panicking, before willing calmness back into his voice. 'No, no it's fine. You wouldn't sue the fire brigade for water damage, would you? Let's just chalk this one up as free drugs. I'll be fine. I'm going to go take that shower.'

'I'm glad you're home and I'm glad you're all right,' she said, blocking his escape.

'You know me, hard as a Russian coal miner,' he said, with an awkward chuckle, a chuckle cut short when she suddenly wrapped her arms around him.

At first, feeling the body of his best friend's wife pressed against his own rendered him as rigid as a frozen cadaver. But even Bob couldn't withstand the warmth of human contact forever. So, despite, or perhaps because of, his inexplicable predicament, his cold heart thawed and he hugged her back. Whether he could admit it or not, it felt good. When the embrace ended, feeling the blood rise in his cheeks, he cast his eyes downward in embarrassment, which is why he was taken off-guard when she kissed his mouth.

It only lasted around two seconds, but it felt a lot longer. The sensation was somewhere between walking in on your parents having sex, and your parents walking in on you having sex. 'I love you,' she said, separating herself, and leaving a pause in expectation of the traditional response. *Oh shit, on a biscuit.*

'And I . . .' Bob began, frantically trying to access and load *the word*. But unfortunately for Kirsty, he decided he was more likely to start speaking Norwegian than make that frightening little pledge. He finally located what he deemed to be the next best thing. 'Ditto, kid,' he offered, following up with a playful fist bump to her chin.

She wrinkled her brow in what looked like complete vexation . . . and then burst into laughter. 'Ditto, kid?! What? That's so weird,' she said. 'You're still off it. Go have your shower.'

Bob opened the medicine cabinet above the shower room sink. He was on the hunt for any kind of painkiller to placate the thumping headache that had bloomed at the centre of his brain. His search was interrupted by a sudden realization that 'his' medicine cabinet was now a 'his & hers' medicine cabinet. Fake eye lashes and a tube of Canesten were amongst a variety of products now rubbing shoulders with his own. Shaking his head in disbelief, he finally found his aspirin behind a pack of sanitary towels.

'Christ, I'm in *The Twilight Zone* . . . with wings.' He

ripped the box open and popped three pills into his mouth. Closing the cabinet, he turned the tap on and drank greedily from the faucet. He wiped his mouth and brought his eyes to meet their reflection staring back at him in the mirror. 'You do look like shit. Your *wife* was right.' He laughed wildly . . . but the humour quickly left him, leaving a scared-looking man staring back. 'Baby steps, Bob. You can figure this out.' He looked to the shower over his shoulder. 'Freshen up, that'll help.'

He took off the black leather and threw it into the corner of the room. A muffled clunk could be heard from within its rolled-up bulk as it hit the tiles. He looked at the black mass for long moments. *Shower first.* He removed his trousers and started to unbutton his shirt, but his attention was pulled back to the jacket and the origin of the clunk.

He picked it up and pulled the phone from the pocket. Dropping the jacket into the corner, he turned the phone over in his hands, scrutinizing it for the first time since he and it were mysteriously united the evening before. A close look at its entire body confirmed what he already knew. It had a little screen. A number pad. A green button to dial and a red one to end the call. *It's wholly unremarkable. It's just an outdated, plastic, stupid old ph— wait a minute.*

He brought it as close to his face as he could without losing focus. As far as he could tell, there didn't seem to be anywhere to load batteries, nowhere to dock, and nowhere to insert a lead for charging. *Weird . . . how is this thing being powered?*

He glanced into the mirror, seeking permission for what he was about to do. His reflection didn't argue. Holding his breath, he guided his finger towards the on button. His finger came to rest upon it. It was cool to the touch and felt more like glass than the rubbery finish he was expecting. He started to apply pressure . . .

KNOCK-KNOCK

'*Fuck me*,' he started, almost dropping the phone to the ground.

'You OK in there? I'm not hearing water running?' Kirsty asked through the door.

'Just about to get in . . . ummm . . .' He looked to his reflection again for inspiration, but all he got in return was a shrug and a look of *you're on your own*. '. . . sweetheart.' His reflection stared back at him, shaking its head with savage disdain.

'OK. Don't be long.'

He listened for the sound of her feet padding away from the door. 'Don't be long?' he said to his reflection. 'Why!?' He placed the phone on the sink and turned the shower lever to the on position. Hot water immediately jetted from the head. 'That should satisfy the guard on the watch tower,' he muttered, returning to the mirror. 'How are we *married* to her?' he asked the haggard mess before him. 'I don't know,' he replied to himself. 'But as hangovers go, this is a doozy.'

He wiped the gathering steam from the mirror and picked up the phone once again, wincing as his wedding band clinked against its casing. 'In sickness and in health,' he said, rolling his eyes. 'OK, let's assume for a moment that I'm not having a catastrophic mental breakdown, last night was real, I am in fact currently married to my best friend's wife and this phone is some kind of time machine.' He leaned in closer to his reflection, as if trying to see into his own mind. 'My memory is patchy. I wasn't super black-out drunk at that point, more super brown-out. I do recollect talking . . .' Even to his own reflection, he felt foolish saying it, '. . . *to my younger self*. Question is, what did I say *to me* that would result in this freakshow?' He mused for a while. 'Come on Bob, *think*.' The furrowed brow and curled lip suggested it wasn't going well. He tapped his head and exhaled in frustration. 'Out of service. Have a hot shower. It'll do you good.'

And it did. The combination of soap and hot water cleansed and rejuvenated, helping the fog in his mind dissipate. Not to the extent that he could remember the conversation with his younger self, but he did formulate a five-point action plan:

1. Bob and the phone leave the apartment.
2. Get to the privacy of his office.
3. Speak to Scotty (what happened to him?).
4. Speak to his younger self and reverse the present hell.
5. *Save his brother, Tom.*

9

Failing the five-point plan, Bob even drafted a one-point contingency plan:

1. Consult a divorce lawyer.

'How was that?' Kirsty asked, startling him again, as he exited the bathroom drying his hair with a towel, another wrapped around his waist.

'Good, thanks,' he said, slightly freaked out to see her sitting on the edge of his bed. Speaking of *witch* . . . in his rush for the solitude of the bathroom, he failed to notice his bed had undergone a transformation from a dark and brooding bachelor's sex arena to a light and airy pillow sanctuary. Thankfully, the Bavarian teak dipped wooden bedside tables were still there, but where a bottle of Blue Label had been yesterday, there was now a picture of Bob and Kirsty as newlyweds beside a mountain lake, looking into one another's eyes, adoringly – *now, that's freaky!*

'There we are,' Bob said, unblinking. She followed his line of sight.

'Best day ever,' she said, wistfully.

'I was just thinking how lucky we are,' he said, sensing an opportunity. 'What a journey we've been on since we got together.'

'It's been a ride,' she agreed.

'Certainly has. It was meant to be. Right from the off the romance was there, wasn't it?'

'I suppose, once you stopped pulling my pigtails.'

'What do you mean?'

'You know, in school. For you it was just childish name-calling and pranks . . . but . . . you were more hurtful than you knew at the time. But then one day it just stopped.' Smiling, she got up off the bed and draped her arms over his naked shoulders. 'And that's when I stopped hating you.'

'I remember,' he said, her face now very close. 'But do you remember what it was about the new me you liked so much?'

'You just started talking to me like a human being.'

'How so?'

'Why are you asking about this stuff?' she said, confused, but still playful.

He shrugged. 'It's nice to reminisce.'

'All right, weirdo.' She took the wet towel he'd been using to dry his hair and walked it to the laundry basket in the corner of the room. Tossing it in she continued, 'You were always asking me if I'm OK. How are you? What can I do for you? Do you need any help with this and that? It was very sweet. It charmed me.' *Holy shit! That's it! That's the advice I gave him. I remember now. He used it on her!*

She stood before him. 'How are you feeling?'

'I am starting to see things more clearly,' he said, his mind racing with this new information. *OK, time to initiate phase one of the action plan.* 'I have to head into the office. I have something important to do ahead of next week.'

'What!? You were just there?' she said. 'Can't it wait? You've just been violated, Robert! You've had a terrible experience. I want to make sure you're all right.'

'I feel perfectly fine. That shower has really energized me. It's all out of my system.'

'You feel fine? Energized?'

'I do.'

'Well, if that's the case . . .' she left a pregnant pause. 'It is Saturday morning.'

'Yes, it is?' Bob replied, raising an eyebrow in puzzlement.

'The most wonderful time of the week?' she smiled.

'I don't follow.'

'It's Saturday.' She curled a finger over the top of the towel around his waist and tugged. 'Gimme.'

'Woah! What are you doing?!' he said, pushing her hand away.

'What am I doing? I'm taking what's mine,' she laughed, quickly removing her T-shirt.

'Kirsty!' He pleaded, as she approached him in her bra and jeans. 'Stop.'

'Stop? That's a new one for you,' she giggled, whilst making another grab for his towel.

'I'm serious,' he said, dodging her grabbing hands. 'I really have to go into the office.'

'I don't give a shit. You weren't here this morning and if I don't get my regular Saturday a.m. fix . . . well, you know how cranky I'm going to be for the rest of the day.'

He started to panic. 'I've just been through a terrible experience,' he said, using her own words from moments ago.

'You said you were feeling fine,' she replied, already slipping into 'cranky'.

'The truth is . . . I still feel a bit odd. I didn't want to worry you. Can you keep it on ice for me until I get back from the office? I'm sure I'll be match fit on my return,' he said, smiling his most sincere smile.

'You seem "match fit", now,' she said, looking down. For all his protests, the erection straining from beneath his towel suggested a very different point of view.

'He's just an employee. I run the show. I want to be present here,' he said, pointing to his heart.

'Fine!' she said, rolling her eyes and snatching her T-shirt off the bed. 'Something feels off with you, Robert. I can't put my finger on it. But something isn't right.' She gave him one last eyeing up and stormed out of the room.

He breathed a sigh of relief and looked down at his rogue petard. 'Are you out of your mind?'

After quickly dressing in an ensemble as close to easy-going as Bob got (brogues, trousers, cashmere jumper and a sports jacket), he took advantage of the moment Kirsty decided to take a shower and slipped out of the apartment unchallenged and unnoticed. The door shut behind him – any other day a mundane practice of security, but today it felt like he'd shut the door on another dimension.

'Step One achieved. Step Two in progress,' he said, quickly walking towards the elevator. He pushed the call button and waited. As the lift slowly started its ascent, he stared at the misshapen reflection of his face in the gold-plated doors.

'This is insane,' he whispered, shaking his head at his reflection. 'Your best friend's wife just tried having sex with you. Christ alive,' he winced, pinching the bridge of his nose. 'Uh, no. Not a chance in hell. Just get to the office, speak to Bobby Jr,' he said, reflexively touching the phone in his sports jacket pocket, 'and straighten this whole mess out. That's the plan,' he concluded, nodding stoically at his reflection, whilst noticing the lift had stopped at level fifteen.

'She looked pretty good in that bra though . . .' he said, as the lift resumed its journey. Lowering his eyes from the digital counter he met his own judgmental gaze once again. 'Don't even think about it!' He gave the lift call button a rapid series of stabs. 'No, siree, Bob! No way. I'm not that guy. I couldn't do that to Scotty . . . even if he would never *ever* know. The point is, I would know.'

The lift opened and he stepped in. The doors lingered for a few seconds, giving him one last look at his apartment at the end of the corridor. Finally, the lift beeped and the doors started to close. '*I* would know,' he repeated, staring unblinking as the gold-plated doors slowly came together, consuming his view until all he could see was a thin strip of colour from floor to ceiling. Just as the corridor was about to blink out of existence, Bob's hand shot out, stopping the doors' union. 'I can keep a secret.'

*

Knock-knock

He heard the rush of water stop, followed by the familiar squeak of the downstairs shower cubicle opening. After a moment, Kirsty opened the door in a thin white robe, her hair still wet. She took in Bob leaning against the doorframe.

'Hi,' he said, with more than a splash of sultry.

'I thought you were going to the office?' she said, coolly, gathering her glistening black hair over her shoulder.

Bob looked her up and down, noting her wet body clinging to the thin translucent material of the robe. 'To hell with the office. I'm match fit now.'

A wicked grin broke out across her flushed face.

What followed was a frenzied ascent to the bedroom. Bob's clothes and Kirsty's wet robe were haphazardly strewn like a trail of breadcrumbs to their lovemaking.

'Holy shit,' she exclaimed, her arm resting on her forehead as she gasped towards the ceiling. 'That was . . .' Words failed her.

'Good?' he suggested, mirroring her ceiling reverie.

'No. The McRib is good. That was . . . *spectacular*. We haven't gone at it like that since we were in our twenties. And even then, it wasn't so . . .'

'So?'

'Raw!' she said. 'Don't get me wrong, you're generally box office. But, I would say, more skewed towards a PG, possibly 15, audience. More tender, romantic. What just happened was like that scene in *Jurassic Park* where they lower the goat into the velociraptor cage. Where did that come from?'

'I don't know. The mood took me, I guess,' he said, smiling into her grinning face. 'Tender and romantic, you say? PG? That's how you normally see me? Good grief.'

'I love that about you,' she said, suddenly concerned she'd offended him. 'But what just happened was also very nice. I'm sure there's a happy medium in there somewhere,' she said, regaining her mischievous edge.

'What's the most romantic thing I've done for you?' he asked, genuinely intrigued.

'Where to begin? I'm a lucky girl, there's a lot to choose from.' She took a moment to ponder. 'Last Christmas at my parents' house still makes me smile. You know how annoying Mum and Dad can be. The constant complaining. Nothing I had made for Christmas breakfast was good enough. I remember washing the dishes, my hand wrapped around a bread knife thinking how I would fare in prison, when I looked out of the kitchen window, and there you are, a big smile on your face in only your tighty-whities, arms outstretched, looking up at me with the words "I love you" written in the snow at your feet.'

'Your father called me an idiot. I'd been out there for about ten minutes waiting for you to look up. I was almost hypothermic.' They began to laugh, but Bob suddenly stopped. *What the hell? How could I have that memory?*

'What's wrong?' she asked.

'Nothing. It's nothing.' He said, logging the thought for further scrutiny later. 'I was just remembering that cold. It was brutal.'

'I loved it. As I said, I'm a lucky girl,' she cooed, snuggling herself to his body, still warm from the lovemaking. 'I love you, Robert.'

'I love you too,' he replied, the words leaving his mouth with such ease it took him a moment to realize he'd said them out loud.

'I love you three,' she replied.

The last time Bob had heard those words of domestic bliss, they were spoken by another husband and wife. 'I wonder what Scotty Pickers-Gill is up to now?' he asked, as casually as he could, half expecting her to jump from the bed screaming, *My real husband!*

'Scotty Pickers-Gill?' she said, with a confused look.

'Scotty. Scott. You know, we went to school with him.'

'Yes, I know who Scott Pickers-Gill is. I'm just wondering why we're lying here talking about him?'

'He just popped in there.'

'Robert, we're having a lovely moment. Why are you bringing up Scott Pickers-Gill? I think it's amazing what you've done for him, helping him the way you have, but I don't want to think about the tragic tale of your old school friend right now. OK?'

'OK,' said Bob, now feeling even more in the dark regarding his friend's fate.

10

Bob stood in the gloom of the half-light from the living room, watching the child's slow, rhythmic breathing. He felt a connection he never thought possible. Somehow, he knew without a doubt that this was his sleeping son. He reached down into the cot and ran his fingers through dark, fluffy hair. The boy, lying on his stomach, shook his head, semi-aware even though he was far, far away in dreams. Bob smiled a smile that hadn't been on his face since he was closer to the sleeping baby's age.

'Well, aren't you a bundle of joy,' he whispered. The baby rolled over and yawned. Bob's smile widened . . . until he saw the name embroidered into the romper suit: his dead brother's name – *Thomas.*

An audible gasp left his mouth, as he suddenly remembered that he was a man where he did not belong. 'I've been here too long. I'm sorry, Thomas. I don't know how or why, but I'm forgetting myself. I have to go.' But the sentiment was not followed through. He reached down into the crib and again started running his fingers through the sleeping infant's hair. '*Thomas,*' he said.

Music started playing from the living room.

Its soothing melody washed over him until a creeping sense of déjà vu pulled his attention away from the crib.

He turned and looked into the empty, music-filled space. There was something about the piece that was familiar to him, it stirred up feelings of . . . annoyance? *Where have I heard this?*

Stepping into the living room the music stopped, and silence (apart from the distant sound of Kirsty resuming her shower) filled the room once again. For a second, he thought he might've imagined it, but it started again . . . and then it dawned on him: *it's the beginning of Tchaikovsky's 1812 Overture on a ten-second loop!*

'It's the doorbell,' he grimaced. 'What have I become?' He opened the door.

'Good afternoon. I brought bagels and whisky . . . and weed,' said Chloe Huxley, beaming from ear to ear, her red hair almost completely concealed by a large white beanie. In one hand she held a brown paper bag, presumably containing the promised bounty, in the other she gripped a lead. Bob followed the length of interwoven rope to the collar of the beast held captive by it – a huge, drooling English bulldog.

'I thought you said you were a cat person?' said Bob.

'I said they had a bad rap. I like both. This is Anvil,' she said.

'Hello Anvil, I'd invite you in but I'm worried your crazy human might take a poop on my carpet,' he said to the clueless dog.

'Ha! Ignore him, Anvil. He gets grumpy when he's been up all night banging your mummy senseless.'

This could be a problem, thought Bob.

He glanced over his shoulder and registered that

the sound of the shower was no longer audible. He attempted to narrow Chloe's field of vision into the apartment by closing the door as much as possible. It was her foot that ultimately stopped him. 'Chloe, what is this? You can't be here.'

'Why did you tell me you aren't married? The more I thought about it, the more it annoyed me. You don't think I'm stupid, do you?' she said, far too loudly.

'Chloe,' he began, lowering his voice in the hope she would do the same, 'I don't think you're stupid. There are forces at work here that you don't understand. Christ, I don't understand them . . .'

'Who are you talking to?' asked Kirsty, entering the living room wearing a thick cotton robe, her black hair wrapped in a towel.

'It's . . . uh . . .' Bob stuttered, panic spreading across his face.

'Chloe Huxley,' she said, stepping around him with Anvil in tow. ' . . . from the office. You must be Mrs Bloomfield. So nice to finally meet you.'

Looking down the long stretch of corridor to the lift, as the scene between his now wife and recent lover meeting for the first time played out behind him, Bob gave flight serious consideration. But an unfamiliar force held him in place. *Responsibility?* He closed the door.

'Nice to meet you too, Chloe. Who's this handsome chap?' Kirsty asked, looking down at the dog.

'This is Anvil. Say hello to the nice lady, sugar bear. *Rello*,' she said, in a gruff voice from the side of her mouth, as if Anvil were a ventriloquist's dummy.

'Precious,' said Kirsty, with a polite yet confused smile. 'What brings you to our home on a Saturday?'

'Yes, I was just apologizing profusely to Mr Bloomfield. But I weighed the options of disturbing you and ignoring a direct order from Miss Pennypacker . . . and, well, here I am.'

'A wise choice,' said Kirsty.

'I thought so,' Chloe said, turning her attention to Bob. 'Miss P asked me to swing by with this. She said it might be of some importance with the upcoming production. You know what she's like – no stone left unturned.' She reached into the paper bag. For a terrible moment, Bob expected to see a whisky bottle and a bag of weed gripped in her pale hand. But to his relief, it was a large white envelope.

'Thank you,' he said, taking the envelope. He tore the seal and removed a single sheet of paper. A crude stick figure receiving a blow job from a fish stared back at him. He quickly pushed it back into the envelope. 'That all looks in order,' he said, as Chloe looked on with a grin. 'I appreciate you coming. But I'm afraid it was a wasted journey as I'll be heading into the office right now. So why don't I walk you out, Miss Huxley.'

'At the office we were placing bets on whether you existed or not,' said Chloe, ignoring Bob and turning to Kirsty.

'Whether I existed or not? Why would you do such a thing?' asked Kirsty.

'Well, to be completely honest . . . we all thought Mr Bloomfield was gay.'

'Robert! Gay!' she said, laughing at the very idea. 'Why would anyone think he's gay?'

'The obsessive cleanliness. The immaculate dress sense. He always smells good.'

'I know how good he smells, I buy his scent,' she said, annoyance creeping into her voice. 'But I can assure you, I am real and if Robert is gay, he hides it very, *very* well.'

'OK. Great chat. It's time I was off. I have to meet the boys down at the YMCA. Miss Huxley, I'll walk you out.'

'Don't forget, Naomi and Ron get here for seven tonight,' Kirsty said.

'Who gets where?' asked Bob distractedly, as he finally ejected Chloe into the hallway.

'My boss Naomi? And her husband Ron? They're coming for dinner this evening. Don't say you've forgotten, Robert?' she said huffily.

'Of course, I haven't forgotten. I'm very much looking forward to seeing Naomi and Ron,' he said, *whoever the hell they were.*

'You're a trip to the dentist, aren't you?' he said, ushering Chloe and Anvil away from his apartment and towards the lift.

'Your wife is lovely. Anvil doesn't normally take to people that quickly,' she replied cheerily.

'What are you talking about? He didn't do anything. He just sat there like a furry balloon. We're getting off-topic. Please don't come to my home ever again. Last night was a mistake. Scotty and I appreciated your hospitality, and in fairness you do throw a hell of a party, but it got a bit out of hand,' he said, as they arrived at the lift.

'Who's Scotty?'

'My friend who was with me last night.'

'Does he work at the office?'

'No. He's an old friend. You met him when we arrived.'

'You arrived with people from the office. Maybe Scotty came later?'

'No, I definitely arrived with him. You remember, he was dressed as Austin Powers.'

'Nope. I didn't meet anyone of that name and description. You arrived with some of the guys from work.'

'Really?'

'Yes, really. I remember it vividly because I was sober and surprised you came. You were apologetic for the "low effort" costume, and you kept saying the guys had dragged you along and that you couldn't stay long. I got the impression you didn't want to be there. Which is why I was shocked to see you still present in the early hours and then surprised furthermore when sweet, polite, butter-wouldn't-melt Mr Bloomfield, followed me to my chamber. Who would have ever known you had such a dark side. You were like two different people.'

The lift signalled its arrival.

'I *am* two different people, and we both regret sleeping with you,' he said.

The doors parted. Chloe and Anvil entered. Bob remained in the corridor.

'Are you not coming?' she asked.

'Chloe, I don't know whether I'm coming or going.'

11

'Good afternoon, Mr Bloomfield,' said Miss Beryl Pennypacker. She delivered the words with the exact enunciation Bob had become accustomed to. For the many years she had worked for him, he'd never quite shaken off the feeling that their relationship was more student and headmistress than boss and executive assistant. The close to twenty-year age difference and her penchant for tweed outfits only served to underline the notion. 'How does the day find you?' she asked, from behind her desk in the reception area of Bob's office.

'I've had better days, Miss Pennypacker. I won't lie,' he said.

'My mother used to say honesty with oneself is the first step to a better day,' she replied, the sentiment eliciting a nod of agreement from Bob. 'I wasn't expecting to see you today?'

'I could say the same for you.'

'Silence is not only golden but productive. I can get a lot done when I'm not interrupted by the kerfuffle of a weekday.'

'Miss P,' he began, sitting down in the seat adjacent to hers, 'can I just say I am very happy that you're still here.'

'Well, I did go home last night,' she said, removing her

glasses, visibly shocked at the sight of her boss sitting in her work area.

'I know. I meant still in my life.'

'Still in your life? Whatever do you mean?' she asked.

'Nothing. Ignore me. I'm being silly. It's just . . . I've recently experienced some changes in my life. It's all a bit confusing.'

'Well, they do say a change is as good as a rest.'

'True. But not all change is for the better.'

'Also true. Ultimately, we are but a leaf on the stream of life.'

'But what if you could change the direction of the stream?' he asked, intrigued to know the thoughts of a woman whose sagacity he admired.

'We do. All the time, by the choices we make,' she replied, perking up.

'I mean, what if you could right a past injustice? What if you could change the past to manipulate the present? Tip the balance of the scales from unfair to fair?'

'What ifs are a waste of precious time,' she said, with a grimace. 'We *cannot* change what has already happened. Ultimately, where the past is concerned, there is but one choice we have.'

'And what's that?'

'Acceptance. We can choose to accept that life is not fair. John and George are dead, yet Paul and Ringo appear to be indestructible. We wanted Biggie but we got Diddy. We wanted Kurt but we got Dave. That is the nature of our reality. Like it or lump it, I'm afraid.'

'But . . . *what if you could change that.* Would you?'

After long moments of deliberation, she replied, 'I would tear Mark Chapman limb from limb if it would bring back John Lennon.'

'Well, I'd say that was a yes.'

A phone rang.

It was not a customized tune or a digital effect, but an actual ringing from inside its large, dull green casing. The phone's outer shell cradled a handset connected to a cord at the rear, with a rotary of numbers from 1 to 9 and 0 comprising its flat, slanting face. The bell's strident pitch dwarfed a radio's efforts to convey Falco's 'Rock Me Amadeus', even though the radio shared the same polished tabletop surface. The only other item between the phone and radio was an automatic personal telephone address book. Its transparent slider rested upon a laddered alphabet that looked well used.

A man, accompanied by a rustling, entered the reception room. The rustling was an unfortunate side effect of the black-and-purple shell suit he wore from neck to ankle, but a quick glance in an adjacent mirror at the fashionable leisure wear complemented by his dark, handsome features reassured him it was a small price to pay when you looked this good. His new Hi-Tech Silver Shadow trainers carried him the rest of the way over the well-worn twist-pile patterned carpet to the ringing phone. He turned down the radio before lifting the receiver. 'Hello, Bloomfields'.'

'*Oh, hello. May I ask who's speaking please?*'

'John. Who's this?'

'*Excellent. My name is Colin and I'm calling from the local council. I wonder if I could have a moment of your time to take a quick survey?*'

'What kind of survey?'

'*It's a very general survey. As you know we have a national census every ten years. We are midway to the next, so we thought we'd get ahead of the curve and have an informal survey of the people of our parish. The better we know you, the better we can serve you, that's our philosophy.*' John rolled his eyes and emitted a heavy sigh, which prompted Colin to add, '*It'll take just a couple of minutes.*'

'It'll have to because I'm taking my sons to football practice in about five minutes,' he said, checking the digital display of his black-and-gold Casio watch.

'*My pen is clicked, we are good to go! I've got the questionnaire in front of me. I'll just quickly fill out the date.*' Colin pauses briefly. '*I can't seem to find my calendar. You wouldn't happen to know the date would you, John? That can be your first question,*' he chuckled.

'It's the 21st of June,' he said.

'*Thank you for that. Now, my records show you are at 231 Grove Hill. How long have you lived there, John?*'

'Ten years.'

'*Which means you moved in . . . you moved in . . . ?*' Silence filled John's ear.

'Maths not your strong point, Colin? Eighty-six minus ten, equals . . .'

It was Colin's turn to fill the silence. '*Seventy-six! Sorry. Maths is my Kryptonite,*' he laughed.

'It's reassuring that there's a . . . what are you, forty?'

'Yup. *Around that.*'

'It's reassuring that there's a man in his forties working for my local council that can't subtract ten from eighty-six. Even the kids I teach would make short work of that simple sum, Colin.'

'*So, you're a teacher?*'

'I am.'

'*That must be very rewarding.*'

'It's a privilege,' he answered with pride.

'*Would you mind if I asked how old are you, John?*'

'Eighty-six minus fifty-three, equals . . . ?'

'*Thirty-three,*' Colin instantly replied.

'That's much better,' John said, sounding impressed. 'There's hope for you yet.'

'*You never know, I might be the next Rachel Riley.*'

'Who?'

'*I mean . . . Carol Vorderman.*'

'The *Countdown* woman. Yes, hilarious,' John said, without laughing.

'*I can see in my records you are married to a Judy Bloomfield, who's also a teacher. You mentioned your sons, who you're taking to football practice. I don't have their names at hand. What are the little rascals called?*'

'Robert and Thomas, who are currently driving me nuts with all this World Cup madness. They're obsessed.'

'*Oh yes, I remember. The World Cup was in Mexico in eighty-six.*'

'I think you mean *is*. It's still going on.'

'*Yes. I meant . . . what a great tournament we're having. It really is the beautiful game, isn't it?*'

'Yeah, wonderful if you're a player. Football – making morons rich since 1888. You know some of these dopes are getting paid £30,000 a year to kick a ball around. That's a lot of money to play a game.'

'*30k? Wow. That is a lot of money.*'

'Dad, come on!' shouted a frustrated young boy as he came barrelling into the reception room. 'We gotta go!' he said, breathlessly. He stood Peter Pan-like, his hands on his hips, a football tucked under his arm and a long, multicoloured knitted scarf wrapped around his neck. Beneath it, he wore an almost identical shell suit to John, and the similarity did not end there. The young boy's features were much fairer than John's, his face less angular, more cherubic, but there was no mistaking that this was his son.

'Thomas! I'm on the phone, and I'll come when I'm ready. You're on thin ice as it is, kiddo. Don't be coming in here shouting and screaming at me. That grounding can be easily reinstated, you hear me? Now, go wait in the car. And take that bloody Dr Who scarf off. It's boiling outside.'

'Yes, Dad. Sorry, Dad,' he said, backing out of the room, his chin resting on his chest.

'Oi! What have I told you about wearing your muddy football boots in the house!' John shouted, noticing the offending articles just before Thomas disappeared from view. Shaking his head, he put the receiver back to his ear. 'You got any kids, Colin?' he asked, exasperated. But an answer was not forthcoming. 'Colin?'

'*Still here,*' he said eventually, his voice sounding fragile.

'What's wrong with you?' asked John.

'*I just . . . stubbed my toe. All good now.*'

'Barefoot at the office? Tut-tut, Colin,' he said, finally driven to distraction. 'I think that'll do it. Best of luck with it all.'

'*Wait! Wait . . . One last thing.*'

'What?!'

'*We have a youth survey that I'd love to get Robert's thoughts on. Could I have just a minute of his time before you head to football?*'

'Goodbye, Colin.'

And the line went dead.

'Charming as ever, Dad,' Bob said, trying to hit the call end button. He finally managed it on his third attempt, such was the moisture clouding his vision and the shaking in his hands after a conversation with his father from thirty-seven years in the past. Ironically, it was the longest conversation they'd had in ages. But that information was lost on Bob because his mind was filled with the voice of his dead brother. So young, so precocious, his only want from life to kick a football . . . and unless Bob could intervene, that would be one of the few pleasures Thomas Henry Bloomfield would extract from his tragically short time on Earth.

Gathering his thoughts, he focused on the positives from the mind-bending conversation with his father, sixteen years his junior, no less. He might have failed to speak to his younger self, but the call had proven useful in regard to establishing a concrete date: June 21st, 1986.

If Bob wanted his old life back (with the inclusion of his brother) he had no choice but to keep calling. His current situation, married with a son (blinked into existence by that first interaction with his younger self) showed that change was possible. That particular change was a mistake, admittedly, but it had happened, nevertheless.

The challenge before him was to establish what he must say to young Robert (or, if it came to it, any other member of his family) in order for them to believe that he was who he said he was. *Hi, I'm your son/brother/you from thirty-seven years in the future* was unlikely to cut it.

Setting his mind to work, his fingers drummed a constant beat upon his desk, which incidentally was no longer the sprawling oak monolith from Bob's pre-phone life. It was now a far brighter and modest modern executive's desk. In fact, the whole room looked like it had taken a cue from the desk's humble simplicity. Gone was the bear-hide rug. Gone was the intimidating dark wood panelling on the walls, in favour of a lighter and far more relaxing complexion. The obnoxious pictures of Bob rubbing shoulders with a Who's Who of British entertainment were also nowhere to be seen.

In fact, the only picture in the office was the one perched on the corner of his desk. And it was of him and Kirsty cradling a newborn baby in their arms. Kirsty was laughing as Bob was pretend-biting the baby's tiny, perfectly formed hand, testing it for authenticity as if it were a gold nugget.

Staring at the unfamiliar image, his attention was pulled away from the conundrum of how he could convince his family of 1986 who he was. He willed himself to remember the moment captured in the picture . . . it felt tantalizingly close. The more he opened his mind to the past, the more the hazy memories of what seemed like another man's life flooded into his consciousness, colliding with his own, mixing like photographs loosely stored in a box. It was only when he closed his mind to the effort that he realized he was breathing in rapid, shallow gasps and his heart was thumping frantically. *I need something familiar.*

'Scotty,' he suddenly said, reaching for his personal phone. 'Christ, I forgot about Scotty!' This time it took a lot more sifting through a multitude of names and contacts he did not recognize before he found his old friend's details. *Alan Goldman? Emma Lance? Nick Elba? Who the hell are all these people?* he asked himself, with another confused swipe.

When he finally arrived at the S's section, he found what he was looking for . . . but not exactly.

Instead of 'Scotty', his oldest friend was under the curiously formal title of 'Scott Pickers-Gill' *How strange.*

He pressed the call button.

After a few rings. 'Hi, Rob?' a voice answered in that familiar faint transatlantic drawl.

'Scotty!' he said, with relief.

'Hey. What's ahhh . . . what's going on?'

'Man, it's good to hear your voice.'

'Oh . . . thanks. Yours too,' he said, sounding uncertain.

'I need to see you. Do you think you could meet me in Soho? The Coach and Horses, twenty minutes?'

A long pause lingered. 'Is this about work?'

'No,' said Bob, his confusion deepening. 'I just need to see you.'

'I suppose I could swing by.'

'Excellent. I'll see you in twenty, buddy.'

'All right . . . buddy.'

12

It was Scotty, but not Scotty.

Impressive would be a suitable adjective to describe Scott Pickers-Gill. Intelligence with a disarmingly laid-back vibe, coupled with a keen dress sense, a regimented gym routine and a penchant for expensive cologne, gave him the bearing of a man who could breeze into any social circle and gain immediate acceptance. At least, that was the person Bob knew Scotty to be.

The moment he stepped into The Coach and Horses, as Bob leaned against the bar, pint in hand, watching the entrance, it was instantly apparent that a great change had befallen him.

His bizarre outfit was the first detail that gave Bob cause for alarm. A severely distressed *Flight of the Navigator* T-shirt (with a long-sleeve T-shirt underneath), a pair of black cut-off jeans, with a cycling cap on his head and Chuck Taylors on his feet, gave the unnerving impression of an ageing student rather than the epitome of middle-class success.

Most shockingly, that well-maintained physique had somehow become a taut and wiry frame of sinew and bone. Ashen-grey skin and sunken eyes completed the look of a man who had lost his sparkle, like a rusting sports car left to the elements.

Scanning the room, he soon found Bob staring (in sheer disbelief) at him. After a nod and the glimmer of a dull smile, he made his way over to the bar.

'Hey,' Scotty said, removing his cap to reveal a full head of hair.

Staring, mouth-agog, at the hairy miracle upon his old friend's once bald head '. . . hi . . .' was all Bob could bring himself to gasp in reply.

'Get you something, mate?' asked the barman.

'OJ, please,' said Scotty, handing him a stack of three pound coins gripped in nicotine-stained fingers.

Close-up, things looked even worse. Bob couldn't stop himself from once again working his way down from the hair to his clothes, to his trainers. *He looked better as Austin Powers,* he thought. Working his way back up, he finally locked eyes with Scotty, who was looking at him quizzically.

'Everything all right?' Scotty asked.

'Fine.'

'You sure? You seem preoccupied.'

'I'm good.'

'OK,' said Scotty, not convinced. 'So . . . why did you want to see me?'

'What the hell has happened to you, Scotty!' Bob shrieked, the words bursting out of him like a jack-in-the-box.

'Excuse me?' Scotty replied, blinking in surprise.

'This . . .' he said, circling Scotty's entire being for clarity, '. . . what has happened?'

Scotty glanced over his shoulder, looking for the candid camera. 'What are you talking about?'

'Your clothes. You look like a roadie for Smash Mouth. You're so thin . . . and the . . .' He couldn't bring himself to speak its name – *the wig!* ' . . . you're drinking orange juice in a fucking pub, Scotty! What's going on?!'

'If this is some kind of practical joke, I don't get it.'

'Scotty. This is not you.'

'What isn't me? What the hell are you talking about?'

'Scotty, I know you and this isn't you.'

'Know me? We're not friends. It's been a long time since school, Rob,' he said, with a grunt of sarcasm. 'I appreciate all you've done for me, hence the professional courtesy of me coming to this pub. Which is exactly where I don't want to be, by the way. I don't know if you're drunk or high, but either way I'm going to head off. This is too weird. I'll see you Monday.' Placing his untouched drink on the bar, he turned to leave.

'WAIT! Wait, Scotty. Please. *I do know you.*'

'Really? When's my birthday?'

Bob's mouth opened and closed almost immediately. 'I have no idea,' he said, cursing his selfish ways.

Scotty gave him an 'I told you so' shrug and started to walk.

'You wipe cutlery obsessively in restaurants. You call bananas monkey bars, which is incredibly annoying,' Bob said quickly, bringing Scotty to a full stop. 'You once broke up with a girl because she said Rage Against the Machine's lyrics were childish. You walked in on your parents having sex as a kid and they told you their 'clothes were in the wash' and they were 'hugging to keep warm'. You stole a Bart Simpson poster from John

Menzies. You refuse to put your seat back on planes and you always give the air hostess your undivided attention in the safety briefing . . . because you're such a good person.

'You have a scar on your left shoulder. You told your parents you fell off a skateboard, but the real reason is you caught it on a fence you jumped over after trying to see your cousin's boobs in the shower.'

A couple of drinkers at the bar turned and gave Scotty a questioning glare.

'She had just got them. I was about nine and curious,' he said sheepishly, before looking back to Bob. 'I never told anyone that.'

'You told your best friend.'

'And that's you?'

'How else would I know?'

'All right, I'll bite,' he said, after what looked like a lengthy internal deliberation, returning to the bar and his glass of OJ. 'How do you know all that stuff?'

'Well, that's where it gets a bit weird.'

'You're telling me you spoke to your younger self in the year 1986, with this phone that you found in a fancy-dress shop,' he said, holding the device in question. 'That's remarkable coverage. Must be a hell of a payment plan, though.'

'I know how it sounds, Scotty,' said Bob, feeling ridiculous, 'but it's the truth. Why would I make it up?'

'Like I said, we don't really know each other, so I have no idea.'

'Just look at the phone for a moment,' Bob said,

ignoring the barb and taking the device. 'There's nowhere to plug in a power source. But when I push this button . . .' – he pressed it on – '. . . it powers up. How?'

'That is odd. I'll give you that,' Scotty replied, taking the phone from Bob and observing it with renewed intrigue. 'You can charge phones by just placing them on a power pad nowadays.'

'Yeah, nowadays. This thing's not from nowadays.'

'How do you know?'

'Look at it.'

'Looks can be deceiving,' said Scotty, handing the phone back to Bob.

'That's a good point,' Bob said, a smile breaking out across his face. 'You always had a way of making me see a problem from a different angle. Classic Scotty.'

Scotty chuckled. 'This is so crazy!' he said, before taking a large gulp of his OJ. 'I admit I don't know how you knew that stuff about me. Not all of it was true by the way. I don't clean my cutlery obsessively in restaurants. I rarely eat in restaurants, and I've never stolen anything in my life . . . ever.'

'Well, I assume there are variables.'

'Variables?'

'When I used the phone to speak to my younger self, I changed the present. Change creates variables.'

'You're saying that conversation resulted in us not being friends any more?'

'Exactly.'

'So, you told your younger self not to be friends with me?' asked Scotty, amused by the notion.

'No, of course not!'

'Then why aren't we friends any more?'

'I . . .' Bob began, struggling to find the right words to navigate a potentially awkward situation. 'I think I accidentally doomed our friendship by shifting the focus of my younger self away from us and towards . . . a girl.'

Scotty laughed. 'Man, there's always a lady involved. Who?'

'Do you remember . . . Kirsty, from school?'

'Kirsty?' he said, furrowing his brow. 'Kirsty? It's not ringing a bell.'

'Kirsty . . . Cummings.'

'Oh! Cummings! Yeah, I remember now. Tough name for a kid,' he said, the memory flooding back. 'Whatever happened to her?'

'She's my wife.'

'You married Kirsty from school? Wow! You know, now that I think about it,' he mused, with a far-off look in his eye, 'I do remember you pair getting pretty chummy.'

'This is what I'm telling you. We didn't get chummy. I didn't marry Kirsty Cummings from school. But after that conversation with young Bob, the next morning I went home and Kirsty was there in my house . . . as my wife!'

'It sounds like you don't want to be married to her,' said Scotty.

'You're damn right!' Bob said, before summoning the barman. 'Two more please, barkeep.'

'Rob, this has been fascinating,' said Scotty, with a

raised hand indicating he did not want another drink, 'but I've got to get going.' He reached for his hat.

'What if I could prove I'm telling the truth.'

'And how would you do that?'

'By calling the past.'

'OK,' Scotty began, with a sceptical headshake, 'if you can defy the laws of nature and the wider universe as we know it, right now, in this crummy bar in Soho . . . you will have my undivided attention,' he concluded with a grin, returning his hat to the bar top.

'Crummy bar? I'll have you know this is one of your favourite boozers.'

Scotty looked around at the weathered decor and various puffy, beer-battered faces. 'I don't think so.'

'I once saw you dip your cock and balls in a jar of pickled eggs in that very corner,' Bob countered, nodding to a grubby area beyond the bar.

'Well, thank God for variables, because that ain't me.'

'It is and I'll prove it.' The barman placed fresh glasses before them. Bob took his pint and guzzled half its contents in one go. Wiping his mouth, he asked, 'How would you like to speak to a young Scotty Pickers-Gill or, because God knows who's going to answer, a member of your family from 1986, right now?'

'Sure,' said Scotty with a reluctant sigh. 'Why not. It's always good to catch up with family.'

'You know what, I'm going to ignore the sarcasm because everything you think you know is about to change.'

'Is it?'

'Oh yeah. In a big fucking way.' He powered up the phone. 'Do you know your old phone number?'

'New York – 212 371 4301. London – 0173 1451. Everyone remembers their first.'

'All right, Mr Wonderful,' said Bob, with a withering look. 'Here's what we're going to do. You're going to ask to speak to your mother; I think Dawn is a better fit for what I've got in mind . . .'

'Why's my mom "a better fit"?'

'Much like his son, Casey is too laid-back, and your sister is . . . shall we say, free from the burden of intellect.'

'I'm starting to think you might actually be telling the truth and you do know me,' Scotty laughed.

'So, we're agreed, your mother's the mark.'

'The mark? Yeah, sure, why not,' said Scotty, very much his father's son.

'I want you to tell your mother of a future event. Something for her that is yet to come in 1986. It has to be something big she won't forget, but it can't be an event she could manipulate or prevent somehow. That could further disrupt this timeline.'

'Jesus, who're you now, Dr Who?'

'Yes, I'm Dr Who and you are my glamorous assistant. Now shut up and listen. I want you to think of a large-scale event that would have been impossible to overlook between now and 1986 – a real "where were you when" moment.'

'Why me? Why don't you think of something?'

'Because then you'll just say I planned all this.'

'Clever.'

'No, it's genius.'

'I'm beginning to suspect you might be a dickhead in the other "timeline".'

'Funny,' said Bob, grinning. 'Now think.'

'9/11?' said Scotty, deciding to go big.

'Too political. Too harrowing. We need more of a cultural event.'

'The Spice Girls?'

'Funny again. You're a dickhead in both timelines.' This time, Scotty was grinning.

'Princess Di?'

'Oh, that might be it. That's good. I mean, terrible, tragic what happened, but for the purposes of this exercise,' he said, nodding with enthusiasm, 'I think that's the one.'

'Great. Now we have a game plan, let's end this madness.'

'Not so fast,' Bob said. 'What are you going to say?'

'Ahhh, something like, "Hey Mom, it's Scott calling from the future. Just wanted to tell you Princess Diana will die in a horrific car crash in an underpass in Paris in 1997 . . . oh, and make sure Dad checks his prostate regularly."'

'Shit, I forgot Casey had prostate cancer.'

'Forgot?' said Scotty. 'I never told you.'

'I suppose you could throw that in,' Bob said, ignoring Scotty's point. He thought for a moment. 'What harm could it do? They'll just catch it early and he won't have to go through surgery.'

'This is getting a little tiresome again,' said Scotty, losing his good cheer and downing the last of his juice.

'All right. Let's do it! Obviously don't say it's you, we want her to remember the event, not that her son called from the future. Just give her the Diana details and mention your dad needs regular prostate exams, and that should do it. Got it?' asked Bob, handing him the phone.

'Roger that,' replied Scotty, inputting his old London home phone number. 'This is so dumb,' he couldn't resist saying as the phone displayed *Calling* . . .

After a few short rings, an accented voice answered '*Hullo,*' in a lazy baritone.

Rather than registering the identity of the voice, Scotty seemed more surprised that the phone actually worked and his old number was still in use. 'Oh, hi. I wonder if I could speak to the lady of the house, please?'

'*Um, ya, may I ask who's calling?*'

'It's . . . it's S . . . Simon from work,' he said, looking into Bob's face, which was rigid with concentration.

'*Oh, right. I'll get her. Give me a sec,*' the voice said, followed by the clunk of the receiver being placed on a hard surface. Moments later, a muffled exchange could be heard between two people, followed by silence and the eventual clunk of the receiver being lifted.

'*Hullo, who's speaking please?*' asked a female voice, also American, but with a raspy intonation very much the polar opposite of the male's.

'Is this Dawn Pickers-Gill?'

'*It is. To whom am I speaking? My husband said Simon from work, but I don't know a Simon at work.*'

Scotty took the phone away from his ear and stared at it in blank confusion, before a smirk formed on his lips.

'Wow. That sounds a lot like her. How're you doing this?' Ignoring the question, Bob grabbed his friend's hand and forced the phone back to his ear, angrily mouthing the words, *speak to her!*

Scotty cleared his throat. 'Hi, Dawn,' he said, with a sarcastically arched brow for Bob's benefit, 'you're right, I'm not Simon from work. But my name's not important. What is important is that I have your attention for the next minute or so. Sound good?' he asked, giving Bob a mocking wink and a thumbs-up.

'*How intriguing! I suppose I can give you a minute of my time, not Simon from work,*' said Dawn.

'She's good,' said Scotty, covering the receiver, before turning his attention back to Dawn. 'Excellent. Then here we go. In 1997, Princess Diana will sadly die in a terrible car crash in an underpass in Paris.' Silence on the other end of the line. 'Hello?'

'*I'm here,*' she said, with a baffled chuckle. '*That has to be the strangest thing anyone has ever said to me.*'

'Well, of course, after all, this is brand new information, right?' he said with more sarcasm, met this time by a light thump on the shoulder from Bob.

'*It is. How awful for her. 1997, you say? I take it Prince Charles won't be with Lady Di?*'

'No. That doesn't work out. So that's part one. Here comes part two, and this one is a bit more personal . . .'

'*OK.*'

' . . . make sure your husband gets his prostate examined regularly.'

'*His what?!*' she asked in a shocked tone.

'Prostate. It's a gland between the bladder and penis.'

'*I know what it is.*'

'Great. Just keep an eye on it.'

'*Is there a punchline coming? Or . . .*'

'Nope. That's us, *Dawn*. It's been fun. All you have to do now is remember this conversation . . . *forever.*'

'*I don't think that'll be a problem.*'

'Excellent. Have a nice day.'

'*You too.*'

'I gotta admit, she was excellent. But you can tell the guy who played my Dad was a bit overdone. A little hammy. Who are they? Actors from the agency?' asked Scotty, handing the phone back to Bob.

'That was your mother and father in 1986. This is really happening, Scotty.'

'Give me a break.'

'Do you honestly think this is how I want to spend my Saturday, Jeremy Beadle-ing a man who apparently I don't even know?' he said, exasperated. 'Phone your present-day mother.'

'No way!' said Scotty, blanching at the very notion. 'Why would I?'

'What do you think we're doing? Call her and ask her if someone rang her in 1986 and told her Princess Diana was going to die, and your dad should get his prostate checked. When she tells you yes, you'll have to believe me.'

'If you knew me, you'd know that my parents and I don't really talk.'

'Why not?'

'Look at me, I'm a forty-eight-year-old bike courier. I'm a colossal fuck-up. I've put them through hell.'

'You're a bike courier?' said Bob, unable to hide his own disappointment.

'Yeah, for you! For Fitz & Bloom. You gave me the job. Jesus! Have you been kicked in the head or something?'

'I can see your life isn't sunshine and rainbows, Scotty, but I'm trying to help you. Don't you understand I can change this' – once again circling his person – 'back into what it should be.'

'And what's that?'

'Happy, successful, well adjusted . . . *bald!*'

'Bald? I'm not bald!' he said, instinctively touching his hair.

'Scotty?' Bob said, in a pleading tone.

'What?' Scotty replied, defensively.

'Scotty . . . I know.'

Scotty turned away from Bob and looked out into the street through the pub's dirty windows. 'Fuck it,' he said after a while. 'You're right, it's a wig. I'm not proud of it.'

'Then why wear it?' Bob asked, gently.

'I started losing my hair when I was young and I felt so self-conscious, you know . . . Jesus, why am I telling you this?'

'Go on,' urged Bob.

With a sigh, he continued, 'I was self-conscious. I thought that would fade in time but it didn't. That insecurity just stayed with me. It never went away,' he said, still unable to meet Bob's eyes. 'But do you wanna know what's funny? All these years later it feels like one of the few things I can control. Look at me, I'm a wreck and what's on my head is the only thing I've managed to maintain. As the rest of me falls to pieces, this 'piece' is as good as the day I bought it. In a way, it's my last nod to vanity.' Breaking off his sad reverie, he turned back to the bar and finished the rest of his orange juice. The action left him staring forlornly into the bottom of the now empty glass.

'That . . . has to be the saddest thing I've ever heard,' said Bob.

Despite himself, Scotty couldn't help breaking into a smile. 'Go to hell, Rob.'

'It must be tough. I get it. I mean, not literally – look at my glorious pelt,' Bob grinned.

'Such an arsehole,' Scotty replied, now laughing.

'I remember when you started losing it, I was there. I also remember *my* Scotty didn't give a flying fuck. You can be him again.'

'You really do believe all this, don't you?'

'Ring your mother.'

They held each other's gaze for long moments. Scotty was the first to flinch, glancing up at the carriage clock nestled amongst the optics behind the bar.

'It's about midday in New York right now, so she's up and around.'

'They moved back to New York?'

'Yeah, years ago.'

'Oh,' Bob said in surprise (Casey and Dawn were still based in London, this time yesterday – before the phone). 'Well, that's even better. How could I have spoken to your mother to set up this 'prank' if she lives in NYC?'

'My mother and I haven't shared a moment's laughter in a couple of decades. We have what I call a weddings and funerals relationship . . . and we're all out of weddings. She's very happy with the three-thousand-mile buffer between us.'

'Christ Scotty, what did you do?'

'You know.'

'I don't.'

'*Stop it, Rob!*' he said, angrily. 'You know what happened. I told you when I came with my hat in hand begging for a job.'

'I can see why you're getting annoyed,' Bob said, holding his hands up in a placating manner. 'We can go back and forth rubbing each other up the wrong way, or you can ring your mother and learn that I am telling the truth. It sounds like you have nothing to lose anyway.'

Scotty's line of sight was pulled back to the street beyond the dirty windows. Bob examined his profile. The knitted brow and slight shake of his head did not look promising . . . 'To hell with it,' Scotty said, taking out his personal phone. 'If only to shut you up.'

'Yes! Thank you, thank you, Scotty. You won't regret it.'

'I already do,' he said, pressing *Call Mom*.

The phone rang interminably as Bob watched, expectation written across his face as he leaned closer to hear the exchange.

In Scotty's mind, he could see his mother staring at his name on her flashing screen, weighing up whether she wanted to answer or not.

'*Hullo, Scott,*' said Dawn Pickers-Gill, choosing to answer on this occasion.

'Hey, Mom,' he replied, matching her underwhelmed tone.

'*What can I do for you?*'

'Just checking in to see how you're doing.'

'*I'm fine.*'

'And Dad and Pip?'

'*Also fine.*'

'Great.' The sound of dead air filled the line between them.

'*Are you in a bar, Scott?*' she asked, hearing the sounds of merriment in the background.

'No, I'm in a café,' he lied. Bob looked on, wincing at the awkward interaction before mouthing the words, *ask her.*

'*What can I do for you, Scott?*' she asked again.

'This is going to sound pretty weird . . .' he began, his eyes screwed shut in embarrassment, 'but did you ever have a phone call from someone in the eighties telling you that Princess Diana was going to die in a car crash in Paris and that you should get Dad's prostate checked regularly?'

The silence that followed drew out to the point where he thought she had ended the call, but the distant honk of a New York car horn assured him she was still on the line.

'Mom?'

'You've been speaking to your father?'

His eyes snapped open.

'Yes, I have,' he said, another lie.

'Jesus, Casey! Why would he tell you about that?'

'Are you saying it's true?' he asked, stunned.

'We said we wouldn't tell anyone. I swear I'm going to kick his ass!'

'Mom, is it true?'

A loud, irked exhalation filled his ear before she finally said, *'Yes.'* Bob sprung from his seat, punching the air in victory, as Scotty gazed unblinking and unseeing at the pub's sticky floor.

'I got a call from some strange man,' she continued, *'and he told me about Princess Di and your father's cancer.'*

'In 1986,' murmured Scotty in disbelief.

'Yes, Scott. In 1986,' she echoed, annoyance in her voice. *'If you've called to make fun or tell me I'm crazy, don't bother. I know what I heard. That call saved your father's life, so I don't care what you think.'*

'Mom, I don't think you're crazy. In fact, you're one of the sanest people I know. Which is why I had to hear the story from you first-hand, it's . . . it's . . . incredible.'

'Oh. Well, thank you . . . for saying that,' she replied.

'I'd love to hear more about that call.'

'Well, I can't remember the day,' she began tentatively, *'but it must have been a weekend because both your dad and I were home. The phone rang and Casey answered. A man asked for me by name, telling your dad he was a colleague of mine from work called Simon. I didn't have a colleague at work called Simon,'*

141

she said, now warming up to recounting the tale, '*so I told him, I said, "I don't know a Simon," and he said, "You got me, I'm not Simon. Who I am isn't important, but what I have to tell you is." I thought it was a joke or something, so I laughed and said, "OK, I'm listening." He said, "Princess Diana will die in a car crash in Paris in 1997." Well, I didn't know what to think. I said, "That's the craziest thing I ever heard." He said, "I'm not so sure, wait till you hear part two." I said, "OK, I'm listening." He said, "You need to make sure your husband gets regular prostate check-ups." At that point, I was lost for words. I was sure it was a joke. I asked, "Is there a punchline?" He said, "No, just remember what I have told you . . . forever." And that was it. He put the phone down.*'

'That's an extraordinary story,' Scotty said, feeling dizzy. 'But there is one detail I'm confused by.'

'*And what's that?*'

'If you were warned by this person to make sure Dad got regular check-ups, how comes he still had to have surgery to remove his prostate?'

'*What are you talking about?*'

'The prostatectomy, Mom. We didn't catch it early!'

'*Scott, I know you drank your way through his entire scare, but this is poor even by your standards. Are you really telling me you can't remember what happened? After Princess Di passed at the exact time and place he told me she would, I was adamant when it came to your dad getting regular check-ups. We argued constantly about it. He called me crazy and obsessed. But I didn't care, I just knew it, I knew it in my bones that that man was real. I don't know how he knew, maybe he was an angel, I don't know, but I couldn't risk anything happening to your dad.*' Her voice quivered with emotion. '*We caught the cancer early. Chemo cured him. He's been cancer-free for fifteen years thanks to whoever that man was in 1986.*'

'It's unreal,' Scott said through strained vocal cords.

'*Are you OK, Scott? Do I need to be worried about you?*'

'I'm fine, Mom. I gotta go.' The tears now openly flowed down his cheeks. 'Love you,' he said, ending the call.

Bob placed a comforting hand upon his shoulder. 'I know how you feel.'

'What's going on?' said Scotty, wiping the tears away with his T-shirt. 'It's real, it's actually real. But how? It's impossible.'

'You're right. It is. Unless you have this phone,' Bob said, holding the device that had saved Scotty's dad from some extremely invasive surgery.

'But what is it?' Scotty asked.

'I've thought about that at length . . . and the only answer I can come up with is this – it's an opportunity! An opportunity for you and me to fix our lives.'

Staring at the phone in wonder, a thought occurred to Scotty. 'Why can't I remember them catching the cancer early? Why am I remembering it differently?'

'I don't know. Maybe if you use the phone to change things, you keep the original memory. Saying that, I've had some pretty strange moments where I've started remembering things I never did. I think they're the memories of the person I've changed into, this new Robert Bloomfield of your reality. It's a head scrambler!' he concluded, signalling the barman for another pint with his empty glass.

'So, what do we do now?'

'Sounds like someone's on board,' said Bob with a satisfied smile. 'You can start by telling me what the hell has happened to you?'

Bob sat in a booth opposite Scotty. The pub was now almost deserted. The regulars had drifted off, making way for the more boisterous Saturday night crowd that would soon descend on Soho.

'I wish I could say he came out of nowhere,' began Scotty, 'but the truth is, I was so drunk I don't even remember hitting him. I do remember waking up in the morning and living the final split second of my previous life before I realized I was in a cell. I had a vague memory of flashing blue lights, angry faces screaming at me, handcuffs too tight. I knew I was in trouble, but . . . when they told me what I had done . . .

'Leo Presser, that's the name of the boy I killed. Ten years old. I destroyed his family, and my own. I can't put the guilt into words but it's wrapped around me like barbed wire. I'll never be at peace. And that's one of the few things that keeps me going, because that's exactly what I deserve. I remember feeling angry when the judge said seven years in prison. It was too lenient.

'I served six years at Her Majesty's pleasure. Apparently, that's enough for killing a kid. I was released back into the world with nothing. No fixed abode, no job, no family and friends waiting for me at the gate. And it felt like more than I deserved because what

I've lost is nothing compared to Leo and his family. I thought about reaching out to them and saying sorry, but it sounds ridiculous: "Sorry I killed your son, sorry I killed your son, sorry I killed your son" . . . just words, meaningless. So, I don't drink for Leo and I don't drive for Leo. I'm sure he's looking down at me oh so proud,' said Scotty, with a bitter snort. 'And that's where I'm at in this "reality", as you put it.'

Bob now recognized, written in the face of his old friend, the familiar agony of the unfathomable sense of loss that had stared back at him from the mirror for so many years. 'I'm so sorry, Scotty.'

'Don't be sorry for me.'

'I'm sorry this has happened to you and Leo. Don't you see? This is all my fault. I changed things. This was never meant to happen. When I first used the phone I . . . I changed things by accident. I didn't have a clue what I was doing.

'Scotty! Do you know what we just did? We used the phone to change your father's life. We removed one of the most agonizing periods in your family's history, not to mention we saved Casey's prostate in the process. We did all that with one phone call. And we are going to do it again!'

'How? What do you have in mind?'

'Get my old life back. Reverse this sad-sack existence of yours and give Leo back the life he was meant to live.'

Scotty nodded in deep thought, before asking, 'What's my other life like?'

'Well, you're not a murderer. I'll tell you that much.'

Bob's joke was met by a stony stare. 'Sorry. You've got a good life.'

'What do I do?'

'Something in finance? To be honest, every time you bring it up, I zone out. But you seem to enjoy it.'

'I am really good with numbers.'

'There you go.'

'Am I married?'

'You are.'

'What's she like?'

'She's . . . very nice.'

'Is she attractive?'

'If that is something that's important to you . . . then, yes, I suppose she is attractive.'

'What does she do?'

'She's a stay-at-home mum.'

'I have kids!'

'Three.'

'Wow,' he said, beaming. 'That's amazing.'

'Yes, you do seem to enjoy it.'

'What about you? What's your life like?'

'I work a lot. Same business.'

'What about marriage and kids?'

'Nah,' Bob's eyes glazed over for a moment. 'Not interested.'

'Come on. Nobody has ever tempted you?'

'There was someone.'

'Who?'

'A girl called Nell.'

'Why didn't you want those things with her?'

'Look, Scotty, we've already done this chat in the other reality . . . my main goal here is to save my brother. That's all that matters to me.'

Scotty looked shocked. 'You're going to try and save Thomas?'

'*We are.* You and I are going to work out how. This is too big to risk talking in riddles with whoever answers that phone when we call. Which is why we need to think of a way to convince the Bloomfields of 1986 that they have to believe me when I tell them their son is going to die.'

'Why not just tell them the truth?'

'I know my parents. They'd never believe me. They'd just put the phone down. No, we need to show them that the man on the end of the line can predict the future.'

'Well, at least we have some time. In '86 it's a few weeks before . . .' Scotty couldn't bring himself to say it.

'Before my brother dies. I know. What we don't know is how long we'll have this "magical" connection to the past. I think we'd better crack on and find a solution so I can level with my family of '86 and guide them in a way that will manipulate the present back to how it was.'

'With the not-so-small inclusion of your brother, Thomas?'

'I've read enough shitty scripts for time-travel films and TV shows to learn that bringing a life into existence that was never meant to be, will "mess with the time continuum", but I really don't give a shit. There is no way that you or anyone else is going to convince me that the world is better off without my brother in it – *understand?*'

'Hey, it's your party,' said Scotty.

*

'Didn't that space shuttle Challenger explode in '86?'

'Yes,' said Bob, after inputting the event into his laptop's search engine, 'January 28th, 1986, way before June 21st.'

'That's a shame,' said Scotty, from the comfort of a chair normally reserved for clients, as Bob tapped away on his computer from behind his office desk. 'What about Chernobyl? That was definitely '86. I remember.'

'Correct. But alas, Russian incompetence won't benefit us on April 26th, 1986,' replied Bob, after another quick search. 'Anyway, we need to be thinking of things that didn't explode. As ridiculous as it sounds, imagine if someone told you it was going to happen – you'd just think they were the ones that made it go kaboom! We need something more subtle.'

'Anybody of note die around that period?'

'I've been looking – Nigel Stock?'

'Who?'

'Hilda Conkling?'

'Never heard of her.'

'Gong Zutong.'

'You're making people up.'

'What? You mean you've never heard of the Chinese optical physicist, Gong Zutong? Jesus, Scotty, read a book!' he said, the glow of the laptop illuminating his sarcasm.

'Going by your kaboom theory, wouldn't your family just assume we murdered Gong, anyway?' said Scotty.

'That's a very good point.'

'I do have them on occasion, Rob.'

'Can I ask you a favour?'

'What?'

'Can you stop calling me Rob?'

'There's no way I'm calling you Mr Bloomfield.'

'No! That's not what I meant.'

'Then what should I call you? He that shall not be named? The symbol?'

'Is Prince alive in this reality?'

'Nah, he died a few years back.'

'Fuck.'

'I know.'

'It was a long shot. Look, where I come from you and everybody else calls me Bob. Not Rob, not Robert. Bob.'

'Bob? That's weird. I've never heard you called that. But if it'll stop you from getting your panties in a twist . . . Bob.'

'Thank you.'

'Lottery numbers?' said Scotty, back to business.

Tap-tap. 'The UK National Lottery was launched on the 14th of November 1994.'

'Ah yes. That rings a bell. What about the pools? Wasn't that big in the eighties, betting on football?'

'Wait a minute,' said Bob, suddenly looking up from his laptop. 'My dad was taking the boys to football practice earlier . . . they're obsessed, he said.' He quickly started typing with renewed vigour. After an urgent scan of the information before him, he seemed to find what he was looking for. 'Scotty, you're a genius,' he announced, turning the laptop to show him the result of his search. 'This is it!'

Scotty looked at the laptop and smiled. 'That's tomorrow night.'

'I know.'

'It's perfect.'

'It is. We can formulate our plan this evening and execute tomorrow,' said Bob, as his iPhone vibrated. 'Oh shit,' he murmured, as he read the text on the display.

Could you pick up a couple of bottles of red on your way home? We're running a little low. Something from Bordeaux works. Hope you are feeling better. Love you, see you soon xxx

He gave the message careful consideration. 'This time tomorrow you and I will be back where we're meant to be . . . so in the here and *incorrect* now, would you like to come to a dinner party, Scotty?'

13

'Kirsty, you remember Scotty?' said Bob, watching her
face drop as Scotty entered from the hallway holding a
weighty plastic bag.

'How could I forget. What's it been, twenty-five
years?' she said, struggling to find her composure.

'I'd say around that,' Scotty said, with an uncomfort-
able grin, extending his free hand. Kirsty took the hand
and they shook. Bob looked on at the interaction with
fascination. Even though he knew in this reality Kirsty
and Scotty were no more than fellow pupils at a school
decades ago, he still could hardly believe they were
strangers to one another in this moment. *This is so weird!*

'Scotty brought goodies,' said Bob, flicking his eyes
between them like a spectator on Centre Court.

'Oh yeah, I brought a couple of bottles of red as
requested.'

'You really shouldn't have,' she said, turning her eyes
(or as Bob felt them, twin laser beams of death) towards
him. 'Robert should have.'

'It's the least I can do. Thanks for having me at your
dinner par—' The words trailed off as he took in the
room and the two other people there besides himself,
Kirsty and Bob. 'Hi,' said Scotty to the smartly dressed
couple sat on the sofa.

'Good evening,' said the man, raising a chubby hand and smiling with a mouth full of disorganized teeth.

'Hi,' said the striking woman, her hand barely making it off her lap due either to a lack of energy or nonchalance.

'Naomi, Ron, this is an old friend of ours, Scott Pickers-Gill,' said Kirsty, taking the bag from him. 'Ron, why don't you pop the cork . . . I mean, twist the cap, on these,' she corrected, glancing into the bag with a huff. 'Robert, a quick word.'

'You're not happy?' he asked, following a seething Kirsty into the kitchen, away from their guests.

'Am I not happy that you've brought a man who's dressed like a fifty-year-old teenager and smells like a car-park stairwell to my intimate dinner evening with Naomi and Ron? Why would you think such a thing!?'

'He's a cyclist. They get a bit ripe.'

'I'm going to kill you. You know that, don't you? I'm going to actually murder you.'

'Come on Kirst. It's not that bad.'

'You mentioned him this morning out of the blue, and now here he is? Strange timing, Robert. What's going on?'

'Just a coincidence. I bumped into him in Soho on my way home and thought it would be good to catch up.'

'First you stay out all night, and now you're bringing home randoms from a million years in our past?' she said, baffled.

'What's so random about inviting a colleague who

happens to be an old friend over for a bite? The more the merrier.'

'Why tonight, the night I have my boss over with her husband, for dinner? Any other night, just not tonight,' she said, as the squawk of a child from a nearby baby monitor took her attention. 'I'll see to Thomas. You get rid of him, or I will.'

'You look good,' he said, taking in her close-fitting green slip dress.

'Much like *Wayne's World*, out there – you do not,' she replied, leaving the kitchen with an aggressive shoulder-barge into the swinging double doors. Feeling his blood rise, he took a moment to re-centre himself before setting off in pursuit.

Entering the living room, he smiled politely to Naomi and Ron who were now sat on the sofa sipping the red from over-sized wine glasses. 'Be with you shortly, guys. Help yourselves to nuts,' said Bob, before turning his attention to Scotty, who was still stood a couple of feet from the front door, awkwardly feigning interest in a framed picture of a daffodil.

'I think I'm going to shoot off,' he said, as Bob approached.

'Why?'

'I want to.'

'Don't be silly.'

'When you said dinner party, I imagined more than two couples and me as king of the gooseberries. I'm going to leave.'

'No, you're not. You're my friend and you're staying

for dinner. We have much to discuss. Plus, as you and I know, none of this is real,' he concluded with a wink.

'I think your wife would disagree.'

'Yeah, my *wife* . . . leave her to me,' he said, his head swirling as he made his way towards Thomas's bedroom.

As Bob entered, he saw Kirsty standing cradling Thomas as he drank from a feeding bottle. He had intended to charm her into changing her mind about Scotty, but the sight of her and the child gently swaying in the dim light took the wind from his sails. Kirsty looked up and the face of a contented mother instantly changed to one of an annoyed wife.

'Kirst—' he said at full volume.

'Shhhhh,' she whispered, 'he's going back to sleep.'

Bob walked over for a closer look. He listened to the child's shallow breathing as he suckled intently on the bottle, tiny bubbles of milk frothing around his mouth in the process. He reached for Thomas's perfectly formed miniature hand and smiled at the warmth of it.

'He's gorgeous.'

'Yeah,' said Kirsty, immediately slipping back into contented mode.

'Can I hold him?' Bob asked. Part of him was expecting an automatic 'no', so he was taken aback when Kirsty guided the precious bundle into his arms.

'We're so lucky,' she said, looping her arm around Bob. 'Our little miracle. I thought our window had closed. But nope, here he is.'

'I never thought I'd have kids,' said Bob, staring in wonder at his son.

'We're as bad as each other – work, work, work. Thank God we came to our senses and realized there might be something more to life.'

'This is more than I deserve,' he said, meaning it.

'Of course you deserve this. We both do,' she said, kissing Bob's cheek.

'Scotty's been dealt a tough hand, Kirst,' he said, remembering the reason he entered the room in the first place.

'Has he?' she asked, suddenly irritated. 'As I remember it, he was dealt a good hand, he just played it badly, Robert.'

'You might be right. But I could have been a better friend to him.'

'A better friend?' she said, taking back the baby. 'You barely know him. What're you talking about?'

'We were close in school . . . but then I started spending more time with you and less time with him.'

'So, it's my fault he hit a kid when he was drunk out of his mind?'

'No, of course not. He's not a bad person is all I'm saying. Take it from me, you two, under different circumstances would get along just fine.'

'Of course, me and the ex-con, peas in a pod,' she said, placing a sleeping Thomas back in his crib.

'Have a heart, Kirst. Let him stay for dinner.'

Satisfied Thomas was settled, she brought her attention back to Bob. 'Just put him downwind of our guests,' she said with a sigh.

*

'So, who do you think she believes to be "so vain"?' said Ron, referencing Carly Simon's 'You're So Vain', which was playing in the background over the apartment's in-built stereo system.

'Warren Beatty is the general consensus, yes?' said Bob, who sat directly opposite Ron. Naomi sat next to Bob and Kirsty next to Ron. Scotty had pride of place at the head of the table on Bob's right.

'I thought Mick Jagger,' suggested Naomi.

'I've always had a sneaking suspicion it was Robert Redford. What about you, Scott?' asked Ron, as he ran his fingers through his thinning hair, the movement climaxing in his short ponytail being drawn through a clenched fist.

'I . . .' Scotty paused, thinking better of it. 'Never mind, it's stupid.'

'Come on, Scotty. We'll be the judge of that,' teased Bob, through a mouthful of Caprese salad.

'Well . . . I always thought the song was about Carly Simon.'

'Really?' said Kirsty.

'I know. Like I said, it's stupid.'

'No, it's not. I always thought the same,' she said, pleasantly surprised.

'You did?'

'Yes. I mean, that's the whole point, right? You're so vain you probably think this song is about you. It's not, the song is about how this vain arsehole hurt Carly.'

'Exactly!' said Scotty, excitedly. 'She really puts herself

out there. She's so brave. She admits in the song that he "had her" when she was young and didn't know better. This guy sweet talks her and tells her how much of a good-looking couple they are. He tells her he'll never leave her, and all the rest of it. But, of course, he does. He's a bastard. She's saying, you're such a vain man you probably think this song is about you and how attractive you are, but it's not, it's about me, and the way you hurt me.'

Scotty and Kirsty looked at one another smiling and nodding in appreciation of their shared emotional intelligence.

'Peas in a pod,' Bob muttered.

'What's that?' said Kirsty.

'I said nah, it's about a man.'

'I'm not so sure. I think they might have me sold,' said Ron, squinting in thought.

'She is literally singing about a man. The song is called "You're So Vain" not "I Was So Dumped". Sorry, it's definitely about a man.'

'I agree with Robert,' said Naomi in her tired way of speaking. 'So glad we finally got to see your sweet little rugrat, Kirsty. He's divine,' she concluded, apparently done with the Carly Simon debate.

'I didn't know you had a baby,' said Scotty, 'congrats.'

'Thank you, guys,' said Kirsty, beaming.

'Yup, he's a good-looking kid. So, what do you do with yourself, Scott?' asked Ron.

'I'm a bike courier.'

'You must be as fit as a fiddle,' replied Ron, piercing a piece of mozzarella with his fork.

'I won't be entering the Tour de France anytime soon. But yes, I suppose it's a good way to keep the LBs at bay.'

'Good, honest work,' Ron said, swallowing his food.

'If you know of any bad, dishonest work that pays better, do let me know,' winked Scotty.

Ron stopped and closed his eyes in thought for a moment, 'I was being patronizing, wasn't I?' he finally said. 'I apologize, Scott.'

'In your defence, no one expects a man in his forties to reply "bike courier" to the question, "What do you do for work?"'

Ron chuckled. 'I like you, Scott,' he said, bracing his hands in prayer and bowing his head. 'Naomi mentioned you work in the entertainment industry, Robert?'

'Work is a bit strong, Ron. The people I manage do all the work.'

'He's being modest,' said Kirsty. 'He works extremely hard representing the great and the good of the showbiz world,' she finished with pride.

'How exciting. Who do you represent?' asked Ron.

'Actors, singers, presenters, influencers,' said Bob.

'Influencer,' snorted Naomi, gulping a mouthful of red wine. 'Isn't that a euphemism for talentless?'

'Well, Naomi, there's talentless and broke and talentless pulling in 150k a year. Guess which one is represented by me?' said Bob.

'How much?! How do I become an influencer?' said Scotty.

'The "influencer" has destroyed my industry,' Naomi continued. 'Social media has replaced the print magazine as the primary means to discover fashion, lifestyle, home style, fitness, the list goes on. It's all-encompassing. We can't compete, can we Kirsty?'

'It is a challenge,' she began, put on the spot by her boss, 'but one I think we are rising to. We have to fight fire with fire and increase our presence online . . .'

'Online!' Ron interjected with his own snort of derision. 'If I had a penny for everybody who entered my office with issues born from endlessly staring at other people's lives, *online*.'

'What do you do, Ron?' asked Scotty.

'I practise hypnotherapy,' he answered, petting his ponytail again.

'Does that mean if you wanted to you could make me cluck like a chicken?' said Scotty.

'It's hypnotherapy Scott, not a night at Butlin's,' Kirsty said.

'Now, that's what I call a snobservation. Butlin's is a world-class resort. You'd know that if you were lucky enough to go there,' countered Scotty.

Surprisingly, Kirsty giggled delightedly at this.

'There's a lot of misunderstanding when it comes to my profession,' said Ron. 'In answer to your question, Scott, most people are susceptible to hypnosis. So, I may very well be able to make you cluck like a chicken.'

'I don't think so. My mind is a fortress,' said Scotty.

'More like a shed with a padlock on it,' said Bob, to a ripple of laughter from Scotty and the rest of the table.

'But I wouldn't use my powers for ill,' continued Ron, turning serious. 'My goal is to create a state of focused attention and increased suggestibility during which positive suggestions and guided imagery are used to help individuals deal with a variety of concerns and issues, such as anxiety, substance abuse, paranoia and so on.'

'Sounds great . . . but there's nothing wrong with a bit of paranoia. What do you think makes you pick up your dog shit in the park?' observed Bob.

'That's lovely, Robert,' said Kirsty, with a clatter of her fork on her plate.

'What? I'm just saying a dab of the devil is sometimes a good thing,' said Bob.

'Ah yes, as Freud told us, "The paranoid person does not project on to the sky, but on to something that is already there." You're talking about prudent paranoia, Robert. That's where an individual considers their impact on society in a positive way. The paranoia I deal with is in most part a pathological condition where sufferers are tormented by delusions of persecution, which manifest in mistrust and hypervigilance.'

Seeing an opportunity, Bob turned to Naomi. 'Do you ever get paranoid?'

'Why would I get paranoid?' she asked.

'You're a beautiful woman and your husband is . . . not quite at your level. No offence, Ron.'

'I'm never offended by the truth,' said Ron with a toothy grin, caressing Naomi's hand.

Bob continued, 'It must have crossed your mind that you didn't marry him with your full consent.'

'I don't follow?' she said blankly.

'Think about it, one minute you're on a first date, the

next you're in a white dress on your way to the church. Maybe at some point Ron sprinkled a little of his suggestive fairy dust on you?'

Along with the rest of the table, she dismissed the notion in good cheer, at least she did at first. Bob watched as a crease of doubt gradually appeared on her conspicuously smooth forehead.

'I'm afraid I had nothing but good old-fashioned charm at my disposal, Robert,' said Ron. 'Am I right dear?'

'Yes,' she said, after a long moment, that crease still wrinkling her brow.

'You'll have to excuse Robert, Naomi. He's not as funny as he thinks he is,' said Kirsty, sensing Naomi's unease and glaring at Bob with her death rays again.

'Cool your nuclear rods, Kirst. Obviously, I'm just messing around. Ron is an absolute catch . . . unless he programmed me to say that, of course?'

At this, the table erupted into laughter. Even Kirsty, seeing Naomi and Ron relax, gave herself to the moment.

'And you're back in the room,' said Ron, clicking his fingers at Bob, to more laughter.

What followed was an undeniably pleasant evening.

'That was a great night,' said Scotty, smoking a roll-up as he and Bob looked out at London's skyline from the apartment's twenty-third-floor balcony, thousands of little lights glimmering back at them in the darkness. 'Thanks again for having me along. It's been a while since I had so much fun.'

'You're very welcome, my friend. It was good to see you laugh,' said Bob, swishing a tumbler of whisky.

'I am a little confused, though,' Scotty added, blowing smoke into London's troposphere of smog.

'Oh?'

'Why? Why do you want to leave this? You've got a great job. You've got an incredible home. Look at this view!' he said, sweeping an arm across the panorama. 'You've got a beautiful kid. Kirsty is . . . she's amazing. Funny, stunning, clever. It all seems perfect. What am I missing?'

'It's not mine.'

'So what? It is now. Why not keep it?'

'Because it belongs to someone else.'

'Have you considered that whoever was meant for all this might actually be having an even better life? That is possible, right?'

'Maybe,' said Bob, a grim expression on his face as he brought the tumbler to his lips. 'But I can't be here. It's not right.'

'You're a better man than me. I'm not sure I could give all this up if I were in your shoes.'

Bob watched Scotty's profile as he looked out on to London. 'Scotty . . .' he began. His friend turned and looked at him.

'What?'

Bob paused. After a long moment he said, 'It's nothing. We've got a big day tomorrow, time to turn in.'

'Of course.'

'What do you say we meet at the office early afternoon?'

'Sounds good. What shall I do with this?' he asked, looking around for a receptacle for his cigarette.

'Put it in here,' said Bob, offering his now-empty whisky tumbler.

Ping!

'It's a text from Naomi saying she and Ron had a great time last night,' said Kirsty, looking up from her phone.

'I'm glad,' said Bob, from over the rim of his coffee cup. 'Scotty asked me to thank you before he left.'

'That's nice of him,' she replied, bringing her attention back to the Sunday supplements laid out on the breakfast bar between them.

Bob had no reading material. He sat eating toast and drinking coffee, completely present in the moment. His wife, beautifully dishevelled in the mid-morning light, sat wearing a thick cotton robe (Bob had already dressed for the day). His son lay squeaking and gurgling from his cot in the adjacent living room, a hanging mobile captivating the child almost as much as the entire surreal situation captivated his father. *So, this is marital bliss.*

He could feel himself drifting into the headspace of Robert John Bloomfield, the man who should be sitting here in this reality enjoying a late breakfast with his wife and son. He instinctively knew that the longer he remained here, the more difficult it would be to hold on to the memory of Bob Bloomfield. Keeping those memories was like holding his breath underwater. Eventually, he would be forced to breathe in and embrace this new reality.

'He wasn't as bad as I expected him to be,' said Kirsty.

'Who?' he said, snapping out of his reverie.

'Scott. I'm sorry I freaked out when he arrived. It's just with Ron and Naomi here . . .'

'No need to apologize. I should've called ahead.'

'He could definitely update his wardrobe,' she said smiling, 'but he's a good guy. Even though he's done a terrible thing, I still find myself feeling sorry for him. It must be a hell of a thing to live with.'

'It is,' he said, breaking eye contact with her.

'Hey,' she said, 'it's very different to what happened with you and your brother. You know that.'

'Is it?'

'It wasn't your fault. You were just a kid.'

And that's all Tom and Leo will ever be. Unless I get on with this day. 'I have to go to the office for a couple of hours.'

'Again? I thought we could lounge around, maybe take the baby to the park for a stroll?' she said.

'You know what, that sounds like . . . a very nice day,' he said, surprised by the lack of revulsion he felt at the very idea. 'But I have to go.'

'Do you really?' she said, adopting a childish pout.

'I do,' he said, as she rounded the table between them and wrapped her arms around him. 'Sorry to be a party pooper. We'll do something when I get back.'

'Promise?'

'I promise.' He rose, kissed the top of her head and gently pulled away. She went back to her supplements in a playful huff. Taking his jacket, he headed towards the front door, stopping en route to look into his son's crib. 'Sorry, little man,' he whispered, running his fingers through the fluffy hair, 'maybe we'll meet again someday.'

Prising himself away he reached the front door . . . but couldn't resist one last look at the people he was about to leave behind. 'Kirsty,' he said, making her look up from her reading.

'Yes?'

'Thank you.'

'For what?' she said, a wide smile lighting up her beautiful face.

'For everything.'

14

'So, first we plant the seed,' said Scotty. 'We wait till it bears fruit. Then we call and tell them what they need to know.'

'Exactly,' said Bob. They were the only people present at FitzSimmons & Bloomfield Entertainment Management on a Sunday.

'And what happens then?' asked Scotty, from one of the comfy client chairs, as Bob paced back and forth along a well-worn trench in the thick shag of his office's carpet – an area once upon a time covered by a bearskin rug.

'I don't know. If they do as we tell them . . . Thomas lives and you get to play happy families?'

'I'm still confused. How does keeping you away from your future wife, Kirsty, turn my life around?'

'I already explained this. Our friendship doesn't happen if I get with Kirsty. You need me in your life to keep you on the straight and narrow apparently,' he said with an arched brow.

'I feel bad. Look at what you're giving up for me. It doesn't feel right.'

'Trust me. It's the right thing to do. You deserve your life back.'

'I'm coming in for a hug,' said Scotty, rising from his chair.

'Please don't.'

'It's happening.'

'I'd prefer not.'

Despite Bob's protestations, Scotty wrapped his skinny arms around his new/old friend. 'Thank you,' he said, inches from Bob's ear.

'All right. Let's not get crazy.'

'Thank you,' Scotty said again, releasing a flushed Bob.

'Don't thank me yet. We've still got to pull the trigger on this thing.'

'What will happen to us? Will it get all swirly like the opening credits to *Buck Rogers*?' asked Scotty, taking his seat again.

'If it's anything like before,' began Bob, with an anxious expression, 'at the moment of change, it's pure agony. It's like being struck by lightning.'

'Jesus Christ!' said Scotty, losing what little colour his complexion still had.

Bob laughed. 'I'm messing with you. You won't feel a thing.'

'That was not cool.'

'I couldn't resist.' He pointed to a large digital wall-mounted clock, which said 2.59 p.m. 'So, 3.00 p.m. has a nice ring to it. You ready?'

'There's no time like the present. Although I'm not sure that saying makes much sense now we have this,' added Scotty, looking at their telephonic link to 1986 that sat at the centre of Bob's desk. 'You know what you're going to say?'

'It's all here,' said Bob, sitting at his desk and opening his laptop. He reached for the old phone as the clock turned 3.00 p.m.

RING-RING

'Not now!' exclaimed Bob, as his iPhone started ringing. He looked at the screen. 'No caller ID.'

'Don't answer it,' said Scotty.

'I don't really subscribe to the whole "If you don't know who it is, don't answer it" thing.'

'That's brave. But we do have more pressing matters at hand, yes?' said Scotty with a raised brow.

'You're right,' replied Bob as the phone continued to ring. 'Nope, can't do it,' he said, grabbing the phone. 'Hello?'

'Hello, Mr Bloomfield.'

He recognized the voice immediately. Holding a finger up, he mouthed the words 'Give me one second,' to Scotty and left the office for Miss Pennypacker's desk-come-reception area.

'Chloe Huxley,' he said, wearily. 'This is not a good time. I *really* can't talk right now . . . even though I would love to ask how you got my number.'

'Lucky guess,' she said, merrily.

'I bet. I'll see you in the office tomorrow. At a professional distance.'

'I'm pregnant.'

Even though he was ninety-nine per cent sure this could not be true, he still felt a primal swell of panic. 'Congratulations. Who's the father, Anvil?'

'He's had the snip. It's you.'

'It's really not.'

'Did you know that sperm can navigate the uterus and fallopian tubes to reach the egg in just thirty minutes. Did you know that?'

'I did. I've walked the route,' said Bob, sitting on the edge of Pennypacker's desk. 'There is no way a pregnancy would register this early. And anyway, I was *very* careful.'

'I'm having this baby. And I want you to be part of its life.'

'You're not pregnant!' he said, as his phone pinged. A banner informed him he had received a picture message from a number he did not recognize. He opened it. The picture showed Chloe sat on a toilet, bare legs exposed, holding a pregnancy test with two pink lines emblazoned across it. 'Really, Chloe? I'm looking at a picture with only two possibilities. Photoshop or you are actually pregnant. If it's the latter, may I suggest you contact the real father as soon as possible. If it's Photoshop, contact a psychiatrist.'

The line went silent before Chloe burst into maniacal laughter. *'You have to get up pretty early to get one over on old Mr Bloomfield,'* she said, with more laughter. *'I'm messing with you! Of course I'm not up the duff. It's a joke!'*

'Good one.'

'But we did have sex,' she said, her voice taking a more serious edge. *'Which would break Kirsty's heart to hear, I'm sure. So, let's avoid that. What do you think about giving me a little boost up the Fitz & Bloom ladder? I think that would be a lovely gesture on your part. Don't you agree?'*

'I swear if you go anywhere near Kirsty . . .' He stopped. *What the hell am I doing?* He suddenly realized where he was and what he was about to do with a waiting Scotty in his office: he was about to say goodbye to this bizarre reality. Which meant there were no consequences. Which also meant he could say what he was about to say without fear of retribution. 'If you go anywhere near Kirsty . . . I'll be very disappointed. Because I want to be the one to tell her about us.'

'*You do?*' she said, on the back foot.

'I do.'

'*And what will you tell her?*'

'The truth. That I'm in love with another woman.' The sentence was greeted with silence. 'It's you, Chloe. From the moment I first saw you, I knew you were the one. I'm all in. I want it all with you. Marriage, kids, the works. I'm going to go home this evening and end it with Kirsty so we can begin our life together.' More silence. He continued. 'God, I'm excited. To have such a young, strong woman, like you, who will look after me, in the future, when I can't look after myself. I'm so blessed.'

'*That all sounds . . . great,*' she finally replied, flatly, '*but maybe we should take a beat for a moment? You know, slow it down.*'

'Ahhh *no*, let's not. I want to meet your parents. Parents? What am I saying? I mean my soon to be in-laws. I've actually got some time right now. Are Mummy and Daddy back from St Moritz yet?'

'*They're not,*' she said, sounding a little panicked. '*I have to shoot off. I have a thing I need to do.*'

'Well, you go do that thing,' he said sweetly. 'And Chloe . . .'

'Yes?'

'I love you.'

'*OK. Bye,*' she said, and the line went dead.

'Into the crevasse,' he said with a big grin, before heading back to his office. 'Where were we?' he asked Scotty, closing the heavy oak door behind him.

'At the trigger-pulling stage.'

'Let's do it.'

Bob hit the 'on' button and dialled.

Calling . . .

Calling . . .

'*. . . Hello.*'

He recognized the voice instantly.

A couple of nights earlier that same voice had been ranting at his younger self, but now it was a lot more formal. To the present day, albeit lacking the slightly higher pitch of youth, she still used the same affected tone when speaking on the phone. It had always amused Bob.

'Hello there, good afternoon.'

'*Good afternoon . . .*' – she paused, trying to work out if she knew the voice – '*Who's speaking, please?*' She does not. She hasn't met Bob post-puberty yet.

'Somebody you're going to want to listen to very carefully.'

'*Oh. OK. Sorry, but whatever you're selling, I'm not interested.*'

'I'm not selling anything. I just want to help you.'

'*Unless you can help clean up the mess in this house before my husband and sons get home, I'm going to say goodbye,*' she insisted.

172

'Judy,' he said, giving it a beat for the use of her name to sink in. 'I want to help you. And all you have to do is listen to what I am about to tell you.'

'How do you know my name? Who is this?'

'I'm a friend, Judy.'

'Wait a minute. It was you who was speaking to my son the other night,' she said, her voice turning angry. *'You told him you were a family friend.'*

'I did.'

'Are you some kind of pervert?'

'Come on, Judy! Use your head. If I was a pervert why would I be talking to you now?'

'Then why were you speaking to my son? What the hell do you want?'

'I've already told you. I just want you to listen to me.'

'Then why don't you just tell me who you are?'

'Because if I tell you, you wouldn't believe me. And it's imperative you believe me. Your family's future depends on it.'

'What's that supposed to mean? Are you threatening me?' she demanded.

'No. Far from it.' He took a deep, focusing breath. 'What if I could predict something that was going to happen today, that no one could possibly know? Any subsequent advice I gave you after that event you would have to follow, yes? No matter how insane it sounded.'

'Why am I listening to this rubbish?' she said. *'This is so absurd.'*

'Because you can hear it in my voice. You know on some level that this is real. Don't you, Judy?' He took her protracted silence as a yes. 'Believe me when I tell you that this is the most important moment of your life. If you give me your complete attention for just a couple of minutes, you won't regret it. Trust me,' he added, with the urgency of a man who believed this to be his own most important moment. He looked to Scotty, who appeared to be holding his breath.

'I'm listening,' she said, the two words met with silent euphoria by Bob and Scotty.

'There's a football match a few hours from now,' Bob continued.

'A football match?' said Judy, as if it were the last thing she ever expected him to say.

'England versus Argentina. It's the World Cup quarterfinal in Mexico. I'm going to tell you exactly what's going to happen in that game.'

'Are you now?' she said, chuckling sceptically.

'Yes. England will lose 2–1.'

'2–1? Extraordinary! How do you do it, Nostradamus?'

'There are some other important details, Judy,' he said curtly, remembering that sarcasm ran through the Bloomfield family like a sewage pipe to the sea. 'In the first half there will be no goals scored.'

'Nul points in the first half. Got it.'

'I feel like you're not taking this seriously, Judy. It's *extremely* important you remember what I'm telling you, do you understand?'

'I'm writing it down!' she snapped.

'Good. That's a good idea. All right, here we go. In the second half, three goals will be scored. The first of which will be in the fifty-first minute by Diego Maradona. It'll look like he scores with his head, but the replay will show it is in fact a hand-ball. The referee didn't see the infringement so the goal will stand. Maradona will call it the 'Hand of God' in the press conference right after the game. Did you get all that?'

'Yup. Maradona is the little one?'

'Yes Mu— Judy, he's the little one,' he said, catching himself in the nick of time. 'The second goal, just four minutes later, is also scored by Maradona. It is one of the greatest goals, *ever*. Maradona puts the ball past Shilton after a sixty-yard dash. It is what will come to be called 'The Goal of the Century'. It's incredible.'

'*Goal of the Century*,' she parroted, clearly writing it down, Bob noted thankfully. '*Yup. Got that. And the third goal?*'

'In the eighty-first minute, John Barnes, who comes on as a substitute, puts a cross in towards Gary Lineker, and Lineker heads it into the net. The game ends 2–1 to Argentina.'

'*Is that it?*'

'Is that it?!' he laughed. 'I wish I could be there to see your faces when all that actually happens.' His laughter stopped when it dawned on him that he would be there, or at least, his younger self would. *Extraordinary.*

'*So, what happens if this comes true?*'

'It will happen. You have to show John and your children all of the details I've given you before the game starts. Otherwise, they won't believe you.'

'*You know my husband's name too? WHO ARE YOU?!*'

'Watch the match, watch everything I've told you come true, and I'll call you after the game with all the answers you need. I have to go.' He hit the call end button.

'Go well?' asked Scotty.

'I think so.'

'What do we do now?'

'We wait.'

He read the prophetic details on the sheet of paper with an amused look. Judy, sat next to him, watching expectantly. He rose from the sofa, chuckled to himself, and walked to the bottom of the stairs. 'Robert, the game is starting!' he shouted, without taking his eyes from the sheet. 'It's a wind-up. It's probably one of the boys from the pub,' he laughed, sitting down next to his wife again after navigating his way around Thomas, who sat cross-legged on the rug between the sofa and television, wearing his Dr Who scarf, playing with an assortment of Matchbox cars.

'You didn't hear this guy, John. He sounded ... serious.'

'As all good wind-ups should,' he said, handing the sheet of paper back to her. 'I can't believe you actually wrote all that nonsense down,' he added, reaching for his can of Skol lager and pack of Silk Cut.

'I know, but it was weird. He sounded so convincing.'

'That he could predict the future?' he said, lighting his cigarette. 'Come on, Jude!'

'I know he can't predict the future, John!' she snapped. 'I'm just saying there was a strange familiarity to his voice.' She paused, deciding whether to speak the next sentence. 'He said it was him who was speaking to Robert a couple of nights back.'

'Really? The same guy?' he said, taking her seriously for the first time. 'Look, if he comes around here, then that's different, but for now, let's agree it's just some bored nutcase on the end of the line. Next time the phone rings, I'll answer it. OK?'

'OK,' she replied, somewhat placated.

'Good, good. Now let's watch England *beat* the Argies three-nil, shall we. ROBERT!' he bellowed.

'I'm here, Dad,' said Robert, from his place standing behind the sofa.

'Oh, didn't see you there. You ready for some footy?'

'John Barnes, top corner!' he said enthusiastically, miming a right-footed volley.

'He's not going to do much from the subs' bench, son,' said John, as his son landed on the chair next to the sofa. 'Thomas, turn the box up for kick-off.'

Dutifully, Thomas did so – and the game began.

By the time the whistle was blown, signifying the end of the first *goalless* half, John appeared to have forgotten the discarded sheet of paper beneath his wife's gin and tonic. Judy, however, felt a quickening of her pulse and a growing unease that drew her eyes to the stranger's prediction she'd written down.

Beverages were replenished, Skol and G&T for the adults, Coke for the boys, and the whistle announced the start of the second half.

Six minutes later, as Maradona's goal was replayed in excruciating slow motion, the ball looping through the air from the wayward foot of defender Steve Hodge, England desperately appealing for offside, John and Judy sat in stunned silence.

'Hand me that piece of paper,' said John, without taking his eyes off the screen. Lifting the G&T, the ice rattling in her unsteady grip, she gave him the sheet. 'Fifty-first minute,' he said, checking the predictions, 'that was the fifty-first minute.' He glanced at the screen again. 'Did that look like hand-ball?'

Before his wife could answer, the commentator announced breathlessly, '. . . *and the goal is given! At what point was he offside . . . or was it the use of a hand that England are complaining about?*'

'What's wrong, Dad?' asked Robert, seeing his stricken parents.

'I'm not sure,' answered John, with a nervous laugh. 'That has to be the biggest lucky guess of all time, Jude.'

'Was it?' she replied flatly, taking the sheet from him. 'According to this, that Maradona is due to score again in . . .' – she looked at her watch – 'about two and a half minutes. And it's going to be the greatest goal ever scored.'

'Come on, Jude . . .' he said, but with far less conviction than earlier.

'What's going on, Dad?'

'Robert!' he snapped. 'Quiet for a moment, please. Just watch the game.' He reached for a calming cigarette.

The seconds ticked by.

The only sounds within the Bloomfields' modest living room came from the TV and Thomas, in his own little world, mimicking engine noises and crashes on the rug, completely unaware that a little Argentinian man on the other side of the world might be about to save his life.

'. . . *it's remarkable how Maradona has been able to control the game in midfield,*' said the commentator. '*And here he goes again, dancing through the midfield, a quick turn and he's away . . . he takes on one, he takes on two . . . he's hurting England again here . . . he's around the keeper, it's a brilliant run . . . AND IT'S IN! IT'S ONE OF THE WORLD CUP'S GREAT GOALS! Leaving a trail of England players in his wake . . . there's no doubt about that one.*'

'Oh my God, oh my God, oh my God . . .' Judy said over and over, beginning to cry. 'John, what's happening?'

'I don't know. I . . . I don't know what's happening. What's next on the list?' he asked, ghostly pale, taking a drag from a cigarette held in a trembling hand.

'John Barnes will come on in about twenty minutes and cross to Lineker who will score with a header. The game will end 2–1,' she answered, wiping tears from her eyes.

'Mum? Dad?' Robert and Thomas asked together.

'It's OK, boys. Mum's fine,' said John, looking from one concerned face to another. It was his eldest son's face that gave him a thought. 'Robert, who was the man you were speaking to a couple of nights back?'

'He said he was a family friend.'

'He didn't give you his name? It's OK, you're not going to get in trouble,' he added, seeing Robert's unease.

'He said he was a family friend. He didn't tell me his name. He knew all of our middle names though.'

'What?' exclaimed John and Judy.

'Yeah. He knew mine, Dad's, Tom's, and he knew Mum doesn't have one.'

'What else did he say?' asked Judy.

'I don't remember.'

'*Robert.* I told you, you won't get in trouble. What else did he say?' said John.

'He told me I had to be nice to people,' he said, scratching at a stain on his shell-suit bottoms.

'Be nice to people? What the hell does that mean?' said John.

'I have no idea,' said Judy.

'Jude, I *need* to talk to this man.'

'Well, you'll get your chance. He said he'll ring us when the match is over.'

The clock mounted on the wall of Bob's office read 7.36 p.m.

'John Barnes just crossed to Lineker. It's ten minutes till full time,' said Bob.

Apart from acknowledging each critical moment (the hand-ball, the goal), they had sat mostly silent through the game, both of them lost in their own thoughts. Their silent vigil now continued, with Bob glancing nervously at the clock, watching the minutes count down.

'Will you tell them who you are?' asked Scotty, the clock now reading 7.41 p.m.

'I've been thinking about that. I don't know if it's a good idea. How will that knowledge affect the relationship between young me and my parents? How will it affect my development? What if I spend the next three decades

180

worrying about how I'm going to save my brother? It's too big a responsibility on those young shoulders. It's too much of a risk. I think the less they know, the better.'

'Yeah, I think that sounds right.' Scotty nodded in agreement.

7.42 p.m.

Bob noted the time. Four more minutes. 'Scotty, there's something I wanted to tell you . . . before we call.'

'OK.' Observing Bob's stern features, Scotty unconsciously adjusted his slouched seating posture to a more upright position. 'What's up?'

'It's stupid, because if what we're about to do works, then this conversation will be redundant because you won't remember it. But I hate having this knowledge over you. It's eating away at me. I want to be a better person. I want to be a better friend and I think in order to do that, I need to be honest with myself and honest with the people who are most important to me.'

'You're starting to freak me out. What's going on?'

7.43 p.m.

'Kirsty is your wife.'

'Errr . . . come again?'

'In the other reality, she's your wife.' Bob watched as Scotty attempted to process the information. His face took on the look of a man trying to solve an impossible equation. 'I had no idea when I told my younger self to start showing people the respect they deserve, that he would apply it to Kirsty. You have to believe me, Scotty.'

'I did think about this, after you told me in that bar that you two were married,' Scotty said with a far-off look in his eye. 'I remember you used to pick on her a bit, nothing terrible, but I suppose some of it was borderline. And then suddenly all that stopped. I even remember you started sticking up for her when anyone else would try and use the jokes that you had made up about her. That's when we stopped hanging out. I thought you were two-faced.'

'None of that was meant to happen. You and Kirsty were meant to be together.'

'If you say so, Bob,' he replied with a snort of laughter. 'I can't see it personally. She's way out of my league.'

'Scotty. I've seen it. It works. It's perfect. You belong with her . . . well, maybe not this version of Scott Pickers-Gill. But the Scotty in my reality, the real you, he should be with her.'

'Thanks . . . I think . . .'

'That didn't come out right. Shit, sorry Scotty. I'm even messing this up.' He rubbed the back of his head for some time before continuing. 'What I'm trying to say is – I stole this life from you. Do you understand? I feel ashamed. I resented her for years for taking you away from me. I was so selfish and jealous. And now I've taken everything from you . . . *everything*. I'm so sorry, Scotty. Can you forgive me?'

Scotty stood, then walked to one of the far corners of Bob's office. He spent long moments with his back to Bob, head bent, his hand on his brow, deep in thought.

'How should I feel? Angry? Hurt?' he said, finally turning. 'I don't know this woman. You're talking about a life I haven't lived. I can't even imagine her being my wife. All I know is everything that's happened to me up until this point, and none of it involves her . . . it barely involves you.'

'That's because . . .'

'Let me finish,' said Scotty, with a raised hand. 'I've made poor decisions in my life, Bob. I've hurt a lot of people. The truth is, I don't think I deserve what you're offering me. I should be apologizing to you. I know what you are about to give up for me. Let's be honest, you could bring back Thomas and still have your life with Kirsty. I don't forgive you . . . because there's nothing to forgive.'

Bob looked at his old friend for long moments with eyes that suddenly looked a little wetter than they had before. He pursed his lips in a tight smile before he said, 'And that is exactly why we're about to restore the life you deserve.'

Bob got up, made his way towards Scotty and wrapped his arms around him. They both held the embrace for a long time. Releasing his friend, Bob said, 'You're the best person I know in any reality. Here, there, anywhere. Let's make things right.' As the tears brimmed in Scotty's eyes, Bob looked to the clock. 'Come on, it's 7.46. It's call time.'

'*Who are you!?*' asked a forceful voice. For a moment Bob was twelve again, shrinking at the authority of John Andrew Bloomfield.

'A friend,' he replied.

'*I know who my friends are and I don't know you.*'

'Don't get bogged down with who I am. It's not relevant.'

'*Well at least tell me how you did that. How you knew that would happen.*'

'It's not the *how*, it's the *why*. Why did I give you that information?'

'*Well, why?*'

'To prove that I can predict the future. After what you've just seen, do you believe me?'

'*It's hard not to,*' he replied, an unmistakable note of awe in his voice.

'Good. That's important.'

'*Why have you been talking to my son?*'

'Because I want to help him. I want to help all of your family.'

'*You told him to be nice. Why?*'

'Because he's about to go down a path that will have a devastating effect on your family. I'm going to tell you how you can prevent that from ever happening.'

'*By predicting the future?*'

'Yes. I've already seen what will happen.'

'*What does he do?*' he asked, sounding like he feared the answer.

'Robert is about to engage in a very bad relationship that will result in him becoming a teenage father,' he said, as Scotty looked on, his jaw clenched in anticipation. 'This will have a catastrophic impact on the rest of his life. You must at all costs keep him away from a girl called Kirsty Cummings.'

'*Robert, do you know someone called Kirsty Cummings?*' John asked, his voice directed away from the receiver. Bob heard a reply, but it was too far away to decipher. '*She's in school with him,*' John said.

'Keep him away from her. He'll do great things if you can keep them apart.'

'*That's all I have to do? Keep him away from her and he'll be fine?*'

'Yes.'

'*I can do that.*'

'Good.'

'*What else?*'

'Thomas . . .' he began, 'This is going to be hard to hear, but hear it you must. Soon you're going to take a trip to Wales to see your sister-in-law. Thomas . . . will die in a biking accident.'

'*No, no he doesn't . . .*' said John, his voice cracking.

'*What's wrong?*' Bob heard his mother ask in the background, her voice fragile with worry.

'You're right, he won't die if you do as I say. Don't let them go out on those bikes. In fact, destroy their bikes and DO NOT go to Wales. If you go and he rides that bike, he *will* die.'

He could hear his mother again in the background, closer than before, asking, *'John? What is it? What's wrong?'*

'You need to tell her everything I've told you. Keep Robert away from Kirsty Cummings and don't let Thomas ride that bike in Wales. Will you do what I'm asking you?'

'This is crazy.'

'Will you do it!?'

'What choice do I have? Of course.'

'Thank you,' said Bob, breathing a sigh of emotional exhaustion, 'I have to go now.'

'Will you tell me who you are?'

'Maybe one day,' he said, ending the call.

He placed the phone on his desk, a desk that had now changed back into its sprawling oak predecessor. He ran his hand over the cool wood as he noted the return of the oak panelling with its framed trove of sycophantic superstars. The bearskin rug completed the picture, confirming that his office had reverted to its previous state of intimidating menace.

'I think it worked,' he said to no one.

Scotty had vanished.

15

The name Scott Pickers-Gill had also vanished from Bob's iPhone, replaced by the original and more familiar *Scotty*.

Bob took this as a sign that they had successfully integrated Scotty back into his correct reality. The next section in his contacts started with a T.

He slowly dragged his shaking thumb up the screen until he came to a name that had sat at the centre of his being, dictating the course of his life for thirty-seven years – *Thomas*.

The blood rushing in his ears, he stared at the name as if seeing a mirage . . . could it be real? Could the weight of impossible grief he had felt for so long be about to be lifted from his soul?

His thumb was poised over the word Thomas. *This is it. This is the moment.*

If this was the moment, why was he hesitating? He willed his thumb to make contact with the name on the screen . . . but it wouldn't budge. His mind began to race uncontrollably. With an unsteady hand, he placed the phone back on his desk.

'What do you say to the brother you killed thirty-seven years ago?' he asked himself, feeling sick. After long deliberations, still nothing was forthcoming. There really was no precedent or instruction manual for the conversation he was about to have. 'Come on. This is ridiculous. Get a grip.' Without thinking, he took the phone and touched the name.

Calling . . .

He waited.

Calling . . .

And waited, until . . . *'Bob-oh! How the devil are you?'*

He tried to reply but the words couldn't get beyond the tightness in his throat.

'Hello? You there?'

'Thomas?' he finally managed, hearing the word leave his mouth minus all the pain and regret for the first time in decades. 'Is that you?'

'In the flesh. How are you doing, big man?'

'You sound fantastic. Just . . . fantastic,' said Bob, elated, even though the adult Thomas sounded understandably different from the nine-year-old he remembered.

'I'm feeling fantastic. I haven't heard from you for a while.'

'I know. It feels like a while for me too,' replied Bob through a mixture of tears and laughter. 'Can I come see you?'

'You sound pumped! I'm loving this energy. I'd have to take a look in the diary but I'm pretty sure I could squeeze you in somewhere over the next week or so. Sound good?'

'I was hoping for sooner.'

'Ummm, sorry, Bob. That's going to be tricky. To be honest, I've got a lot of regulars and I can't really bump them for a . . . I hate to say it, a flake.'

'A flake?' Something wasn't right, 'Sorry, I'm a bit confused now.'

'*You're not as committed as you should be, my friend.*'

'To what?'

'*The programme. For the best results, you have to stick with it.*'

'What programme?'

'*My shred programme,*' he replied, a little offended.

'This isn't my brother Thomas,' said Bob, in a desolate tone.

'*No. It's Thomas Aaron,*' he replied, laughing, '*your personal trainer. At least I was a while back. I think you might have dialled the wrong Thomas.*'

'Thomas Aaron,' repeated Bob, now remembering the trainer he had had a few sessions with about eighteen months earlier. If he hadn't been so heartbroken, he would have felt like a perfect idiot. 'Sorry to have bothered you, Thomas. Goodbye.'

'*Wait! Did you still want to book . . .*'

Bob ended the call, silencing the only Thomas in his phone contacts.

'FUCK!' he screamed at the top of his voice.

How had his father managed to keep Bob and Kirsty separate (a quick look at his bare wedding ring finger confirmed Bob was a bachelor once again – something that should have made him happy, yet strangely, it did not) but somehow fail to stop the tragic events of that holiday to Wales in 1986. How? *HOW!?!?*

It made no sense.

Thankfully, he had the means to speak to his father of 1986 and ask him what the hell went wrong. Why hadn't he stopped Thomas from getting on that bike on that fateful day?

He could still save his brother.

He reached for the old phone . . . *wait a minute.* A thought suddenly occurred to him. He switched the old for the new and brought up his contacts.

There it was.

With a deep sigh of relief and unimaginable joy, without hesitation, he pressed his thumb to the word *Brother.*

Calling . . .

Calling . . .

Calling . . . straight to voicemail.

The voicemail service did not have a personalized message. Bob did not leave a message of his own. Instead, he pressed *Brother* again.

Calling . . .

Calling . . .

'Hello, Bob,' answered a man's voice.

'Thomas?'

'*Yeah. Hello. What's up?*'

'It's you. It's really you?'

'*You called me, Bob. Who else were you expecting?*' He sounded amused but also distracted.

'Ha! Yeah, I know. Sorry.' It was him. It truly was him. He could hear it in his voice. It had that distinctive Bloomfield ring to it.

'*Listen. It's difficult to talk at the moment. I'm in the middle of something. Can we catch up another time? I'd rather give you my full attention.*'

'I . . . ahhh . . . I was . . .' His voice faltered with emotion.

'*Are you OK, Bob? You're sounding a bit strange.*'

'Yes. Everything is all right,' he replied, wiping his nose on his sleeve. 'Everything's all right now.'

'*Look, like I said, I can't really speak now . . .*'

'Can I see you?'

'*Ummm, yeah. That would be great. When are you thinking?*'

'Now.'

'*Now!?*'

'*Please.* I have to see you,' said Bob.

'*Give me a second.*' Bob heard a short, muted exchange before Thomas returned. '*Why don't you meet me for supper at Moxy in Soho in an hour, sound good?*'

'Perfect. Can't wait to see you.'

'*Looking forward to seeing you too,*' Thomas said, ending the call.

The only thing that could be heard in the empty hallways and offices of FitzSimmons & Bloomfield Entertainment Management was the sound of a man weeping tears of redemption.

Bob had frequented Soho for twenty-five years. He knew all its nooks and crannies in intimate detail. In that time, there wasn't a bar or restaurant he hadn't stumbled out of, been politely asked to leave, or been forcibly ejected from. He belonged to Soho as much as it belonged to him. Which was why he now stood on Greek Street, sick with nerves and excitement, but also confused. Because during his entire patronage of this hallowed part of London, he had never seen, let alone entered, a restaurant called Moxy.

He stepped into the restaurant's revolving door, almost too weak with apprehension to push himself through. Breathless and shaking, he stepped into a dimly lit reception area, essentially a corridor-come cloakroom with coats hanging on either side. At the end of the short corridor, stood a man behind a lectern. Red curtains hung directly behind him, dulling the voices and commotion of dining within. Bob stood there frozen as the corridor in his mind's eye stretched out before him like an image in a funhouse mirror. His breathing became laboured as spots of light danced in his vision. Feeling utterly overwhelmed, he placed his hands on his knees and breathed deeply.

'Sir?' said the man from behind the lectern. 'Are you OK?'

'I'm fine. Just felt a little dizzy,' said Bob, bringing himself upright.

'Oh, Mr Bloomfield! Forgive me. I didn't see it was you. We've been expecting you,' said the smartly dressed maitre d'. 'Are you sure you're OK? Could I get you some water?'

Bob looked at the man who appeared to know him and searched his mind for some kind of recognition. 'Thank you but I'm fine,' he said, drawing a blank.

'Well, if there's anything you need, please let me know. I'll take your jacket and then show you to your brother.'

'Thank you,' said Bob in a whisper, looking towards the red curtains as the maitre d' took his coat.

'Splendid.' He hung it up and presented Bob with a ticket. 'If you would like to follow me, Mr Bloomfield.'

The curtains were drawn back and Bob stepped into a lavish space of carved mahogany panelling (a favourite of Bob's), cherub statues and soaring pillars of marble that climbed to a ceiling where a huge crystal chandelier cast its glittering light. The place was relatively full for a Sunday evening, with pockets of diners spaced evenly around the room.

Bob saw his brother almost instantly.

Even though he was sitting alone with his back to Bob, the smart suit, his hair, the shape of his shoulders, left Bob in no doubt that he was looking at Thomas Henry Bloomfield.

'If you'll follow me,' said the maitre d' with a guiding gesture.

'It's OK, I can see him. I'll take it from here.'

'As you wish,' replied the maitre d', before disappearing back behind the curtain.

Bob walked the winding route between the tables, too scared to take his eyes off his brother in case he suddenly disappeared, in case this was all just a dream and he might wake up with a start at any moment, reaching for the bottle on his bedside table.

But it was not a dream and Thomas really was now just an arm's length away from him, sitting there, completely oblivious to the events his older brother had brought about to bring him back from wherever dead children go.

As if needing the physical touch of his brother's body to confirm he was actually there, Bob reached out his hand and rested it on his shoulder.

'*Thomas.*'

'And here he is. Exactly on time. Punctuality has always been a Bloomfield minor superpower,' he said, rising from his chair and turning. 'It's good to see you, Bob.'

For Bob, nothing but himself and Thomas existed in that moment.

The noise of the surrounding diners faded to silence as Bob looked upon the wonderful face of his long-dead brother with an indescribable joy.

Since he had last seen him, all those years ago, adulthood had ushered in the trademark Bloomfield angular features, the Roman nose and high cheekbones, but they couldn't quite obscure the cherubic innocence of his youth. Long-lashed, wide eyes and pinched, rosy-pink lips made sure there was enough of their mother in him to draw in anyone who might enter the gravity of his warm, welcoming gaze.

'Are you going to say something or are you going to continue to stare at me in this peculiar manner?' Thomas finally asked.

'I'm . . . just so happy to see you,' he answered with a quivering lip, before throwing his arms around him. Bob being wider and a full head taller than Thomas, meant the smaller man was almost completely enveloped by the embrace.

'I could do without the bear hug, thank you, brother,' Thomas said, prising himself away and smoothing the lines of his suit. 'Why don't you take a seat and tell me what's going on?' He pointed to the chair opposite his own.

Bob sat down, his back against the wall so he could

see the entire room. But he only had eyes for his brother. 'It's so good to see you, Tom.'

'Yes, you've said,' Thomas chuckled, taking his own seat. 'You've maybe had a few drinks today, Bob?' he added with a wry little grin.

'No. Not a drop.' Bob returned the grin.

'Then perhaps you should have one.' Thomas flagged a passing waiter. 'What'll it be?'

'Champagne.'

'You heard the man. Champagne.' The waiter nodded and left. 'What are we celebrating?'

'This moment.'

'OK, I can live in the moment,' Thomas replied, smiling.

'That's all I've ever wanted for you,' said Bob, his bottom lip quivering.

'That's a lot of sentiment for a man who once told me he'd throw our grandmother into a volcano if it meant he'd make partner? You're either getting sentimental in your old age, or you're a stranger wearing my brother's skin as a suit.'

'It's me, Tom,' said Bob, earnestly. 'I've been through some . . . stuff lately that's led me to re-evaluate my life. If I've been selfish and distant, I'm sorry. Whatever has happened between us up until now, good or bad, isn't important. Things are going to be different from now on. I'm going to be the best brother I can be.'

'Sorry, Bob,' Thomas said, shaking his head in bewilderment, 'I'm just trying to process all of this. What's brought on this new outlook?'

'Pilates,' Bob grinned, after a few seconds' hesitation.

'Pilates? OK, sure. That was the missing element. Well, whatever has got you so giddy, if it means we can get on and see more of each other, it's very welcome. Will there be a feast at this celebration of your metamorphosis?' he asked, indicating the menu.

'I'm not hungry,' said Bob as the champagne arrived. 'I want to hear how you've been? You look fantastic.'

'Thank you,' Thomas replied, taking both freshly poured glasses and handing one to Bob. 'What should we drink to?'

'To new beginnings,' Bob proposed.

'To new beginnings,' repeated Thomas.

'So how is work?' asked Bob, thinking *What is your work?* would be more apt.

'You know how it is, get rich or die trying,' Thomas replied, idly watching a woman at a nearby table taking pictures of her starter from various angles. 'How are things at the agency?'

'No complaints. But forget that, I want to hear about you,' insisted Bob, frustrated that his brother's attention seemed to be elsewhere.

'Do you chronicle the meal's entire journey?' Thomas asked, leaning towards the table where the photo shoot was going on.

'I beg your pardon?' said the woman, in surprise.

'Do you chronicle it?' he repeated, raising his voice over the room's din. 'A good documentarian follows their subject to its natural conclusion. You've just photographed that beautiful smoked salmon with goat's cheese on a bed of carpaccio beetroot for your eager fans on your social media outlet of choice, so why only give them half the story?'

'How is this only half the story?' she said, giggling in confusion as Bob and her husband watched on, equally confused.

'What happens after that first picture is taken? Tell the full story of the smoked salmon. You put it in your mouth, you chew, you swallow, you digest the masticated salmon in your small intestine with all those glorious stomach acids swishing about in your gut. The salmon is stripped of its nutrients before the detritus your body doesn't need forms a turd that you then shit into your toilet at home. I'm sure your phone will be close at hand, so just open your legs and voilà, there's your conclusion staring back at you. Ready for its moment of fame on the unflushable toilet that is the internet.'

'That's disgusting,' said the woman, utterly appalled.

'How dare you speak to my wife that way!' said her husband, throwing his napkin on to the table in protest. 'You're revolting. Don't talk to us again or I'll have a word with the maitre d' and have you removed.'

Thomas turned back to his brother, gave a shrug of indifference, and sipped his champagne. The fuming couple carried on their evening as if Bob and Thomas were not there.

'That was a bit harsh.'

'Just having some fun,' Thomas replied. 'Come on, you can't tell me that doesn't annoy the hell out of you, watching Annie Leibovitz over there shooting the cover of *No One Gives a Shit* magazine?'

'It wouldn't make my list of favourite things,' Bob agreed. 'But I'm not sure I would have gone at it quite so hard.'

'Goodness me. Where has my sushi knife-sharp big brother gone? You've become a Lamborghini with a roof rack,' he laughed.

Seeing his brother laugh so heartily, Bob couldn't help but join him. 'Don't you worry, I can still slice tuna wafer-thin when I need to.' At that exact moment, a glass smashed, and the table behind Thomas (a table of men who were recent arrivals and very drunk), erupted in jeers.

'Taxi for the twat!' they shouted at one of their own, with boisterous glee. Bob noted them and rolled his eyes. Thomas didn't seem to register the ruckus.

'Are you sure I can't tempt you with a bite?' Thomas asked.

'Actually, maybe I am a bit peckish.'

'Allow me,' said Thomas, reaching for the menu as a flustered waitress brushed up the fallen glass behind him to loud applause from the pack of drunkards responsible. After a few moments' study, Thomas raised a finger. A waiter materialized before his finger had barely reached its zenith.

Bob watched in wonder as his brother ordered. He was still struggling to believe he was here, he was back – he had saved him. Bob looked around the room, it was *real*. The people in it were really there. He reached out and touched his champagne flute, the glass cold in his fingers: it was real. Thomas was really sitting in front of him, ordering dinner, blissfully unaware that he had been dead for the last thirty-seven years.

'You're looking at me in that peculiar way again,' said Thomas, as the waiter hurried off.

'Am I? Sorry. Have you seen Mum and Dad lately?' he asked, trying to appear relaxed as he took another swig of his drink.

'No, I haven't seen them lately, Bob,' replied Thomas, resting his chin on his fist. The crease that began to form on his brow suggested he was still uneasy, or at least confused, by this self-proclaimed new-and-improved Bob Bloomfield sitting opposite him.

The silence that had stretched out between them ended suddenly with an explosion of high-pitched howls from the table of drunk men behind Thomas, the clamour punctuated by the hammering of five empty shot glasses against wood.

'Any chance you gentlemen could turn the volume down,' Thomas said over his shoulder, without taking his eyes off Bob.

'Fuck off mate. You have your night, we'll have ours, yeah,' said the most vocal of the bunch, his cohorts bursting into another ear-shattering bout of laughter.

Thomas smiled at Bob and raised an apologetic hand. The smile had left his face like an unwelcome guest by the time he'd swivelled in his chair to face the five drunk men.

Those who met Thomas's stare froze mid-laugh. The two facing away from him, including the most vocal, confused by the sudden silence, turned and looked into his blank emotionless face.

Bob watched in amazement as the colour drained from Mr Vocal, pint by bloody pint, fear stretching over his face in a chalky mask. 'There . . . there's . . . there's been a miscommunication,' he stuttered 'I . . . we apologize. We were just blowing off a little steam. You'll hear a pin drop over here from now on, I promise,' he added, the words high-pitched and strained like the whining of an animal struggling in a snare.

Thomas took a moment to meet the eyes of each member of the group in turn. 'I recommend you leave a very generous tip for the poor girl who's been coping with you pack of arseholes since you arrived. If you don't, you'll all be leaving through the back door in carrier bags. Do I make myself clear?'

'Yes, Sir,' they all whispered in unison.

They did not stay for food.

'What the fuck was that!?' asked Bob, his own colour now a little less than rosy.

'Pack mentality,' said Thomas, with a bored shrug. 'They always crumble if an individual challenges them. They just can't believe anyone would be that brave, so they assume you're a total nutcase. Psychology 101.'

'That was one of the most badass things I have ever seen. They were terrified of you.'

'Imagine being terrified of little old me,' he shrugged, as their food arrived.

'Yeah, imagine,' said Bob, noticing a glint in his brother's eye.

'All right, let me explain the feast we're about to be

blessed with.' He began introducing Bob to the various dishes that started to arrive at their table.

As they ate and drank and talked, Bob hung on every word his brother said. He had never known happiness like it. He felt a connection that went deeper than any he had ever had in his adult life. He had always assumed the love he felt for Scotty was akin to the love one might have for a brother, but now, sitting opposite his actual brother, he felt a love that was on another level, a love that existed in every fibre of his being. The part of him that had died the same day Thomas had in 1986 had returned. He felt whole again.

'Tom,' he began, as they finished the last of their meal, 'I'm sorry how I treated you when we were kids.'

'Don't get all nostalgic on me, Bob.'

'I mean it. I was a bad kid. And you got the brunt of that. I've always regretted it.'

'Well don't. The past is the past. You can't change it, can you?'

Bob thought of the phone that currently sat locked in his office desk drawer, and for a fleeting moment felt a compulsion to tell his younger brother everything. But a warning light flashed in his mind, telling him to exercise caution, that it was too soon. 'You can't,' he lied.

Thomas checked his watch. 'I have to be somewhere.'

'Really? You have to go?'

'I'm afraid so,' he said, rising. 'This new-and-improved Bob was very good company. We should do it again soon.'

'I'd like that. Go on, get going, I'll settle the bill.'

'Don't be ridiculous,' he said with a laugh. 'It's all sorted.'

'You shouldn't have,' said Bob, genuinely touched.

'It's what brothers do. See you soon,' he winked. Bob watched him walking away until he stepped through the curtains.

The combination of utter euphoria pleasantly amplified by the champagne meant he barely registered the long walk to his home. It was only when he stepped into his darkened apartment and switched the lights on that he felt the loss of what he had left behind that very morning.

He looked around the empty, lifeless space, calling out, 'Kirsty!' But he was met only with silence. There was no trace of the life where he had been a husband and a father. Everything was as it had always been. He switched the lights off and made his way to bed, aware that on a day he had brought his brother back, he had also lost something precious that would never return.

16

It had been niggling away at him all morning.

From the moment he awoke, during his shower, break-fast, the commute to the office, every time he basked in the joy of the memory of seeing Thomas once again, he felt the creeping sensation that something wasn't quite right.

His best guess was that it was too early for memories to form of his life with Thomas over the last thirty-seven years. But there was a . . . feeling, an emotion that he felt in connection with him. And it was incredibly confusing because it couldn't be true – Bob felt *fear*.

Stepping out of the lift into the corridor leading to his office, Bob walked with a troubled brow. Was he scared to lose Thomas again? Scared that Thomas might find out that Bob had once put him in a situation that had resulted in his death? No. That wasn't it. The fear he felt was one of danger, something deadly, something you would run from.

'Mr Bloomfield.'

Roused from his anxious musings, he found himself looking into a pair of green eyes. 'Chloe,' he said, startled.

'I'm glad I bumped into you. Can I just say I'm sorry for my drunken behaviour on Friday night. I was completely inappropriate,' she said.

Not sure how the evening had unfolded in this reality, he went with, 'Chloe, I think it's more than appropriate to be jolly at your own party. Think nothing of it.'

'But I do. You were good enough to come and I just got a bit tipsy and excited,' she said, blushing. 'And ended up scaring you off.'

'So, I didn't . . . sleep over?'

'Sleep over?' she said, with a note of surprise. 'No, you left.'

'Well, no harm, no foul,' he said with relief. 'Thanks for having me over, Chloe, I had a great time. If you'll excuse me, I should be getting to my office.'

'Maybe you'd give me a chance to make it up to you?' she said, blocking his escape. 'Perhaps we could grab a coffee sometime?'

'Chloe,' he began with a sigh, 'you are clearly a very special woman. Maybe in another life we could've had that coffee and taken Anvil for a stroll through the park . . . but I think in this one it's not such a good idea.'

'Fair enough,' she said, crestfallen. 'You know where I am if you change your mind.'

'I do. Now I should be . . .' he gestured towards his office.

'Of course,' she said, stepping aside. As Bob walked away, she suddenly had a thought. 'How do you know I have a dog called Anvil? I never told you that.'

'Lucky guess,' he said and kept walking.

He sat behind his desk with the ancient phone, released from the locked drawer, in front of him, continuing to ponder what this fear that was blooming inside him could mean.

He opened his laptop with the intention of typing the words Thomas Henry Bloomfield into the search engine.

BUZZ-BUZZ

'I said I wasn't to be disturbed, Miss Pennypacker,' he said, pressing his intercom with one hand whilst the other hovered over his laptop.

'Apologies, Mr Bloomfield. Usually that would mean none shall pass, but Mr Thacker is here to see you. He says it's urgent.'

With a frustrated huff, Bob closed the laptop. 'All right, show him in.'

A few moments later, Miss Pennypacker presented a rarely seen unshaven and dishevelled Roger Thacker. Stepping around his desk, Bob extended his hand. 'Good to see you, Roger,' he said, gripping the clammy, perma-tanned hand of one of the agency's oldest clients, and possibly Britain's favourite TV presenter.

'You too,' he replied, minus the inexhaustible saccharine enthusiasm he was famous for. He took a seat before he was offered one. 'Thanks for smoothing over that . . . ahhh . . . misunderstanding at Debenhams.'

'Sticking your dick through a glory hole in the changing rooms at Debenhams is not a misunderstanding. Foolhardy, yes,' said Bob, sitting down, 'misunderstanding, no.'

'Old habits die hard, I suppose,' said Thacker, forlornly.

'Old habits? Just how many glory holes have you . . . engaged?'

'I'm not here for judgements, Bob. I get enough of that at home. I swear, that fucking shit weasel Ian Sommer at *The Print* has had it in for me for years,' he said, becoming agitated.

'Relax. It's contained. Now, why don't you tell me why you're here.'

He ran a hand over his face. 'Got a bit of a problem brewing,' he said, with a haunted look.

'What kind of problem?' Bob could already feel his stomach sinking.

'It's probably easier if you . . . see it.' He handed over his phone. 'This was sent to me last night. Just press play.'

Bob did so.

Darkness filled the screen, but two voices could be heard between the crack of a whip. One belonged to a husky female who said, *'You like that, don't you, ya dirty little bastard.'* The other was a man's, but his words were muffled and incomprehensible. *'Ya filthy worm!'* the same husky female shouted, followed by another crack.

Turning down the volume, he glanced at Roger, who smiled apologetically back at him. Bob looked to the screen again. The camera had been faced down on a surface of some kind, but now it was picked up and directed at the source of the moaning: *Mr Roger Thacker.*

In the centre of a small, bare-walled concrete base-ment, his naked, pale, toneless body, dimly lit by a solitary exposed bulb screwed into a low ceiling, swung steadily from side to side suspended in a sex swing.

Another silent crack of the whip saw the swing revolve Thacker's face directly into the camera's lens. The white ball-gag that filled his mouth highlighted perfectly his preposterously orange face. There could be no doubt that this was the host of prime-time hits such as *Kids Do the Cutest Things* and *Grandma We Love You* bucking and writhing in masochistic ecstasy.

The whip was thrown to the ground and the person who had been delivering the whipping walked into shot. Bob saw a thick-set woman who wore a scant outfit of chains and leather straps . . . but the part of the costume that caught his eye the most was the prosthetic hanging between her legs. Grabbing the phallus, she stepped to Thacker's prone form from behind and steadied him . . . Deciding he had seen enough, Bob pressed stop. 'This is going to be a problem.'

'Come on, Bob, don't say that,' Thacker whined. 'I don't want to hear that. We can fix this, right? A couple of NDAs, a bit of pocket money and a stern talking to. You can make this go away.'

'Why did you let them film it?' said Bob, ignoring his pleas.

'I had it recorded on my phone,' he replied, bowing his head with as much shame as he was capable of. 'They must have sent it to themselves.'

'Who're they?'

'She drives a black cab . . .' said Thacker.

'Jesus Christ! Classy, real classy.'

'And the guy filming it is her husband. I'm not sure what he does. You know how it goes. We got talking in the cab; she seemed lovely, discreet. She invited me back for a drink . . . and one thing led to another.'

'What's wrong with you? I've never known anybody with less command of their impulses. You're like a shaved monkey. That video is not a normal conclusion to an evening for a married man with four children.'

'Yeah, you're right, Bob. You're right,' he said, nodding in contrition.

'Oh, you think so?'

'I do.'

'Roger, you've already done the wrong thing. You're not qualified to tell me I'm right. I already know I'm right,' Bob said.

'I said I didn't come here for judgements,' growled Thacker, his patience waning, 'You don't know what it's like, Bob. Everything I do is so wholesome. Mr Clean Cut. Mr Family Man. For decades I've been that sickeningly sweet grinning idiot on TV. Think about it. What's the last thing you want when you come home from the chocolate factory?'

'If only you worked in a chocolate factory, Roger. If only. How much do they want?'

'100k by the end of the week or they send that video to the press . . . and I should tell you,' he took a breath, 'full disclosure, it gets worse.'

'How could it possibly get worse?' Thacker scratched an invisible blemish on Bob's desk with his finger. 'How can it get worse!' Bob demanded.

Thacker drew a deep breath. 'The husband . . . he took a . . .'

'Stop!' pleaded Bob. He looked at Thacker's orange face for a long moment. 'I can't do this any longer,' he finally said, shaking his head.

'What do you mean?' said Roger, confused. 'What are you saying?'

'You're never going to learn. I've done some terrible things over the years in the pursuit of trying to keep your career above water.'

'And now we're suddenly in the deep end you're going to bail on me?'

'It's all deep end with you, Roger. You're going to have to own it. I can't do this any more. I don't want to be the monster you unleash to destroy anyone who's unfortunate enough to cross your path. I'm sorry, we're done, Fitz & Bloomfield will no longer be representing you moving forward. Best of luck.'

Roger stared at Bob in disbelief. 'You cocky prick. Who the fuck do you think you are? The foundations of this agency are built on my career. I'm the golden goose!' he said, jabbing a thumb at his chest and rising from his chair. 'I'm going to go speak to Fitz and by the time I'm finished, you'll be in the mail room and I'll have this entire office turned into a museum for my awards. You just fucked up – big time.'

Bob shrugged. 'Do your worst. But don't forget to show Fitz that video in its entirety, just so he has all the facts at his disposal. You might want to take a bucket with you – he's a bit more squeamish than me,' Bob concluded. A furious Thacker slammed the heavy oak door to Bob's office as he stormed out. 'Well, that felt good,' Bob said to himself, surprised by the feeling of satisfaction the altercation had given him.

But that joy soon disappeared when he remembered what he'd been doing before the interruption. He flipped open his laptop and typed Thomas Henry Bloomfield into the search engine. It wasn't long before a handful of hits featuring his younger brother's name filled his screen:

TOMMY BLOOMFIELD, ON NIGHT CLUB AND RESTAURANT EMPIRE – 'I'M A LEGITIMATE BUSINESSMAN'

PRETTY BOY TOMMY OPENS UP LATEST RESTAURANT 'MOXY' WITH STAR-STUDDED EVENT

'Pretty Boy Tommy?' said Bob, scratching his head. 'My God . . . *that was his restaurant.*'

THOMAS BLOOMFIELD HELPING POLICE WITH THEIR INQUIRIES INTO THE MURDER OF HITMAN, ENFORCER AND DRUG TRAFFICKER, JASON DENSLEY AKA 'JAY THE TANK'

'What the hell . . .' he said, dread suddenly spreading through him.

PRETTY BOY TOMMY DENIES BEING INVOLVED IN ORGANIZED CRIME SYNDICATE 'THE BAND CLUB'

'Fuckin' hell!' he yelped, almost jumping out of his seat in fright. With a shaking finger, he pushed the intercom button. 'Miss Pennypacker, you can tell Thacker I'm done with him. Enough's enough. I'm not going to change my mind. Now please, no more disruptions, I'm in the middle of something.'

'Apologies once again, but Mr Thacker has left. It's your brother.'

'What about him?' he asked, staring at his laptop in horror.

'He's here.'

'He's here!? At the office?'

'Yes. He's sitting in the waiting room.'

'Shitshitshitshitshit . . .' He slammed the laptop shut. He took a moment to compose himself before pushing the speak button again. 'Did he . . . did he mention why he's here?'

'No. He being your brother, I didn't ask. Would you like me to?'

'No! No. Don't do that. It's fine. You can bring him in.'

'Right away.'

Looking at the door his brother would soon step through, Bob smoothed the front of his suit and tried to subdue the anxiety in his stomach. He heard the approach of footsteps and voices.

The door opened.

'Well, this is a lovely surprise,' said Bob, in a voice that was slightly too high. 'To what do I owe the pleasure?' he asked, rising from his chair as Miss Pennypacker exited, closing the door, and sealing them in.

'I was in the neighbourhood,' said Thomas, adjusting the cuffs of his immaculate grey suit.

'Take a seat,' said Bob, taking his own. But Thomas ignored the offer, choosing instead to meander over to Bob's gallery of superstars mounted on the wall. 'I call it the gallery of grotesques,' Bob said with a nervous laugh. But Thomas ignored him still, as he silently examined each image.

'Is she as much of a bitch as everyone says?' he eventually asked, pointing to a picture of Bob and a woman dressed in a skimpy outfit, who was grinning into the camera.

'Ha! No,' he said, struggling to keep his voice steady. 'She just has one of those faces.'

'She certainly does,' Thomas nodded, moving on to the next picture. 'I recognize him. He plays a tough guy in all those mockney gangster movies. Hilarious. I'd love to see him try to make it through one day of clink.'

'Oh, I don't know, he does quite a lot of his own stunts actually.'

'*Stunts?*' Thomas repeated, as if it was the most ridiculous thing he had ever heard. 'Good-looking boy like that, he'd be on his hands and knees by mid-morning, Bob.'

'What can I do for you?' Bob asked, hoping to change the subject.

'You've changed your tune,' Thomas replied, turning from the gallery and coming to sit opposite Bob. 'You were desperate to see me last night, now I'm getting the "what can I do for you" treatment.'

'Not at all. I'm excited to see you. I'm just surprised.'

'*Surprised*,' Thomas said, seeming to ponder its meaning. 'You're surprised to see me. That is interesting. Interesting you should say that. Remember when we were kids, living at Grove Hill,' he said, inspecting his finely manicured nails, 'and I beat the shit out of that kid who tried to steal my football. The old man went berserk. You remember?'

'Yeah. He wasn't happy.'

'He was not.' His eyes glazed at the memory. 'What a dick. What was I supposed to do? Let that little shit take what was mine? What kind of message would that send? Hey, fellow pupils, I'm a little weakling. Feel free to use and abuse me . . . not a fucking chance.' A flash of anger came over him, but it quickly disappeared as if it had never happened. 'Anyway, that was round about the same time as the World Cup when our dear parents got that phone call.' He lifted his eyes to meet Bob's gaze. 'You remember that?'

'I think I do, yes.'

'Mum called him our "guardian angel who could predict the future". He saved us, she would say. If it wasn't for whoever that was on the end of that line, you would be married to some whore and I would be dead.' He laughed. 'I mean, it's insanity, right?'

'Complete insanity,' Bob agreed, feeling his jaw tighten after hearing Kirsty described that way.

'But the fact is, he *did know* the details of that game.

The things Mum had written on that piece of paper went beyond coincidence. Every detail was exactly correct, down to the minute. How could that be? *Impossible*. Pure science fiction.' He paused, to rub his chin in thought. 'Which is probably why I just couldn't stop thinking about it. You know I loved sci-fi as a kid.'

'Dr Who,' said Bob, quietly.

'Yes! Exactly. Dr Who. Fantastic. I was bloody obsessed,' he said wistfully. 'School was so dull, so restrictive for a mind like mine. But Dr Who, it was like having your skull cracked open. The mind could roam free, unfettered, it could *fly*. It got me thinking in a different way. Anything was possible. I think I learnt more from that show than I did from the entirety of school. The way Physics and Chemistry and English were taught – unbelievably dull. History!? How can a syllabus make history – that's the history of *everything* – fucking boring? No wonder kids nowadays are all fat, lazy and stupid.

'Anyway, I digress. I couldn't get beyond the questions: Who was the person on the end of that line? And how could they have known the details of that football match? So, I put my mind to work.'

1986

Optimus Prime, now fully transformed from a mild-mannered six-wheeler into a towering Cybertronian nightmare, stood menacingly over GI Joe. Joe's attention was split between Optimus's unreadable glowing blocks for eyes and the gigantic black hand cannon he had levelled at him.

'It's the end of the road,' said Prime. Joe looked longingly at his Striker Jeep that was but a short dash away. Prime read the thought written all over his chiselled face. 'Don't even think about it,' he growled.

'Last time I checked, thinking isn't a crime,' replied Joe.

'That's true. But being a Decepticon is.'

'You're crazy. I'm GI Joe,' he said, flabbergasted.

'*No*,' Prime extended the cannon so it was millimetres from his head, 'you're not.'

Joe took one cautious step backwards, before he screamed, 'DEATH TO THE AUTOBOTS!' Suddenly, his limbs began to turn in on themselves. Jagged sharp metal tore through his skin, tearing and breaking the flesh and bone that had hidden his true form. Prime watched silently as the silver metal that had lain in wait beneath the heroic form of GI Joe transformed and multiplied before him. Soon his nemesis of old, Megatron, stood defiant before him, laughing his wicked laugh. 'Yes, it is I . . .'

'Aren't you a bit old to be playing with moulded polymers?'

'Not really,' said Thomas, who held in his hands Optimus Prime and Megatron in a stand-off of epic proportions. The arena for this duel to the death was the windowsill of his bedroom, which looked down on to the modest but well-kept garden of 231 Grove Hill. GI Joe and the Striker Jeep lay at his feet on the carpeted floor.

'*By your age, I had already traversed my first black hole.*'

'Cool,' said Thomas, dropping the toys and turning to the man who was sat on the end of his bed.

'*That depends on the size of the black hole. But I would have to say my first was not cool. In fact, it was almost absolute zero, but not quite, if I remember correctly. And I probably do.*'

'I don't mean cool like the temperature,' said Thomas, sitting with his legs crossed at the man's pointy brogues, which were just about visible poking out beneath the stripes of his incredibly long scarf. 'I mean cool, like, impressive.'

'*Ohhhhhhh,*' said the man, in a rich baritone. With a wide tombstone smile, and wild, seemingly lidless eyes, he leaned down and pointed a long finger at the print on Thomas's T-shirt. '*Cooooool,*' he said, trying the word as if it were the first time he had spoken it.

Thomas looked down at his TARDIS T-shirt and smiled, 'Cool,' he said in agreement.

'*Now,*' – sitting up straight, he lifted the scarf and crossed his legs – '*you would like to discuss something with me. Tell on.*' He removed his hat, revealing a mop of disarrayed hair, and dropped it on to the bed.

'I want to know who called my mum and dad and told them about the football match before it happened.'

'*Yeeees. I imagine you would,*' he said, resting an elbow on his knee and a fist under his chin. '*I think best we start at the end and work backwards. So, forget the "who" for now and focus on the "how". How does a feeble of mind and body Homo sapien know the future?*'

'Build a time machine?'

'*There is no such thing.*'

'As a time machine?'

'*Silly boy! No* – time. *There is no such thing as time.*'

'I don't understand.'

'*How could you? Your only means of intelligence is that pink blob in your head,*' he said with a pitying frown. '*It's all happening at once, dear boy. The only reason you think there is a past is because that pink blob holds memories. Think about it – the past is something you examine in the present. The future is something that never arrives, yet you all blindly believe you are moving towards it. It's actually quite humorous,*' he chuckled, with a fiendish grin. '*The past, the present, and the future – are now. It's all happening in the same moment.*'

Thomas opened his mouth to speak, but then closed it in confusion. After a while he said, 'But you're a Time Lord?'

'*Yes. But not in the primitive way you think you understand. It's not a question of travelling backwards and forwards through time. It's a question of where one is at the same moment as someone here, in what you call* 1986. *For example, the year* 3178 *exists alongside* 1986. *Much like this room exists alongside your brother Robert's bedroom. You see?*'

'Sooo . . . whoever rang Mum . . . is living alongside 1986, but maybe in 1987 or 1999? They've already seen the football match!'

'*Capital! Well done, dear boy. Your mind is expanding,*' he said, flaring his biggest eyes yet. '*It's entirely due to my influence, of course. So don't get ahead of yourself.*'

'Still doesn't answer how they called 1986?'

'*Well spotted. The universe is full of annoying anomalies that* even a supreme being such as myself am not initially privy to. This is one of them. But rather wonderfully, if we can answer the question of who, the answer of how will follow.'

'OK. So, who was calling?' asked Thomas, scratching at his scalp. 'Why did they want to save me?'

'*Well,*' he began, momentarily confused by the question, '*because you are a good boy.*'

'What if I'm not,' replied Thomas averting his eyes to the worn carpet he sat on. 'What if I have bad thoughts. Really bad thoughts.'

'*Perhaps they are unaware of your predilection for mischief.*'

'Hmmm.'

'*However, if they are fully aware, then I can think of only one kind of person who could overlook and want to save someone with such . . . monstrous tendencies.*'

'Who?'

'*Family.*'

'Family?' echoed Thomas, with a thoughtful nod. 'Yeah, that sounds right. Who else would care about me and Robert?'

'*Indeed. It's a short list I'm afraid, dear boy. Let's assume, for a moment, that in order to bring you back from the dead this member of your family would have had to have lived through your death. How long beyond your demise is difficult to say, but consider that, for them, in their reality, you would suddenly pop back into existence. Can you imagine that? A loved one returning from the dead . . . that would be an extremely emotional experience. Utterly overwhelming. For a human.*'

'So, if one day, an uncle or a cousin . . . if someone is "utterly overwhelmed" by me . . . it's them?'

'*It stands to reason,*' he said, drawing his hand along the woollen weave of his scarf.

'Who are you talking to?' asked Judy, with an amused look on her face, as she peered around the door frame at Thomas sat alone on the floor of his bedroom.

'No one. Just playing,' he said with an innocent smile.

Bob nodded along, his pulse quickening as Thomas, with the aid of a Time Lord, connected the dots with frightening accuracy.

'Makes perfect sense, doesn't it? He had seen the football match and he had seen my death. He was desperate to bring me back. I couldn't for the life of me work out how he came by the means to contact Mum and Dad in 1986 . . . but I soon realized it wasn't important. The most important discovery I made was the conclusion that, for him, after that phone call, I would magically pop back into existence. Can you imagine the raw emotion of someone you loved returning from the dead?

'So, armed with that knowledge, I said to myself, just bide your time, Thomas, that day will come. And I waited and waited and waited, so long in fact that I had completely forgotten about my crazy theory . . . until yesterday, when you walked into my restaurant. And you were so *surprised* to see me. *Utterly overwhelmed,* you might say.'

Bob looked into Thomas's unblinking eyes for long moments, 'Wow!' he finally said. 'That's a wild theory. Personally, I always thought Mum and Dad were winding us up.'

Thomas's face lost all expression. 'Don't do that, Bob. Don't do that. My lie detector is so finely tuned it can sniff a single drop of bullshit from a mile away. I've known people who were very good at lying, better than you, and they still couldn't beat my lie detector. They were stupid to even try,' he added icily. 'So, let's not pretend that wasn't you on the phone in '86.' Thomas took Bob's uneasy silence as confirmation. 'Good man,' he said, his face regaining some of its warmth. 'Now, let's have a nice conversation. How does this work? Is my brother Bob in there somewhere or has he been replaced by this new clueless version? You asked me last night if I had seen our parents lately. They disowned me years ago. Everyone knows that. But somehow you don't. I was right, wasn't I – I just popped into existence for you. Do you know anything about me?'

'I think you might be a bad man, Tom, but I'm trying really hard not to believe it.'

'Me, bad?' He pressed his hand to his chest, feigning hurt. 'After all I've done for you, brother dear.'

'What do you mean?'

'I mean, look around. This office, your name on that wall out there . . . you're welcome.'

'What are you talking about? I worked my balls off for this.'

'You might have. But *my* Bob was clever – he took a shortcut. He asked me to . . . *have a word with FitzSimmons,*' he said in a conspiratorial whisper. 'That Bloomfield on the wall out there is you *and me.*'

'I don't believe you,' said Bob, in a voice that suggested he did.

'Believe me, don't believe me, it doesn't change anything. You seem to be lost.at sea here, so allow me to explain the details of your current situation. You are going to give me what I want or I am going to burn this entire place to the ground. I'd actually enjoy it. Frankly, all this . . .' – he looked around the room – 'it's always looked like more of a hobby than a real profession to me.'

'What are you?' asked Bob, clutching at his desk to steady the now spinning room.

'I'm your sweet little brother,' Thomas replied, with taunting innocence.

'What do you want?'

'Whatever it is you used to make that call. That's what I want.'

Bob realized his mistake the second his eyes landed on the phone that had been quietly sitting on his otherwise nearly empty desk.

'So that's it. That's the anomaly,' said Thomas, following his line of sight. 'That's responsible for my resurrection? How novel. Give it to me.'

Bob picked up the phone and, as Thomas extended his hand, Bob placed the phone in his own inner jacket pocket.

'I really wish you hadn't done that,' said Thomas, retracting his hand with a 'tut'. 'I'm going to give you something I am not in the habit of granting, that rarest of opportunities in my world – a second chance. *Give it to me*,' he snarled.

Bob looked past his brother to the door.

'You're considering options that aren't available to you. Don't make me hurt you, Bob.'

'You would really hurt me, Thomas? Your own brother? I brought you back. If it wasn't for me, you'd be dead.'

'Which explains the second chance I just offered you.'

'I can't believe this. What has happened to you?'

'I'd be more concerned with what's about to happen to you.'

'I'm not going to give you the phone.'

'You've come to a decision. Good for you. Now we can move this along,' he said, rising from his chair. Bob did the same.

'What are you doing?' asked Bob.

'You won't give, so I must take.'

'I'm walking out of this office. Keep away from me or I will beat the shit out of you.'

Thomas laughed heartily. 'We aren't children any more, Bob.'

'True, but the last time I checked, I'm a lot bigger than you, little brother.'

'The door is right behind me,' said Thomas, positioning himself between Bob and his exit.

'I'm serious. If you come anywhere near me . . .' Bob warned.

'You'll do as I say, Bob. Everybody does,' said Thomas, with unwavering authority. 'One way or another, you're going to reach into that pocket and give me the phone.'

Bob started walking to the door. Thomas took one step towards him, which Bob took as permission to drop his shoulder and barge Thomas aside. But his little brother saw the assault coming and used Bob's momentum against him. A flat palm, wound from the hip, brutally fast, slammed with the force of a lump hammer into Bob's solar plexus.

Every cubic centimetre of air in his lungs rushed from his mouth like a hull breach on a starship, leaving nothing but a silent scream in its wake. Unable to breathe, the veins in his neck ugly knots of agony, Bob dropped to his knees.

'There, there, big brother. You've had a bit of a tap to the abdomen. Just try to relax and breathe. It'll pass,' soothed Thomas, resting a comforting hand on Bob's convulsing shoulder. 'It's funny, isn't it. Who relaxes after being told to relax? It probably creates more pressure on the poor sod who's in trauma. Still, it's the thought that counts, so my recommendation stands.' He rubbed the area between Bob's shoulder blades as he finally started coughing and spluttering for oxygen in wrenching gasps. 'Good. That's progress.'

But no sooner had Thomas praised Bob for managing to breathe again, when the contents of his stomach cascaded out of his mouth, leaving him coughing and spluttering once again. 'Oh! That can happen. No shame in it.'

'*You little shithouse,*' Bob hissed in strained, gurgling gulps, 'you just made a big mistake.' He spat, staring through bloodshot eyes at the puddle of vomit pooling on the floor before him.

'You've got air back in your lungs and a mop and

bucket will see to the floor. Don't make me break something you can't fix.' Almost before Thomas had finished speaking, Bob swung his arm at him, fist clenched like a wrecking ball. But with incredible speed, Thomas ducked the incoming blow and launched his own counterattack – an arcing chop with the side of his hand, which met Bob's Adam's apple with deadly accuracy. Bob's hands instantly went to the point of impact. He clutched his throat in disbelief as his airflow came to an abrupt halt.

'They say the Adam's apple serves no specific function. I disagree. When hit right, it can be a marvellous pain-delivery system, and that terrifying swelling blocks the airway for a disconcertingly long period. Horrible, isn't it?' Watching Bob's protruding tongue and eyes bulging from their sockets, Thomas gave a mirthless chuckle. 'It's crazy, isn't it? You aren't underwater, you're not in the vacuum of space, here you are on Earth, and yet no air for you.' Bob collapsed on to his side, his bright red face and some of his jacket now resting in the vomit. 'I may have been a little over-zealous in my defence,' Thomas admitted, observing Bob's hands still locked around his swollen throat. 'Let's give it a beat. Worst-case scenario, I'll pop a little hole in your windpipe there.' Taking a knee, being careful to avoid the vomit, Thomas brought his ear closer to Bob's now purple face. 'There we go,' he said, noticing desperate wheezing, like air escaping from a punctured inner tube. 'There's a hole in the dam.' He stepped away from Bob's crippled form.

Like a man breaking the surface of a watery grave, Bob breathed in a great torrent of air, his burning lungs and throat releasing a high-pitched howl in the process. Such was the relief of being able to breathe, he forgot for a moment what had brought him to this wretched state (sobbing, face-down in his own vomit) until Thomas's hand-crafted Italian brogues stepped into his field of vision. 'You're back in the room,' he heard, as a handful of his hair was gathered in a vice-like grip.

'Wait a second,' Bob said, feeling his head being yanked off the floor. 'STOP!' he yelled, on his knees, looking up at his brother's cocked, white-knuckled fist.

'Are you ready to reach into that pocket?' Thomas asked.

'Wait a sec . . .' The sentence was cut short by a fist being driven into his face. At the centre of Bob's brain a searing white light exploded, accompanied by the ringing of a deathly gong. Dazed and confused, he brought a shaking hand to his eye socket and felt a burst of pain. 'YOU PIECE OF SHIT!' he wailed, blood gathering in his vision whilst he tried to loosen the hold on his hair. But his weakened hands were easily batted away.

'That eye is going to shut up shop for a while,' Thomas said. 'It's going to swell up beautifully. That's me at about a five, possibly a six. I could turn up the dial for your other eye, but you're not going to like that because the socket is going to cave in. And you can't fix that with a cold steak. So, let's try one more time . . . before I have to lose my temper. Reach into your fucking pocket and hand me the phone.'

'I can't,' Bob said, barely audible.

'What did you say?'

'You're evil, Tom,' he said more loudly, bloody tears now flowing from his eyes. 'I can't give it to you.'

'Incorrect,' said Thomas. 'That is not the answer we're looking for. But not to worry, nobody leaves this show with nothing, so I'm going to cave your face in.'

Bob braced for impact.

'*GET AWAY FROM HIM!*'

Bob and Thomas both froze mid-strike. Opening eyes that had been closed in terror, Bob peered past his attacker. '*Thank God,*' he moaned, as Thomas swivelled to see who had interrupted their meeting.

Standing in the open doorway, with a phone held aloft in her willowy hand, was Miss Pennypacker, fire and brimstone etched across her face.

'UNHAND HIM!' she demanded.

'Ah, the receptionist,' Thomas said, giving her a warm smile.

'Executive assistant, actually. This phone is connected to the police who are currently en route. So, I'm telling you again, step away from him, NOW!'

Thomas turned his grin back to Bob. 'Don't you hurt her,' grimaced Bob, through laboured breaths.

'Hurt her? You think I'd harm an old woman? What kind of a person do you think I am?' replied Thomas, releasing Bob from his grip. Stepping aside, he allowed him to get to his unsteady feet and make his way to the protection of Miss Pennypacker.

'Are you OK?' she asked.

'I think so,' he said, trying to wipe the red sheen from his bloody eye.

'The police are coming.'

'I have to go.'

'Go?' she replied in shock. 'You should be here when they arrive.'

'Miss P,' he said, taking her cool hand in his, 'I can't explain it . . . but I have to go.'

'OK, go,' she said, seeing the look in his eye, 'I'll make sure he's here when the police arrive.'

'Thank you,' he said, squeezing and releasing her hand.

Thomas had been quietly watching, wiping the blood and vomit from his hands with a black handkerchief. 'Let's do this again soon,' he said.

Fleeing his office building as quickly as his legs would carry him, Bob found himself in a local park with his hands on his knees panting with fear and exhaustion. He saw a public restroom and decided to assess the damage there.

As he entered, his battered face and blood-and-vomit-caked jacket drew judgmental stares from the other patrons, so it was no shock to him when he saw the mess staring back at him from the mirror.

The eye, as predicted, was very much on its journey towards 'shutting shop'. An engorged purple and black welt hung beneath his eyebrow. Blood ran down his cheek and throat, gathering at his shirt-collar and over-flowing in grizzly streams along his shoulder and arm.

He grabbed a fistful of hand towels, wetted them and started dabbing at the vomit and blood.

Unsurprisingly, a man covered in blood quickly emptied the facility. Bob was soon alone. Free of interference, he focused on trying to clear as much of the sour-smelling bodily fluids from his person as possible. In fact, he was so focused, he hadn't noticed he was being watched by a man standing in the entranceway.

'Ouch. That has to hurt,' he said.

Bob turned his good eye in the direction of the familiar voice. 'How did you find me?' he said, dropping the now red hand towels into the sink.

'Wasn't hard. I followed the trail of bloody breadcrumbs.'

'And Miss Pennypacker?'

'I threw her out the window.'

'What!'

'I'm kidding,' he laughed. 'She's an old woman. How did you imagine she'd keep me there? I just walked out and didn't harm a grey hair on her head.'

'Thank you for that.'

'It's not too late for you and me, you know. We want the same things.'

'And what are they?'

'Money. Power.'

'Does this make you feel powerful?' asked Bob, gesturing to his face.

'You've only yourself to blame. That could have been easily avoided if you had just given me the phone.'

'What do you want it for?'

'He asked Lazarus. Which would make you Jesus. *That is power*,' he said, choosing that moment to attack.

Thomas covered the ground between them with a startling speed. Bob dived into the only sanctuary available – the disabled toilet behind him. He locked the door just as Thomas launched himself like a compact battering ram. The thudding impact made the hinges creak in the doorframe.

'How long do you think two inches of wood can delay the inevitable?' Thomas asked calmly through the door.

Bob looked around the surprisingly large space. Noting the toilet, sink and sanitary bin, he crossed the room to the window. He lifted the lever, but it only opened a few inches. Even if it had opened all the way, it was too small for his large frame to fit through.

'Shit!' he said, slamming the window shut.

'Not big enough, eh?' said Thomas, his ear pressed to the door. 'You're trapped, Bob. Open the door or I promise you I will see to it that you legitimately need the disabled toilet for the rest of your life. Do you hear me? Just open the door.'

Bob knew Thomas was right on two accounts – he was trapped, and the phone was a tool of immense power. At all costs, he could not let it fall into Thomas's hands. Bob removed the phone from his pocket . . . and held it above his head. One hard and fast strike to the corner of the sink would neutralize the threat of his brother having access to the past.

'It's quiet in there . . . you're *thinking* again, aren't you,

Bob,' said Thomas, his voice still unnervingly calm. 'You have a simple choice – open the door and give me the phone or I break down the door and take it from you. The first is a far more elegant solution. The second would see me breaking a perfectly good door and the rest of your face.'

'You're a monster!' Bob shouted, the phone still poised above his head.

'Again, you've only yourself to blame. If it wasn't for you bullying me when we were kids, I never would have learnt how to look after myself.'

'I told you! I regret that.'

'I don't. Oh, you were better after that phone call, but the damage was already done . . . and I wouldn't change it for the world. I actually thank you for it, Bob. You taught me at a very young age that no one can be trusted. Even family.'

Wait.

Bob slowly lowered the phone. *I never would have learnt how to look after myself.*

An idea started to take shape in his mind.

'Open the door!' shouted Thomas, rattling the handle, his patience now wearing thin.

Bob switched the phone on and dialled.

'Come on, come on. *Please,* answer. Pleasepleaseplease . . .' he said, as it started to ring.

'OPEN THE FUCKING DOOR!' Thomas scream-ed, followed by a violent thud.

'Hello, Bloomfields'.'

'YES!' said Bob, in equal parts joy and relief. 'It's you!'

'Yeah . . . *it's me*,' the voice said in slow confusion. '*Who's speaking, please?*'

'It's your friend from the other night. You remember, yes? I spoke to your parents too about the football match. I told them what was going to happen. You know about all that, right?' he said, trying his best not to sound terrified.

'*How did you know about the game?*'

'I have a gift, Robert. I can see into the future.'

'*That's so cool.*'

'Yes, it is.'

'*How do you do it?*'

'I don't have time to get into that. I need to tell you something about your future.'

'*My future?*' he replied, excitedly.

There's another almighty crack on the door.

'I'm afraid it's not good.'

'*What do you mean?*'

'I don't want you to be scared,' he said, looking up at the door's creaking frame, 'but I have to tell you something that's not going to be nice to hear.'

'*Maybe I should get Mum or Dad?*'

'NO! Don't do that. I have to speak to you. It has to be you, and you have to keep it secret.' CRACK! Another ferocious attack on the door saw it teetering on the verge of destruction. 'I don't have much time. I'm sorry, but there's no easy way to tell you. You saw that I knew what was going to happen in that game. So, believe me when I say that someone is going to hurt you in your future. I can see it.'

231

'*W . . . w . . . why?*' he asked, instantly scared.

'It doesn't matter. It's going to happen unless you do as I say. Can you do that?' he asked, but all he heard was sobbing. 'ROBERT!' he shouted, hating himself for scaring the boy. 'Don't cry. Just listen.' Another deafening thud echoed off the walls. Bob tried his best to tune out the assault, which was now looking more imminent than ever. 'Robert, you need to learn how to protect yourself. Boxing, martial arts, kick boxing, all of the above, anything! Just learn to protect yourself! Train at that stuff like you're expecting the worst, because *it is* coming. Someday somebody is coming to hurt you, *do you hear me!*' The wood around the doorframe started to groan and splinter, giving Bob his first glimpse of daylight on the other side. Thomas immediately renewed his attack with even greater ferocity.

'*Who's going to hurt me?*' asked Robert, still sobbing.

'My time's up. Don't tell anyone about this conversation. Keep it secret,' he warned, as the door finally blew off its hinges, sliding across the tiled floor. 'It's up to you now,' Bob said.

Thomas stood in the destroyed doorway, the little man as composed as ever, not even short of breath.

'I hope you don't mind me popping in like this,' he grinned. 'Who were you talking to?'

'Wrong number,' Bob quipped, attempting to project confidence but sounding more like his scared twelve-year-old self. He went to put the phone back in his inside pocket.

'Uh, uh, uh,' Thomas said, wagging a finger, 'that belongs to me.' But Bob ignored him, tucking the phone

232

out of sight. 'That makes no sense to me. Look around, there's no old woman here to save you. This all could have been so easy.' Thomas sounded full of pity as he stepped through the shattered doorframe and began a slow amble towards Bob.

Stepping over the remains of the door, Bob skirted the toilet's perimeter, edging nearer to the exit . . . but it was a futile effort. In a flash, Thomas made his presence felt – an explosion of pain erupted in Bob's rib cage, sending his grunting body clattering into the toilet's water tank and back to the furthest point from the exit.

Slumped over the cistern, he looked up to see where his attacker was, only to be met with a steam train to the jaw, his head snapped back against the porcelain with ferocious force. Groaning in pain, the sound of an animal being feasted on by a lion, he slid on to the bathroom floor.

'From an office in the clouds to the floor of a public restroom,' Thomas tutted.

Pulling himself up off the floor with the aid of the sink, Bob sat half slumped against the wall, defeated and broken. After coughing up a great mouthful of blood, he brought his good eye to try and focus on Thomas. Blearily, he could see that he had turned to address a teenage boy, frozen in horror, who looked in at the scene.

'Occupied,' Thomas said, with a blank stare that sent the boy running for the exit. Satisfied, he turned back to Bob with the intention of concluding their business – and for a millisecond his entire field of vision was filled with five knuckles.

The next thing Thomas saw was the ceiling of the main restroom area passing rapidly above him as he slid along the floor on his back. He came to rest between the line of urinals and sinks. His nose was without doubt broken – he could already smell and taste the metallic tang of blood. Propping himself up on his elbows, he looked at Bob standing beyond the shattered doorframe, staring at his own clenched fist in disbelief.

'Interesting,' said Thomas. He was quickly back on his feet and dusting off his suit as best he could. He pinched his nose between his index finger and thumb and pulled down rapidly. A pair of loud clicks echoed around the restroom producing a guttural growl from him.

'I'm . . . I'm sorry, Tom,' said Bob, assuming that was the right thing to say after you had broken your brother's nose.

'Hitting a man when his back is turned,' said Thomas, caressing his swollen but now straightened nose. 'I'm impressed.'

'Sorry.'

'Don't be,' he said with a bloody smile. He wiped the tears from his eyes, rolled up his sleeves and cocked his fists before crossing the restroom towards his brother. Bob raised his own fists in preparation, the act providing little comfort as Thomas lunged, knuckles flashing, towards Bob's startled face.

Bob braced for impact.

But instead of an explosion of pain, something else happened. He was a passenger in the events that followed. Like a marionette manipulated for lethal purposes, Bob watched, dumbfounded, as his body, seemingly independent of thought, moved with deadly precision, deflecting the incoming rapid hook with an even quicker forearm block, parrying the motion and knocking Thomas off-kilter.

Capitalizing on the smaller man's shock, Bob drove his free arm with devastating speed into his chest. A sickening thud was followed by a yelp of pain, as Thomas grabbed at his chest as if he were having a heart attack. Like before, Bob's immediate reaction was to reach out and apologize, which he soon realized was a mistake when his opponent instantly turned his buckled anguish into a rocketing uppercut. Thankfully, reflexes he didn't know he had kicked in, helping to make what could have been lights-out, simply a glancing blow.

Commitment to the uppercut left Thomas's defences exposed. Stealing the opportunity, Bob brought his own uppercut into play. He felt the impact of Thomas's teeth slamming shut through the underside of his jaw, then he felt nothing, as Thomas became airborne.

This time, giving him no quarter, Bob pressed his advantage. Releasing a gladiatorial roar, and before Thomas's fluttering feet had even reconnected with terra firma, he unleashed a kick that sent him flying into the wall and then crashing on to the sanitary bin, its contents spilling out on to the floor. Panting with exertion and seeing his brother's prone body slumped amongst the detritus, Bob relaxed his fighting pose and stood amazed.

'Holy shit! It worked! It actually worked,' he said, clenching and unfurling what felt like another man's fists.

'So that's who you were speaking to . . . *yourself.*'
Thomas winced, wiggling his jaw from side to side. 'We
did a bit of martial arts together as kids, but I thought
you gave it up.'

'Apparently not,' said Bob, in further wonder. 'That
was incredible.' He unclenched his fist and offered it to
his brother. Thomas took it and was pulled to a seated
position, slumped on the toilet.

'Thank you,' he wheezed, in pain. Bob tried to remove
his hand but Thomas gripped it harder, pulling him
closer to his bloodied face. 'This isn't over,' he rasped in
a deadly whisper. 'I have to have that phone.'

'That's not going to happen,' Bob replied, wrenching
his hand free and backing away towards the exit.

'You've only won the battle,' said Thomas, spitting
blood on to the floor.

Bob ignored him and kept walking.

'Bob! BOB!' Thomas shouted after him. 'You're not
at the top of the list of people I'll see dead . . . but you
are on the list!'

17

'Oh, my God!'

'Sorry, Kirst. I didn't know where else to go.'

'Did you consider a hospital?' she said, aghast at the state of the man standing on her doorstep. 'What happened?'

'My brother.'

'Jesus. You'd better come in,' she said, stepping aside.

'Thank you, Kirst.'

'Go to the kitchen,' she said, as he limped by her. 'My God, you stink.'

Entering the kitchen, the purple monkey amidst the fridge art greeted him. It was all as it was a few days back. Except for a playpen at the centre of the room containing a baby excitedly hitting two wooden alphabet blocks together. Bob stopped in his tracks. The baby reminded him of a child he once knew in another life.

'Ches, say hello to Bob. Or at least what's left of him.'

'This is Chester,' he nodded, as the baby gurgled and smiled up at him. 'He's gorgeous.'

'A compliment? How hard did he hit you?' she said, with mock concern. 'Take a seat.'

'Where's Scotty?' he asked, gingerly lowering his aching body on to a chair at the kitchen table.

'It's midday on a Monday, Bob. The kids are at play

group and he's at work. His hangover has just about dissipated after your night out on Friday,' she added, annoyance creeping into her voice as she ran some hot water into a bowl. 'Take the jacket off.' Bob did as he was instructed, groaning in the process. 'What the hell were you two fighting about?'

'We were playing video games and it got out of hand, you know how brothers are.'

'Funny.' She placed hot water, some towels, and a first-aid kit on the table. 'That eye looks like it needs stitches.'

'Nah, it'll be fine.'

'I suppose you're right. Your looks are fading anyway.'

'Funny,' he said, returning her grin.

'All right, this is going to hurt.' She started to wipe away the streaks of congealed blood. A gash, which now sat on top of what looked like a purple marshmallow filling his eye socket, elicited a sharp stab of pain.

'Arrrrgh,' he winced.

'I have some butterfly stitches I can use to try and hold it together. But unless you get it properly stitched up, you're going to have a nasty scar.'

'Do what you can.'

She took the stitches from the kit and started applying them. Bob watched her attend to him, his face inches from hers.

'There. That doesn't look too bad,' she said, applying the last stitch.

'Kirsty,' he said, her eyes meeting his.

'What?'

238

'I'm sorry for the way I treated you over the years.'

She looked at him with a raised brow. 'I think you might be concussed.'

'I'm serious. I've been such an angry arsehole. You didn't deserve it.'

'That's nice of you to say,' – she walked to the sink and emptied the bloody water – 'But why? Why have you been so angry?'

'I always felt like you both took something away from me.'

'What exactly do you think we took from you?' she said, turning to face him.

'Scotty took you away from me. And then you took Scotty away from me.'

'I was never yours, Bob.'

'I know. I was a jealous idiot,' he said, casting his good eye downwards.

'You are an idiot,' she said, sitting next to him. 'You didn't lose either of us. We were always here for you.'

'I recently figured that out,' he said, reaching for her hand, 'and I'm telling you I'm sorry. I'll be better.'

She gently patted his hand. 'I'll see if I can find something of Scott's for you to wear.'

Kirsty went upstairs, leaving Bob to quietly sit and watch her son energetically crawling around his pen, little hands and knees thumping the cushioned flooring in a pleasant patter, grabbing toys, playing with them briefly, before discarding them and moving on to find the next thrill. After Chester had pushed aside a stuffed teddy, Bob was amused to see him reaching for a toy phone that looked vaguely similar to the one he had found on a shelf in Soho.

'Careful who you call with that thing, Chester,' he whispered to himself. Chester seemed to answer with a high-pitched squeal. Bob smiled, but the smile soon faded as he reached into his trouser pocket and removed his iPhone.

He typed a text.

Meet me on Westminster bridge in one hour.

He pressed send.

Kirsty came downstairs holding one of the only items that might have fitted Bob. It wasn't exactly what you might expect to find a 'rich and successful Entertainment Manager' wearing, but beggars and choosers and all that, she thought.

As she entered the kitchen, she was surprised to see Bob leaning into Chester's playpen laughing and giggling, waving a teddy at him, Chester apparently delighted with it all.

'Will wonders never cease. Could this be the man who said it was pointless being godfather to any of our children because if Scott and I die in a car wreck, the child would most likely be with us?'

'I don't remember saying that,' he replied, sheepishly.

'You'd had a few.'

'I've said some shitty things.'

'You have. But it's never too late to change. So why

don't you change into this.' She unfurled one of Scotty's baggiest jumpers, which just happened to have Mickey Mouse and Eurodisney emblazoned across the front.

'Do you have anything . . . sane?'

'Not in your size,' she said, throwing him the jumper.

'How the mighty fall,' he muttered, shaking his head at its brightly coloured hideousness.

'The purple matches your eye,' she said.

'Why do I get the feeling you're enjoying all this?'

'Because you're a perceptive man,' she grinned. 'You can change in the bathroom behind you.'

He pulled the jumper on, his ruined suit jacket, shirt and tie in a heap on the bathroom floor, and looked at his reflection in the mirror. He mused that this was the face and attire of a man who had succeeded in getting the one thing he had always wanted – his brother back. The maxim 'be careful what you wish for' had never seemed more fitting.

He felt no pity for the man in the mirror. Frankly, he deserved everything that had been inflicted upon his damaged face. But as someone had once told him, it was never too late to change. And change things he must. He already knew what he had to do, and he was scared and daunted by the prospect. Whether it would work or not – and there were many potential pitfalls – he had to try and do the right thing for once in his selfish, miserable life. He had to try and put the monstrous genie back in the bottle.

He rested his hand on the phone tucked into his

waistband, concealed perfectly under the baggy jumper, checked his watch and saw it was time to leave.

'Do you have a bag I could put these dirty clothes in?' he asked, exiting the bathroom.

'Just leave them on the floor there. I'll get them cleaned.' She pointed her phone at Bob and snapped a picture. 'Wow. That's one for the mantlepiece. You look . . .'

'Like hammered shit?'

'Vulnerable. Human even.'

'Thank you . . . I think.'

'For a bright guy, you're pretty dumb, Bob. You think it's all about stature and success, but it's not. It's about making a connection, letting someone see behind the mask.'

'So, you're saying you find me more attractive right now than ever before?'

'I'm not.'

'But maybe in another life?'

'Never,' she said, breaking into laughter. Bob joined her but quickly stopped.

'Man, that stings,' he said, gently touching his split eye.

'Are you going to be OK?' she asked. 'Do you want to talk about what happened with your brother?'

'I appreciate that. But it's . . . complicated. And you've already done more than I deserve. I have to get going. Thank you, Kirsty,' he said, extending a hand.

She looked at the hand for a moment before batting it away and embracing him. He hadn't realized how much he'd needed it until her arms were around him. He returned the gesture with an intensity that might have surprised her, he had no way of knowing, but her hug in that moment meant everything to him, and he tried to draw strength from it for what was to come.

Disconnecting, she pulled away. 'Be careful,' she said with a sad smile.

18

The Millennium Wheel spun its never-ending circles, the sun steadily reflected off each pod in clean flashes of dazzling brilliance. The same could not be said for the River Thames, however. Even though the light danced and flickered on its surface, it still failed to add any whimsy to its murky-brown flow.

En route, Bob had made a more expansive investigation of Thomas Henry Bloomfield via the internet. The clearer picture of his brother's notoriety only served to intensify the nightmare he now found himself in. At a distance, Bob could already see him stood at the exact halfway point of Westminster Bridge, the Houses of Parliament providing an ironic backdrop for the man who had chosen to ignore and break the laws made from within its imposing Gothic revival walls.

Closer now, he noted his brother's change of suit (another immaculate ensemble, all-navy with a baby blue shirt) and sunglasses, no doubt concealing a pair of black eyes. Thomas held himself in a way that did not suggest he had recently been beaten into submission on a restroom toilet floor. In contrast, with one eye out of commission and gingerly holding his ribs, Bob limped his way along the bridge.

A group of Japanese tourists who had amassed

between them, blissfully unaware of how close they were to one of the most dangerous men in London, finished their selfies and departed. Seeing Bob limp towards him, a broad grin spread across Thomas's face. 'This is not a good advert for Euro Disney,' he said.

'Or siblings,' replied Bob.

'You're wrong. It's the opposite. If you weren't my brother, you'd have a pair of pliers in your mouth and nails through your feet by now.'

'That sounds about right. I've been reading about you,' said Bob.

'Oh, have you? Did you enjoy?'

'You're an animal.'

'Don't ruin the ending for me now,' said Thomas, with the return of that arrogant grin.

'Animal,' Bob repeated.

'You have to be in my world, Bob,' he said, with a sigh. 'Nothing's crueller to animals than other animals.'

'I wish I'd never brought you back.'

'Nonsense! You've done this country a great service. Because of me a lot of bad people are dead. Which means because of *you* a lot of bad people are dead.'

Bob looked out on to the Thames in anguish. 'I would never kill anyone.'

'You're no stranger to death. What about your little brother? I always wondered how he died. I know it was on a bike ride in Wales. But how did it happen? You never told us when you called.'

Bob turned, and even now he could see his long-festering guilt reflected back at him in his brother's sunglasses.

'It was my fault,' he said, barely above a whisper. Thomas removed his glasses. His eyes were indeed heavily bruised, but it was also the first time Bob had seen them without that omnipresent air of superiority. 'I made you cycle down a hill you weren't ready for. You were going too fast and . . . you went over the edge. Seeing your body on those rocks . . .' His voice wavered as he saw the image in his mind as clearly as the day it had happened. 'It was the worst day of my life. I've felt such guilt all these years.'

After a long moment, Thomas said, 'For what?'

'Did you not hear what I just said?'

'I did. Did you barge him off the road?'

'No.'

'Did you cut the brakes on his bike?'

'No.'

'Then I fail to see how any of it was your fault,' he said, putting his glasses back on.

'How can you say that?' Bob blinked in disbelief. 'You were too young to be on that road. You were terrified.'

'No, I wasn't. I never went to Wales.'

'No, you didn't,' said Bob, coming to a realization. 'The Thomas I knew would never have become the man you are.'

'Oh, Bob! Five hundred thousand words in the English language and those are the ones you choose to use,' said Thomas with a patronizing smirk. 'Can you really be this stupid? I didn't *become* the man you see before you. I was born this way. What I am, is in my bones. It can't be taught. It's like breathing: it's automatic. I'm just lucky, I suppose,' he finished with a shrug.

247

'I don't believe it.'

'Even when the proof stands before you,' he tutted.

Sickened, Bob took a step back. 'I can't believe the guilt I have harboured all these years for you.'

A bus slowly and noisily passed them. They stood watching each other until its rumblings had faded into the distance. 'Let's conclude this family trip down memory lane and get to the real business of the day. *The phone.* I assume that's the reason for this incredibly hammy "meet me on Westminster Bridge" request. Christ, who're you, *The Man from Uncle*?' he laughed contemptuously.

Bob took another step back, reached under his jumper and took out the phone.

'Good. You brought it.'

Bob took the phone . . . and held it over the murky waters of the Thames.

'Bob. *Don't test me*,' said Thomas, in a chilling, emotionless tone. 'I have terrible means at my disposal. Don't force me to use them against my own flesh and blood.'

'I can't let you have it, Tom.'

'The moment that hits the water, everything you have will disappear with it. I promise you, I'll take *everything*.'

Bob clenched his jaw resolutely.

'Don't be stupid!' said Thomas, sounding uncharacteristically panicked. 'You know the power that thing has. Why don't you join me? Think of the things we could do together.'

Bob looked at the phone and then his brother.

For a moment, it seemed to Thomas as if Bob was actually considering his offer of a partnership, until . . .

'*Never,*' said Bob, releasing the phone.

'NO!' screamed Thomas, making a futile lunge at the barrier just in time to see the phone hit the water. He watched with dismay as it sunk out of view, lost to the Thames forever. When the last of the bubbles had disappeared, he turned to Bob with unbridled rage written across his face. 'You're finished,' he spat.

'I couldn't let you have it. I'm sorry, Tom,' said Bob, his hands raised in contrition. For a moment he thought Thomas might attack him. But thankfully he didn't, choosing instead to look over the barrier again at the point of impact.

'You idiot,' he said, more calmly, seeming to have found his composure. 'Now I have to ruin you, Bob.'

'You do what you have to do.'

'There is one good thing to come out of this,' Thomas said, still staring into the Thames.

'What?'

He turned. 'At least now I know you haven't got the power of life and death over me.'

'No. I haven't. You hold all the cards.'

'Yes. I do.'

'I'm going to go now,' said Bob.

As he walked away, he could feel his brother's eyes on his back. Glancing over his shoulder, the feeling was confirmed. Thomas stood motionless, watching Bob's limping form hobble along the bridge.

'I'll see you around, Bob. Say hi to Mum and Dad for me,' he shouted, just before Bob disappeared from view.

19

'3-7-2-3-1' he said, and the metal panel slid up sound-lessly, revealing a wooden box in the wall cavity. He reached in and removed it. 'Lock,' he commanded, and the panel slid back into place. He swung the hinged painting of a daffodil back flush to the wall, concealing the safe behind it.

He entered the kitchen and looked up at the clock for what felt like the thousandth time in the last thirty minutes.

7.36 p.m.

Close. But not yet.

He placed the box on the kitchen table, opened it, and removed folded sheets of old yellowing paper. The pages were frayed and thin, threatening to come apart. He gently smoothed them flat, laying them out before him, revealing scrawled text.

He read over their details out of habit rather than need. He had read it so many times over the years that he could recite it from memory. But at his age, it was a necessary safety precaution to have it written, just in case his memory failed him.

He looked out at the setting sun's golden rays reflecting on the windows of the next tower block to his own. It felt fitting that the day was drawing to a close. It would have been nice to have seen the sunset one last time, but his flat wasn't lucky enough to face west, and it was best not to be on the ground this close to nightfall.

His view was suddenly obscured as the sight of a rising drone-pod filled his window. The occupant's eyes met his own as they peered directly into his kitchen.

'Windows blackout,' he said with annoyance, and the glass instantly went from transparent to solid black, throwing the room into complete darkness. 'Lights.' And the small but neat kitchen was instantly illuminated. Being high up in a tower block provided him with a sense of security, but his privacy was often compromised by passing drone-pods, allowing any stranger to see into his living space.

7.40 p.m.

Watching the clock, he gently stroked the scar above his eye, a habit he had developed over the years when nervous. He had waited a long time for this moment, and it was finally here. He had once counted the years stretching out before him with a deep sense of dread, uncertainty an ever-present companion through the decades. Now the moment had arrived, time seemed to have gone by in an instant.

He looked around his living space. Its frugal layout

provided little insight into its owner's life. But what was the point of acquiring things when ultimately you intended to abandon them? Plus, don't you need money for possessions? He had enough to feed and clothe himself, but an excess of cash was a luxury he had had taken away from him a long time ago. As for a female presence, he had adopted the same attitude: why start a relationship that you would one day have to end? No, regardless of how quickly they had seemed to pass, the truth was that the years had been long and lonely. He was ready to end it all.

7.43 p.m.

'Kirsty is your wife.'

'Errr . . . come again?'

'In the other reality, she's your wife.' Bob watched as Scotty attempted to process the information. His face took on the look of a man trying to solve an impossible equation. 'I had no idea when I told my younger self to start showing people the respect they deserve, that he would apply it to Kirsty. You have to believe me, Scotty.'

'I did think about this, after you told me in that bar that you two were married,' Scotty said with a far-off look in his eye. 'I remember you used to pick on her a bit, nothing terrible, but I suppose some of it was borderline. And then suddenly all that stopped. I even remember you started sticking up for her when anyone else would try and use the jokes that you had made up about her. That's when we stopped hanging out. I thought you were two-faced.'

'None of that was meant to happen. You and Kirsty were meant to be together.'

'If you say so, Bob,' he replied with a snort of laughter. 'I can't see it personally. She's way out of my league.'

'Scotty. I've seen it. It works. It's perfect. You belong with her . . . well, maybe not this version of Scott Pickers-Gill. But the Scotty in my reality, the real you, he should be with her.'

'Thanks . . . I think . . .'

'That didn't come out right. Shit, sorry Scotty. I'm even messing this up,' he rubbed the back of his neck for some time before continuing. 'What I'm trying to say is – I stole this life from you. Do you understand? I feel ashamed. I resented her for years for taking you away from me. I was so selfish and jealous. And now I've taken everything from you . . . *everything*. I'm so sorry, Scotty. Can you forgive me?'

Scotty stood, then walked to one of the far corners of Bob's office. He spent long moments with his back to Bob, head bent, his hand on his brow, deep in thought.

7.44 p.m.

'How should I feel? Angry? Hurt?' he said, finally turning. 'I don't know this woman. You're talking about a life I haven't lived. I can't even imagine her being my wife. All I know is everything that's happened to me up until this point, and none of it involves her . . . it barely involves you.'

'That's because . . .'

'Let me finish,' said Scotty, with a raised hand. 'I've made poor decisions in my life, Bob. I've hurt a lot of people. The truth is, I don't think I deserve what you're offering me. I should be apologizing to you. I know what you are about to give up for me. Let's be honest, you could bring back Thomas and still have your life with Kirsty. I don't forgive you . . . because there's nothing to forgive.'

Bob looked at his old friend for long moments with eyes that suddenly looked a little wetter than they had before. He pursed his lips in a tight smile before he said, 'And that is exactly why we're about to restore the life you deserve.'

Bob got up, made his way towards Scotty and wrapped his arms around him. They both held the embrace for a long time. Releasing his friend, Bob said, 'You're the best person I know in any reality . . .' as his office phone started ringing. Separating himself from Scotty, they both looked at the phone.

'That's strange,' said Bob.

'How so?' asked Scotty.

'That's my direct line. Which I do not give out.' He reached across his desk and lifted the receiver. 'Hello?'

'*Bob?*'

'Yes?'

'*Are you with Scotty?*'

'Yeah . . .' he said, giving Scotty a confused sideways glance.

'*Thank God. Stop what you're about to do and listen to me.*'

'Who the hell is this?'

'*You're about to call your family in the past to tell them how to save your brother and restore Scotty's former life.*'

'How do you know that?'

'*Only two people on Earth know what I've just told you, and I'm one of them. I'm you, Bob. In the future.*'

'Bullshit!' said Bob.

'*Too far-fetched? Fair enough. Sorry to bother you. I'll let you get back to calling your family from thirty-seven years in the past. Don't be stupid, Bob. I'm you and you are me.*'

'You sound . . . different.'

'*I'm a bit older.*'

'How much?'

'*Thirty-seven years.*'

'Bullshit,' he said again.

'*You don't sound so sure.*'

'So, you're me from 20 . . . 58?' said Bob, but the statement was directed at Scotty.

'What!?' said Scotty.

'I'm gonna put you on speaker phone.' Bob pressed the hands-free button.

'*Hello, Scotty,*' said the voice from the speaker.

'Hi . . .' said Scotty, cautiously. 'How did you know I was here?'

'*Because I stood next to you in that very room thirty-seven years ago.*'

'It's impossible,' said Bob. 'The future hasn't happened yet?'

'*Assuming you're in the present is astoundingly arrogant.*'

'Hey, dick. I'm just trying to get my bearings here. It's a lot to take in.'

'*You just called yourself a dick.*'

'And you called yourself arrogant.'

'*I know, I was.*'

'But I definitely become a dick though, yes?'

'Guys, please. This is not helping,' Scotty interjected, attempting to bring some order. 'What did Bob just tell me before you rang?'

'Scotty, *you always were the voice of reason.*' The line was silent while Bob and Scotty stared at the speaker in anticipation. '*I told you that Kirsty is your wife in the other reality.*'

'*Holy shit,*' said Scotty, finding he needed to sit down. 'It's true. It's you.'

'You've had the phone all this time and it still works?' asked Bob, sitting at his desk, the phone in question in front of him.

'*It does.*'

'Then why did you wait so long to call me?'

'*The connection is fixed at a distance of thirty-seven years. So obviously I had to wait thirty-seven years to talk to you at this exact moment.*'

'Man, that's a long wait for a chin-wag,' said Scotty.

'*You have no idea. I couldn't know for certain what reality the phone would connect me to . . . but somehow, and I can't explain it, I knew the phone wanted to help me. I think it wants to help all of us.*'

'When I was a kid,' began Bob, ignoring his future self's musings, 'and Dad would be particularly tyrannical, what did I do to his car?'

After a moment's thought, the answer came, '*I would put a little bit of dogshit on the door handle.*'

'Correct. Just wanted to double check. Never told anybody that.'

'You did what?' said Scotty, in shock. 'That is diabolical.'

'*I'm not proud of it.*'

'Yeah, it's not a cherished memory,' admitted Bob, equally embarrassed. 'So, what's the future like? Are you smearing dogshit on hover boards yet?'

'*No,*' he replied sternly. '*The future . . . my future, is the one you are about to create. And it must be stopped.*'

Bob and Scotty looked at one another, perplexed.

'What is it you want to stop?' asked Scotty, nervously.

'*The phone call you're about to make.*'

'That's not going to happen,' said Bob, matching his resolute tone.

'*I knew you would say that, Bob, because that's exactly what I would have said in the same circumstance. But you haven't heard what the phone call you are about to make will unleash. I'm begging you to listen to me first.*'

'Unleash? What are you talking about?'

'*I'm talking about the evil that is Thomas Henry Bloomfield.*'

'I'm sorry. I know it's hard to hear,' he said, into the ancient phone, which felt heavier in his old hand than it ever had before.

'*What are you talking about? Thomas isn't evil!*'

Bob stroked the scar above his eye. He ignored the anger and accusation in his younger self's voice and instead chose to remind himself that what was on the weathered old pieces of paper before him on his kitchen table had been written by the same person. Whether he knew it or not, the Bob on the end of the line wanted the same thing as the Bob of 2058.

'Of course, the nine-year-old you remember wasn't evil. He had issues, we both know that. But the man he will become, if you stop that trip to Wales in 1986, *he is evil.*'

'*I don't believe it. There's no way.*'

'It's already happened. I've lived it,' he said sadly. 'I made the call you are about to make. I brought him back. The thirty-seven years he lived, in the blink of an eye for me, crafted and nurtured a dark heart.'

'*What happened to him?*' asked Scotty.

'After I created a new reality with my brother in it, in time the memories of our life together appeared in my mind and the details of Tom's grim story invaded my thoughts like a waking nightmare. I'd always remembered him as sweet and mischievous, but now I know that's something that happens when you lose someone . . . you cling to the positives, the good. Re-examining my youth, whether we admitted it to ourselves or not, I think we all knew that Thomas had always been a strange child – introverted, brooding, intense, lost in his own little world.'

'*That's not the way I remember him. That's not true!*' Bob cried through the phone.

'Are you trying to convince me, or yourself?'

'*It's not true,*' Bob repeated.

'If I know it, then you know it. It's inescapable.' His statement was met by silence, so old Bob continued, 'As a teenager, he lashed out at anybody who had any kind of authority over him: our parents, teachers, anybody who dared to try and control him. It wasn't long before he had his first taste of captivity for stealing cars, at the age of seventeen. Even then, my mother and father still held out hope that they could get him back on track, but all they could do was watch that teenager grow into a cruel and unfeeling man.'

'*Did you two get on, at least?*' asked Scotty.

'Not really. I don't think he ever forgave me for how I had treated him when we were much younger. Which I probably deserved. The days of me exerting my will over his were long gone. I was scared of him. I knew he was dangerous. And he proved that when he went back to prison for assault by the age of twenty-three. Any humanity he took with him into that place was gone by the time he was released.'

'*What about Mum and Dad? How did they react?*' asked Bob.

'They couldn't do it any more. They washed their hands of him. I was there that day. He just laughed at them. I'm still not sure what broke them more: turning their backs on him, or the fact that he didn't care. They were never in the same room with him again.'

'*Never!?*' said Scotty in surprise. '*Why not? Where did he go?*'

'He had made friends in prison, like-minded people you could say, who were more than happy to put a roof over his head. The story of what happened next has been told many times over the years. None of it provable of course. He's far too cunning for that.

'These new friends revelled in that part of him that was missing. They saw that it gave him a special ruthlessness, a willingness to do whatever was necessary, a significant advantage in the criminal underworld. But my brother was never going to be satisfied with being just a soldier. He covets power above all else.

'When this version of myself first met Thomas in our merged realities, he had already progressed through the criminal ranks. He was a powerful, dangerous man, but still a man who served and answered to a superior power – The Boss. At least that's what everyone but Thomas called him. He thought of him as more of a businessman than a gangster, a stressed-out, paranoid control freak, who spent most of his time worrying about doing time. Thomas suggested he lacked the minerals. And everyone privately agreed with him. Which is why Thomas decided to kill him and become their leader. But Thomas didn't just murder him, he erased his family from existence, burning the boss, his wife . . .' Old Bob wavered for a moment. Even now, after all these years, hardly believing the words he was about to speak, 'and their three children to death as they slept in their beds.'

'*No . . . I can't believe it,*' he heard the younger version of himself mutter in a hollow voice.

'You must,' he replied in the same voice, 'because if you make that call it's going to happen.' Long moments passed. He could feel his younger self reeling.

'*You have the phone! Why didn't you call Mum and Dad and tell them all this?*' asked Bob, in desperation. '*Surely they could have done something. Got him help . . . anything.*'

'I couldn't risk Thomas knowing I have the phone. If I called our family in the past, he would know it still exists. He thinks I destroyed it.'

'*How?*'

'He saw me drop the phone into the Thames. At least he thought he saw me drop it. In actual fact, it was Chester's toy phone. I packed it with coins to make sure it sank when it hit the water.'

'*Who's Chester?*' asked Scotty.

'Your son in the correct reality,' he replied.

'*Chester Pickers-Gill? Why the hell would I call a kid that?*' asked Scotty, baffled.

'*Scotty. Please.*'

'*Yup. Sorry, Bob. Not important right now.*'

'I couldn't risk Thomas having the phone,' continued old Bob. 'Can you imagine what would happen if he possessed the power to speak to the past? It was a risk to even keep the phone. But I had to try and undo this hell I've created. I kept it in the hope that I could call you in this very moment, to fix this.'

'*If I don't make the call . . . you're asking me to let my brother die.*'

'Our brother, Bob. *Our brother.* And I wouldn't ask you to do this if I didn't think it was the right thing to do.'

'I can't believe this is happening,' said Bob, holding his head in his hands.

Scotty looked on, angst-ridden. 'I don't know what to say, Bob.'

'Maybe I could speak to Mum and Dad. Come clean, tell them it's me . . .'

'*Bob! Stop!*' came a shout from the speaker. '*Don't do it to yourself. You know what needs to be done. Thirty-seven years ago when you duped Thomas into thinking you'd destroyed the phone, you were worried that the memories you had accumulated skipping between realities would cloud your mind. You were worried that you might forget what the phone represents and this new reality you had created, with your brother, would become all you'd ever known. So, you wrote a letter to yourself detailing most of what I've just told you. You see, the words you've heard were written in your own hand on paper I have in front of me in 2058. I've kept it and read it many times over the years. I've watched the clock ticking down to this moment. I need to put right what I have broken with this blasted phone.*

'*I know the guilt you've lived with, Bob. You want to save your brother.*' The line went silent for some time. '*But I know there's another reason why you want to bring him back,*' he continued, his voice now thinner, weaker somehow. '*I thought if I could bring back Thomas it would fix me, but it didn't. Everything was the same. Only then was I able to see that I'd been using his death as an excuse for my own shortcomings, and they were all still there even when Thomas came back. I'm still a lonely, angry and selfish man. But you can be different. You can be better than me. That's why I called you now, and not as soon as you found the phone. I wanted to give you a chance to find your humanity. Our time with Kirsty, the baby, helping Scotty . . . we were starting to be better. You saw the man you could be. Be better now, Bob. Don't make that phone call.*'

'What will happen to you if I don't?' asked Bob.

'*I'm not really sure. But I think, along with this whole night-mare, I will cease to exist.*'

'And you're OK with that?' said Scotty, incredulous.

'*Ending my life today has been the only thing that has kept me alive for the last thirty-seven years. Yes, I'm OK with it, Scotty,*' he said, his love for his old friend evident in his voice.

'OK. I'll do it. I won't make the call,' Bob said suddenly. But there was no reaction from the speaker. 'I said I'll do it,' he repeated.

'*I don't believe you,*' said a sad voice.

'Why?'

'*Because I'm still here. If you were truly not going to make that call . . . I think I'd be gone.*'

'NOOOO!' Bob screamed at the speaker. 'I'm not going to let my brother die!' He slammed the call end button.

In 2058, Bob lowered the phone from his hot, aching ear, took the old letters in his hand and crushed them into a ball.

20

'What are you going to do?' asked a bewildered Scotty.

Bob picked up the phone his future self had just called on. 'How do we know he's not lying? He could be trying to manipulate us for his own ends?' he said, staring at the phone, confused and angry.

'Do you think you're capable of that?'

'Thirty-seven years from now? I don't know.'

'He sounded kind of legit to me.'

Bob studied Scotty and loathed the sincerity etched across his face. 'What would you do, Scotty?' he growled. 'Do you want to stay here trapped in this life? Or do you want to get back to your wife and kids? I know I want to see my brother again.'

'He's gone, Bob,' said Scotty, quietly. 'And it sounds like that might be for the best.'

'That's my fucking brother you're talking about. It's not true!' Bob shouted, banging his fist against the desk.

Scotty recoiled, and then a great sadness came over him. 'You asked me, do I want to stay here trapped in this life or do I want to go back to my wife and kids. The one thing I want more than *anything* is to stop me from getting in that car on that awful night . . . and to bring back Leo Presser. But if it means three kids have to die . . . I can't do that, Bob. I won't. I've hurt enough people. No more. I choose to stay here.' He got up. 'So, if you're going to make that call, I can't be part of it. I'm leaving.'

'Scotty, wait!' said Bob, rising himself. 'Don't go. We're in this together.'

Scotty had reached the door. 'It's your party, Bob,' he said with a sad smile, and left.

'Scotty!' Bob shouted as the door closed.

He stood alone in his recently transformed office, its bright cheer only serving to heighten the sense that he was a man lost. He craved the familiar comforts of his sprawling oak desk and bearskin rug.

He fell back on to his seat with a thud, and then propped the phone on its end before him. He regarded it with a mix of wonder, resentment and hatred. Why had it come to him? What was the point of it? If bringing his brother back would unleash torment and darkness, why had he been presented with the opportunity?

Thomas was his brother, and that meant something, they had a bond. If his future self was telling the truth, and that was the course Thomas's life would take . . . maybe he could reason with him. Point out the error of his ways. Unite him with Mum and Dad. Yes, that was why the phone had come to him. To save Thomas. Just because things had got a little complicated didn't mean he could turn his back on him now. His brother needed him. As a family they could rid him of his demons . . . surely.

He took the phone and dialled.

*

266

'*Who are you!?*' It was his father's voice.

'A friend,' said Bob.

'*I know who my friends are and I don't know you.*'

'Don't get bogged down with who I am. It's not relevant.'

'*Well at least tell me how you did that.*'

'It's not the *how*, it's the *why*. Why did I give you that information?'

'*Why?*'

'To prove that I can predict the future. After what you've just seen, do you believe me?'

'*It's hard not to,*' he replied, awe in his voice.

'Good. That's important.'

'*Why have you been talking to my son?*'

'Because I want to help him. I want to help all of your family.'

'*Why did you tell him to be nice?*'

'Because he's about to go down a path that will have a devastating effect on your family. I'm going to tell you how you can prevent that from ever happening.'

'*By predicting the future?*'

'Yes. I've already seen what will happen.'

'*What does he do?*' he asked, sounding as if he feared the answer.

'Robert is about to engage in a very bad relationship that will result in him becoming a teenage father. That will have a catastrophic impact on the rest of his life. You must at all costs keep him away from a girl called Kirsty Cummings. Do you understand?'

'*Robert, do you know someone called Kirsty Cummings?*' John asked, his voice directed away from the receiver. Bob heard a reply, but it was too far away to decipher. *'She's in school with him,'* he said.

'Keep him away from her. He'll do great things if you can keep them apart.'

'That's all I have to do? Keep him away from her and he'll be fine?'

'Yes.'

'I can do that.'

'Good.'

'What else?'

'Thomas . . .' he began, the name triggering a swirling mass of emotion in his mind. He sat for some time, frozen, unable to push the voice of his future self from his thoughts.

'Yes . . . Thomas?' he heard his father prompt, the fear rising in his voice again. Bob stared unblinking, the sting of tears in his eyes. *'Hello? Are you still there?'*

'I'm still here,' the tears started to flow as he tried desperately to contain the torrent of emotion that threatened to overwhelm him.

'What about Thomas?'

'Thomas . . .' Could he really be this evil villain in waiting? Could he unleash that on his family . . . on the world?

'Is it a girl? Do I have to keep him away from someone?'

'Thomas . . . will be fine.'

'So, he's safe?'

'. . . yes,' he closed his eyes, his face contorted in agony. 'You don't need to worry.'

'*Thank God. Is there anything else?*'
'That's all.'
'*Will you please tell me who you are?*'
He ended the call.

Opening his streaming eyes, Bob placed the phone back on his desk and stared into space, hardly believing what he had done. After a long time, he started to become aware that the office had changed. His desk was now back to being its sprawling oak predecessor. He ran his shaking hand over the cool wood as he noted the return of the oak panelling with its trove of sycophantic superstars. The bearskin rug confirmed that his office had reverted to its previous state of intimidating menace. He was back in a world without Thomas in it. He started to sob uncontrollably, his chest heaving in great bouts of heartbreaking grief. He had lost him all over again.

'*NOOOOOO!*' he suddenly screamed, reaching for the phone. 'TOM!' He wiped his eyes. 'I can't do it.' He pushed the on button and . . . nothing. He pushed it again. *Nothing.* No illumination, no activity whatsoever. He manically jabbed at it to no avail. The phone was lifeless. It was over. His brother was gone forever.

21

Bob left the building of FitzSimmons & Bloomfield Entertainment Management and walked, broken and dejected, in a directionless haze . . . when suddenly, a name came to him – *Scotty!*

He opened his iPhone and made a frantic search for his old friend. And to his relief there he was: '*Scotty*'. Gone was the confusing formality of the other reality's Scott Pickers-Gill. It appeared that his father had successfully kept young Bob and Kirsty apart. He pressed a thumb to Scotty's name.

'*Hey Bob,*' he answered after a few rings.

'Scotty! Where are you?'

'*Ah . . . home.*'

'With Kirsty and the kids?'

'*Yeah. Everything OK?*' he asked, hearing the concern in Bob's voice.

'Not everything. But some things are,' he said with a sigh of relief.

'*Hmmm, that's cryptic. Are you still drunk from Friday?*'

'So, we were at Chloe Huxley's bash together?'

'*Jesus, Bob. How smashed were you?*'

'SBOD. Did we leave together?'

'*That bad, eh?*' he said, laughing. '*Yes, we left together. Chloe was on the hunt and your resolve was wavering. You said*' *you needed to get home and attack your . . . er, technical area, I think is how you put it,'* he finished with another chuckle.

'How's Kirsty?'

'I'd say she's close to forgiving me for my inebriated state and the ungodly hour of my return on Friday night – I mean, Saturday morning. Only now am I starting to feel normal again. That was some night!'

'It was,' said Bob, who had stopped momentarily to check the road for cars before continuing his aimless ramble. 'I'm sorry I've been distant of late, Scotty.'

'That's OK. I know you're a busy man.'

'It's not OK. You've always been there for me and I've taken that for granted for far too long. I'm going to be a better friend from now on, I promise, because you're the best. I love you, Scotty.'

'Wow. I love you too,' he said with surprise. *'What's brought all this on?'*

'If I told you, you wouldn't believe me.'

'Try me.'

'Maybe one day. Can I come see you, Kirsty and the kids, soon?'

'I'd like that. Are you sure you're OK? You sound kind of odd.'

'Don't worry about me,' he said, noticing a red light up ahead. He stopped in his tracks . . . maybe he knew where he was going all along? 'Scotty, I have to go. See you soon.' Putting his phone back in his pocket he looked at the red glowing neon sign at the end of the alley.

The doorbell's dainty chime signalled his arrival. The proprietor, true to form, sat behind the counter, smoking his pipe whilst reading his tatty paperback. But that was the only familiar sight that greeted Bob from three nights earlier.

'Welcome to *Always in Style*, feel free to browse. I'm here if you need any help,' said the old man with a welcoming smile, before turning back to his book.

Bob looked at what was before him in abject confusion. Its previous dusty, ramshackle muddle had been transformed into a neatly organized modern retail space. Strip lighting above illuminated each aisle with clinical accuracy, leaving nothing hidden away in the shadows.

Even the old man had changed. The burgundy dressing gown was gone, replaced by a leaf-print blue shirt and a khaki Harrington jacket. The fez had also been replaced by a white fedora, completing the fetching look.

'What the hell happened here?'

'Excuse me?' he said, looking up from the paperback.

'This place. It's had a bit of a re-vamp since Friday.'

'I'm not sure I follow.'

'I was here on Friday night. This all looked completely different. It was dusty, dirty, lit by candlelight. It was a proper mess. Even you looked different.'

He shook his head slowly. 'I don't think so. Maybe you've got me and my store confused with somewhere else?' he said, bringing the pipe to his thin lips. Bob did a double-take, suddenly realizing it was not a pipe, but a vape stick.

'You don't remember me?'

'Sorry. My memory isn't what it was, and I get a lot

of customers in,' he said, blowing a dense, fruity cloud from a crack in the corner of his mouth.

'Clearly,' replied Bob, gesturing to the empty shop.

'Mondays are usually quiet.'

Bob approached the counter and placed the matt-grey eighties mobile phone on it. 'Maybe you remember this?'

'No refunds, I'm afraid,' said the old man with an apologetic shrug.

'I'm not here for a refund. I bought this off you on Friday night.'

'OK. What's the issue with it?'

'Issue?' Bob repeated with a laugh. 'What the hell *is* it? That's what I want to know.'

'A cordless communications device,' he said, stroking his fluffy beard.

'You know what I mean. I saw that look on your face when I bought it. What is it?' he asked again.

'It's just a useless old phone,' the man said, bemused.

'But it was working.'

'You could call people on this?'

'Yeah, you could say that.'

'Well, that is surprising.'

'It stopped working a short while ago.'

'I don't make them, I just sell them. But still . . . no refunds.'

'Like I said, I'm not here for a refund.'

'Then why are you here?'

'I was hoping you might have some answers. You could tell me what it all means. What's its purpose?'

'I don't know what to tell you. I'm just an old man who owns a shop,' he said, pushing the phone back across the counter. 'I'm sorry.'

Bob nodded, taking the phone. 'So that's it? It's over? And I'll never know why it all happened. Christ, maybe it didn't happen. Maybe I've lost my mind.'

The old man, engrossed in his book once again, gave no sign he had even heard him.

'Sorry to trouble you,' said Bob, dejected, and turned to leave. He took one last frustrated look into the well-lit aisles of tat and sighed.

'Do you feel different?'

'Sorry.' Bob stopped and turned. 'What was that?'

'A change within ourselves is the only true measure of experience. Do you feel any different?' The old man asked again, without taking his gaze from his book.

'I do.'

'Then I would say something happened,' he said, finally meeting Bob's eyes. 'Thank you. Come again. Bye-bye.'

Bob stood for a long time, considering his words, as the old man sat reading. 'I think I understand. Thank you,' he said eventually, before walking out.

22

Resuming his aimless wandering of Soho's darkening streets, he did feel different.

He had begun to question if recent extraordinary events had happened or not, but, as the old man had suggested, he did feel an unmistakable change within himself. That corner of his soul that had been filled with screaming guilt and rage since the loss of his brother was still there, but it had been turned down to a sad, dull murmur. It would always be with him, he had to accept that. But maybe he didn't have to accept the man it had made him become.

Maybe it wasn't too late to become the man he told his younger self he wished he was. The kind of man a woman like Kirsty would want to marry. The kind of man who could patiently wait thirty-seven years to fix a broken future, sacrificing himself for the greater good.

It was time to stop wandering aimlessly. It was time to take control of his life and start living. And he could think of only one person he wanted to do that with.

He removed his iPhone and dialled.

After many rings, a cold voice finally answered. *'What do you want?'*

'I just want you to listen to me for a moment. I'm an

idiot. A moron. I'm a selfish, arrogant man who couldn't see the wood for the trees. I now realize I had it. I had what we are all looking for. I had it! I see that now. I threw away the one thing that makes it all worthwhile. And that means I never deserved it in the first place. You might feel I still don't, and you would probably be right. The man I've been up until this point doesn't deserve you. But I want to be the man who does. And I think I'm ready to become that man if you give me a chance. So, the answer to your question, "What do you want?" I want you. I want it all – marriage, kids, everything. I want it all with you, Nell,' he finished, holding his breath.

After an agonizingly long wait, he finally heard her reply, pushed out through an emotional sob. 'Really?'

'Yes, really.'

Another sob. 'You've got me crying here, Bob!'

'Good tears?' he asked.

'Yes . . . good tears,' she said, with a sniffle.

'Can I come see you?'

'You'd better.'

'OK. I'll be there as soon as humanly possible. I can't wait to see you, Nell.' Wearing a broad, joyous smile without any hint of cynicism, he ended the call and slipped the phone back into his pocket. 'Yes,' he said, turning and stepping into the road.

By the time Bob heard the horn, it was already too late. A blinding flash of headlights was instantly followed by the terrible thud of metal on bone. As his world rotated on its axis, Bob's helpless body arced through the air, finally landing motionless, fifteen feet from the now stationary car, in a crumpled heap.

He stared up at the starless sky. A voice shouted, 'Call an ambulance.' Someone must be hurt, he thought, when all at once the sky was filled by the face of a kid, eighteen, maybe nineteen. 'Ohnonono! I'm so sorry . . . Jesus, no. Are they coming!?' he shouted to someone Bob couldn't see. He took his jacket off and draped it over Bob. A nice gesture, Bob thought, but wasted on him as he couldn't feel a thing. 'Someone is coming,' the kid assured him, his face full of panic and anguish. 'Stay with me. I'm so sorry. You just stepped out . . . what's your name?' Bob tried to speak but his chest didn't seem to want to work. He must have had the wind knocked out of him, he thought, it'll pass in a moment.

Blue flashing lights now filled his fading world. He saw a hand rest on the kid's shoulder. 'Step back please.' And the next face he saw was a paramedic's. 'Can you tell me your name? Can you hear me?' she said. He could, but he still couldn't speak. 'You're going to be OK,' she said, but he couldn't see her any more. All he could see now were blue flashing lights, flashing and flashing and flashing. And then those blue lights became flashing green lights.

Green grass and trees flashing by.

He took a deep breath and tasted the piney wind filling his nose and lungs. He looked down and saw his hands gripping handlebars. Looking up he felt the sunshine on his face and the road rushing by beneath his bike.

He suddenly heard a shrill cry. 'Robert!' Fearing the

worst, he turned. But instead of tragedy, he saw his brother's euphoric smiling face. 'This is so cool!' he yelled joyfully, now riding alongside Bob.

'*Tom!*' Bob shouted, as they rode together side-by-side on a road that never ended.

23

'Are you the driver of the vehicle, Sir?'

'Yeah,' he said, distractedly watching the man he had just hit being loaded into the back of an ambulance.

'I'm going to need to ask you some questions.'

He turned to face the policeman, 'Oh, yeah, OK.'

'What's your name and address?'

'Leo Presser. 15 Burrows Road, Kensal Rise.' The policeman wrote the information down in a small notepad.

'Do you have your driver's licence and insurance with you?'

'I do.'

'OK, Leo. Have you been drinking at all?'

'No.'

'Would you be OK doing a breath test?'

'Yes. Is he going to be all right?' he asked, looking back to the ambulance, as the back doors were slammed shut and the sirens switched on.

'He's with the best people now, Leo. Why don't you come sit in my patrol car. It's a bit quieter in there and you can tell me what happened.'

The whole street had been cordoned off, but, as he followed the policeman to his car, he could still feel the many eyes of the curious bystanders, drawn by the flashing lights, standing behind a length of tape that read 'POLICE LINE DO NOT CROSS'.

It was the first time he had ever sat in a police car. It was possibly the first time he had ever spoken to a police officer. Although, as he took his first breathalyser test and answered the various questions being levelled at him, he found it hard to believe any of this was actually happening. He should be home by now, his father teasing him about spending so much time with his new girlfriend, while his mother attempted to force-feed him a meal he didn't want, but that he would eat anyway because he knew she hated him eating anyone else's cooking.

'*Leo*,' said the policeman. 'You drifted away there. Are you all right? Is there someone I can call to come and get you?'

'My Dad,' he said, quietly. He gave him the number. 'Can I get some air?'

'Yes. I'm done with you for the moment. But don't go far.'

Leo got out of the car, walked a few paces away from the gathered crowd and sat on the pavement, his own car shielding him from judgmental eyes. With his feet in the gutter, he stared at the spot where the man had lain. Blood, black in the streetlights, lay on the tarmac in a vague circle. He couldn't stop thinking about the horribly unnatural angle his leg had been at beneath his body. He put his head in his hands and started to cry. For a while he sobbed, scared for the man he had hit, and for himself, until the tears eventually stopped. Drying his eyes with the bottom of his T-shirt, he looked again at the spot where the man had lain, this time noticing his jacket lying bloodied in the gutter a few feet from him. He got up to retrieve it. Bending down to pick it up, he saw that there was something beneath it – a black . . . no, dark matt-grey rectangle. He picked it up and turned it in his hand.

It was a phone. But not a modern one, it was an old phone, like the ones he had seen in some of the films his dad watched. It was beaten up pretty badly, one side of its plastic casing was scratched in an ugly burr like it had slid across the road. And its small screen had a faint crack in it. *Why would anyone carry around an old broken phone,* he thought, as he idly pushed the on button. To his surprise, its display sprung into life.

'It works,' said Leo Presser.

Directly beneath the green illuminated display, two buttons – one red, one green – began to pulse invitingly.

Epilogue

'No way.'

'Come on.'

They faced one another in the hallway like a pair of gun slingers.

'No,' he replied, resolute.

'Please!' He knew there was a limit to how many times he could say no to him.

'I don't mind taking you.'

'How lame am I going to look turning up with a babysitter.'

'A babysitter? More like a cool chauffeur. You know, like Alfred. Which means essentially you would be Batman.'

'Dad . . . please,' he begged. 'You must have been in a similar situation with grandad?'

'Grandad?!' he laughed. 'Your grandad wouldn't give me the bus fare.'

'And how did that make you feel?' he replied, with a look that suggested he had struck a decisive blow.

After long moments, his dad gave a great sigh and removed the keys from his pocket. 'If there is a dent, a scratch, a single hair that isn't grey on my headrest . . . so help me God in heaven, I'll . . .' He tossed the keys, which were snatched out of the air in triumph.

'You're the best dad ever,' he beamed, wrapping his arms around him in a quick embrace as he skipped towards the front door.

'Well, make sure you're the best driver ever when you're on the roads, OK.'

It had taken days of coordinated badgering of his father in order to get the keys to his beloved car. As he drove the return journey from his girlfriend's house in Brixton, he intended to eke every last drop out of the experience. The sat-nav showed Park Lane and up through Edgware would be so much quicker . . . but far less enjoyable. As the night lights of the city came to life in the twilight, cruising through Soho would be *epic*, he thought excitedly.

Ignoring the exit for Park Lane, he guided the car on to Piccadilly. With his window wound down, the cabin was flooded with a delightful cacophony of car horns and excited voices. He marvelled at the sights of The Ritz and Piccadilly Circus, having to squint as the huge digital advertising board blinded him with its colourful message. Here he was, grinning from ear to ear, cruising through central London after spending a very pleasant afternoon with his new girlfriend. He had never felt more grown-up. Life was good.

The car's central dashboard lit up. *Incoming call* flashed on its digital display.

He hit *answer* on the steering wheel.

'Hello.'

'Leo.'

'Yeah. Hi.'

'*Where are you?*'

'I'm driving,' said Leo, distractedly turning the car to go left.

'*Where?*'

'Where am I? Where are you?' he said with a chuckle, fancying the voice sounded familiar to him now.

'*LEO! Where are you exactly?!*' came the voice again, but more aggressive . . . panicked even.

'I'm in Soho,' he said, his smile now fading, confusion taking its place.

'*What street?*'

'Why? Who is this? I'm so confused right now.'

'*THE STREET!*' the voice shouted into the phone.

'Wardour,' he replied, instantly annoyed that he had capitulated so easily. 'I'm going to hang up unless you tell me who this is.'

'*Leo, you are about to hit and kill a man with your car,*' the voice said in rapid desperation.

'What the hell are you talking about?'

'*On your left! A man is about to step into the road! On your left!*'

'WHAT?!'

'*AtallmanonyourLEFT! LOOKNOW! LOOKNOW!*'

'I DON'T UNDER . . .' Leo began to shout back, but as he did so his eyes were drawn to a tall man he was bearing down upon rapidly, tucking a phone into his pocket.

'*STOP! STOP! STOPTHECAR!*' screamed the voice.

The tall man turned and stepped into the road.

Tyres screamed.

Time slowed.

Through the windshield, Leo saw every detail of the tall man's face, his pupils lost in the huge whites of his eyes, his mouth aghast in a petrified oval, his hands outstretched in a futile attempt to stop the inevitable impact that would end his life. At the last moment, the man closed his eyes, bracing for impact.

Tyres stopped screaming.

Time resumed its normal flow.

The man opened his eyes and looked down at his hands, which were resting on the bonnet of the car. Breathing heavily, he slowly tilted his head and peered in through the windscreen at Leo, frozen in terror. The man's face broke into a wide smile. Tears brimmed in his eyes. He staggered to the driver's side, one hand still on the car bonnet and looked in at Leo through the open window.

'I . . . I thought that was it,' he said, the tears now rolling down his face. 'I thought I wasn't going to get my chance.'

'I'm . . . I'm . . . I'm sorry,' stuttered Leo.

'No, I'm sorry. I should have been looking where I was going.'

'Are you OK?'

'Yeah,' he said, wiping tears from his eyes and bursting into laughter. 'Yeah, I think so. Sorry to give you such a scare, kid.' He raised his hand in a farewell gesture and turned to walk away.

'Hey!' Leo shouted after him. 'You said you didn't think you were going to get your chance. A chance at what?'

The man stopped. 'To live a good life,' he said, smiling back over his shoulder.

Leo watched the man walk away until he turned into an alley and was gone from sight. A horn sounded from behind. He put the car into drive and pulled off. As he was doing so, he suddenly remembered the mystery caller. He looked to the dashboard. There was nobody there. Just a map that was showing him the way home.

Acknowledgements

Thank you to my wife, Phylicia, who started this whole thing with just six words: 'Why don't you write a book?' I love you, Sweet P.

Laura Hill, my wonderful friend, who also happens to be my agent, talked me off the ledge on more than a handful of occasions. Being told 'don't give up' by someone you love and respect goes a very long way. You're the best, Lau.

It was Laura who introduced me to Paul Stevens. He is the literary agent extraordinaire who's been thanked in acknowledgements like this in more books than you and I have had cooked dinners. Having Paul in my corner makes me feel like a child in a school play who has Denzel Washington as an acting coach.

Paul looked over my first eighty pages and to my surprise and delight chose not to set them on fire and jam them in a bin. Instead, he introduced me to Bill Massey.

Quite simply, if it wasn't for Bill, who I am proud to say is my editor, you would be staring at your empty hands right now and not this book. Bill, thank you for your patience, thank you for that masterful editorial brain and thank you for never sugar-coating it. Bill reached into my chest and crushed my heart on more than one occasion but always helped me get back up on the horse.

It's because of all of the ridiculously talented people above I had the best phone call of my life. Enter – Rowland White from Penguin Random House. Thank you for taking a chance on me, Rowland. That first thirty-minute chat we had is still the best phone call I have ever received. I'll cherish that memory for ever. Getting *Call Time* Penguin-ready with you and the excellent Ruth Atkins was an indescribable joy . . . just so bloody exciting from start to finish!

I'd like to add a special mention and thanks to Nick Lowndes and Kay Halsey who had the unenviable job of deciphering my hideous grammar, which must have been like trying to crack the Enigma code.

And lastly, thank you Formula 1. Thank you for all the long-haul flights and lonely hotel rooms. You gave me one of the things I needed the most in order to write *Call Time* – time.